IT HAD BEEN
A FINE BEGINNING

The ships had gone out—to the moon first, and then to Mars, Venus, and Mercury. And Murchison ventured into the asteroids, and Quintero dared the sun's flaming atmosphere.

Men—all heroes—ranged the new frontier.

But then the politicians killed it. They dragged home the venturous ones—the ones who dared—and took away from them Man's most challenging frontier.

But it would come back. It *had* to come back. Even if Joe Webber had to build the rockets with his own bare hands. Even if he had to snatch men off the streets, and seal them in the rockets, and shoot them off at the stars.

The high, cold stars.

for
DAVE and his JANE
unafraid to think different

COMPLETE AND UNABRIDGED

THE
MAN
WHO
WANTED STARS

DEAN McLAUGHLIN, Jr.

LANCER BOOKS • NEW YORK

A LANCER ORIGINAL • 1965

LANCER BOOKS, INC. • 185 MADISON AVENUE • NEW YORK 16, N.Y.

PART ONE

"MAYBE I CAN do it," Roger Sherman admitted. "I don't know. If I had a choice, I'd say no. I wouldn't try. But . . . oh, the hell with it."

"Any other way, we don't have a chance," Captain Milburn reminded him. "Don't worry. Forget it. We think you can do it."

"Well I'm not so sure," Sherman said. He was a big man—rare among spacemen. His blocky face was clenched and grim.

"If anyone can do it, Rog, you can." The Captain was firm.

"It's asking a hell of a lot," Sherman reminded him. "This ship wasn't built for it."

"We know that, Rog," Milburn said. "We don't expect miracles."

A crewman with a cutting torch drifted up nearby and caught a hand-hold on a beam. "What about that bulkhead there?" He pointed at a section of the wall.

Captain Milburn glanced at it for only a moment. "Yeah. Take it," he decided. "Take the whole damn wall."

"Right," the crewman responded. He pushed off.

"This ship isn't built to hit atmosphere," Sherman repeated. "It's like trying to fly a plane under water."

"But you think you can do it," Captain Milburn insisted.

"I don't know. I think *maybe* I can, but I don't know."

The Captain shrugged. "We'll just have to try. *I* think you can do it."

"It's your decision, Bill. God knows, I wouldn't want to make it."

"It's your job, Rog. If you say no, I won't argue. You think there's a chance—I say try it. If we don't, we're dead men anyway."

He broke off there. The man with the cutting torch was attacking a thick beam that cut across the face of the wall.

"Hey, leave that," he yelled.

The crewman looked up guiltily.

"That beam's what braces this piggy bank against the jet," Captain Milburn told him. "Without it, when Rog puts the shove under us, it'll mush this ship together like a tin can somebody stepped on."

"Well then, whattaya want me to do?" the crewman demanded.

Wayne Staples drifted into the compartment. He was wearing a spacesuit and he had the helmet under his arm. He waited unobtrusively while Milburn finished with the crewman.

"Take the plates," Milburn ordered. "Take every damn plate in the whole damn ship, but leave those beams alone!"

"Yes sir," the crewman said meekly.

Milburn turned to Staples. "Yeah? What is it?"

"We've finished searching the orbitbase, sir," Staples reported.

"Well?" the Captain demanded. "Find anything?"

"Oh, yes sir," Staples said quickly. "God, sir. It's like walking in a tomb. They left everything there. I even found a guy's toothbrush."

"I didn't send you to look for toothbrushes," the Captain reminded him.

"I know that, sir," Staples said, quashed. "It's been empty a long time, sir. The air's all gone out of it."

Sherman couldn't wait any longer. "What about the tanks?" he asked. "Did you find any water?"

He wasn't really hopeful, but he had to ask. The *Jove* needed water if he was going to pilot it down. Every drop was worth its weight in blood.

"Not much," Staples admitted. "Most of it was evaporated away, but there was a little left. Frozen, of course, but that's all right. It'll be easier to handle that way."

"How much?" Sherman persisted.

6

Staples shrugged. "I don't know," he said carelessly. "A couple, three tons. Something like that."

"Every ounce counts," Milburn said. "Get it aboard. Can you manage it all right?"

"It'll be some trouble," Staples admitted. "But we'll do it. Somehow."

"Good," Milburn said. "And try to get a better figure how much there is. It may be the difference between making it and not making it. What about the black plaster? Any of that?"

"Oh, sure. Lots of it."

"Is there *enough*?" Milburn prodded.

"Enough to cover the ship five times," Staples assured plainly.

"That's what I wanted to know," Milburn snapped. "We'll need every bit of it. Get it aboard. What else did you find?"

"There was a stock of scout projectiles and mounts," Staples offered.

"We'll want those, too," Milburn said.

Roger Sherman got tired of it. He kicked off and drifted over to the astrodome. The cover plate was off and the view was faced toward Earth. Earth was big. It filled all the view except a crescent rim of night-and-stars in the upper left hand side, and there was a lot more of Earth he couldn't see.

Only three hundred miles down, he thought, and it was good to see. After being away for so long, after having gone so far, it was a welcome sight. The oceans were blue and the land was green and brown and gray, and the rivers were thin lines of blue through the richest green. It was Earth, and it was beautiful.

He felt sick. Disgusted. It was so terribly unfair. They'd gone farther than any men had ever gone—all the way out to Jupiter—and come home again. Come home like Ulysses, after seven years.

And they had been forgotten. The orbitbase was empty. Even the air was gone from it. There was no ship to carry them the last three hundred miles. They had only the *Jove,* which had borne them for all the millions of miles they had gone, but which had not been built to go that terrible last three hundred miles home.

7

Three hundred miles and the barrier of atmosphere—atmosphere that burned a meteor to nothing in the flick of an eyelash—atmosphere that had destroyed half a hundred ships without a trace before men learned how to build them and how to pilot them down from safe, sterile space.

So they would try it anyway—try going down in the *Jove*. Maybe it was suicide, but they had to do it.

Because there were no other ships. Because there wouldn't be any other ships. Because the groundhogs had scrapped every ship there ever was, and left the orbitbase to float alone and empty out in space like the cast-off shell of a sucked egg.

Sherman wanted to hit something. Smash it. The stupid . . . stupid . . .

. . . and the fearful three hundred miles. Earth spread below him, just out of reach, three hundred miles down. As unattainable as a mirage in the desert.

"What are the chances?" Captain Milburn asked soberly.

"Damn them," Sherman muttered bitterly. "Why did they have to do it?"

"Scrap the ships?" Milburn wondered. "Abandon the orbitbase? . . . I don't know, Rog. Maybe they were afraid—because space was something they didn't understand. But I don't think so. That never was much of a reason for men to give up a thing. No—I guess they just didn't care. It didn't mean anything to them."

"Didn't mean anything!" Sherman cried. "But . . . I"

"Oh, in the beginning it meant something. It was a challenge—a dare. But once we'd proved we could do it . . . well, it was expensive, and politicians can always think of better things to do with money. I remember, now, there was some talk around Washington before we left . . . and no man's ever climbed Everest twice. I guess there's a point there, somewhere."

"Yeah. Somewhere," Sherman muttered.

"So what are the chances, Rog?" the Captain asked again.

"I tell you, Bill, I just don't know."

"But there *is* a chance."

"Of course there's a chance. If there wasn't, I wouldn't try."

"That's what I wanted, Rog. If anyone can do it, you can. If any man can do it, Rog, you're the man."

"I wonder if Blair and Ellis knew that."

"Haven't you got over that yet? Hell, man. That was three years ago!"

"But I didn't try!" Sherman protested. "I didn't even try!"

It was out there—all the way out there—where Jupiter filled half the sky. It was an ugly thing—striped like a kid's ball with dirty colors, and the red spot like the mouth of some unspeakable beast.

While the *Jove* held its orbit around the planet, its shuttles carried the explorers to its moons and even to the fringes of the planet's atmosphere. And one of the shuttles blew up.

Royce, at the communicator, was the first to know about it. He was talking with the shuttle when it followed its orbit around behind Jupiter. He waited the proper length of time for the shuttle to come back into line-of-sight, and then tried to re-establish contact.

He couldn't do it. The shuttle wasn't there. Half an hour later, he picked up the suit-radios of Blair and Ellis, the two men who had been in the shuttle. The signals were weak and mushy, and Royce didn't need to hear what Blair and Ellis were saying to know what had happened.

For one thing, they were in too close to Jupiter—much closer than the shuttle's orbit would have put them.

Sherman ordered the other shuttle got ready the instant he heard about it. He hurried to the communications cell. Captain Milburn was already there.

Royce managed to fix their positions by tracking their signals and figuring the distance by the time between a signal-over and a reply. With a couple of fixes, Sherman roughed-out their trajectories, and a third fix on each confirmed his figures.

Sherman was already jotting more figures when Captain Milburn said, "Can you pick them up?"

"No," Sherman muttered, and went on jotting figures.

9

"Blair says he's got four and a half hours' air," Royce reported. "He wants to know how soon you'll pick them up."

"Tell him he's got plenty," Sherman said. "He'll hit atmosphere in three and a quarter."

To the Captain, he said, "I can't do a thing." He passed over his sheet of figures. "The only orbit that would get me to them before they hit air would burn more than the shuttle's tanks hold. I'm not going after them."

"Shall I tell them?" Royce wanted to know.

Milburn gestured, shushing him. "Don't tell them." And to Sherman, "You're sure?"

"I'm sure."

"Check the figures again."

"I checked them, sir."

"I said check them again," Milburn ordered.

Sherman took the paper and checked his calculations. There was nothing wrong with them. He gave the sheet to the Captain. "You check them, sir."

Milburn crumpled the paper and threw it away. Weightless, it floated in the air.

"What do I tell them?" Royce asked.

"Tell them . . ." the Captain began, and stopped. He nudged Sherman. "You tell them."

It was something he couldn't do. It was hard enough to think of the men adrift in space with nothing to hang on to—falling helplessly toward the great, ugly mass of the planet. He couldn't tell them he had plotted their orbits and the orbits ended at death—that there was nothing else possible, and it was only three hours away.

"No," he whispered hoarsely. "No. God! Don't make me."

"Tell them," the Captain instructed Royce, "to make whatever peace they can with themselves and their gods. They've got three hours."

Royce told them.

"They want to talk to you," Royce told Sherman after a moment.

"No," Sherman said. It would be like talking to men he'd killed. "I won't. Don't make me."

"It's the least you can do, Rog," the Captain said, looking solemnly at him. "Talk to them."

Royce held the microphone and earpiece out to him. He took them with numb fingers.

"Mike . . . Owen . . . I'm sorry." He meant it as he had never meant anything in his life.

And Owen Blair's voice came through, mushy with the interference, accusing no one and reproaching no one, "If you can't . . . you can't . . . way it is . . ." and Mike Ellis was murmuring, ". . . Mary, Mother of God . . ."

Sherman gave the set back to Royce.

"I'll have to announce it to the ship," the Captain said. "Jim—warm the PA."

"It's warm already, sir," Royce said, and passed him the PA mike.

The Captain spoke into it. "Attention. Attention." And the words echoed through the *Jove*.

Mike Ellis hit atmosphere first. He burned out in half a minute. Owen Blair didn't go in for another fifteen minutes, but he didn't last any longer.

"I didn't even try," Sherman repeated. "That's the thing, Bill. I didn't even try."

"There wasn't anything you could do," Milburn said. "So shut up about it. If you don't think you can take us down, say so and we'll try to think of something else. But for God's sake quit mumbling about it."

Sherman backed off as if he'd been slapped. "I'm willing to try," he repeated. "But if I can do it or not . . ."

"God damn it! Shut up!" Milburn roared.

The crewman with the cutting torch had burned a plate out of the wall. Grappling it with heavy gloves, he towed it slowly toward the air lock.

"It depends on too many things," Sherman tried to explain. "How much weight we can drop—and how much we have in the tanks—and whether I'm up to the job . . ."

"And how calm the atmosphere is," Milburn interrupted disgustedly. "And how much the ship can take. And whether it sinks or floats when we hit the water . . . Ahhh! You make me sick."

He turned away, then turned back again. "Listen, Rog. There's just one thing that's going to make the

11

difference between whether we make it or we don't. And that's you, Roger. You. You wouldn't have been with this expedition if you weren't the best pilot there is. But if you don't think you can do it, now's the time to say so."

"I'm going to try it, Bill," he said. "I don't promise anything more."

The Captain made an exasperated face. "What can you expect?" he wondered helplessly, almost to himself. And aloud, "Another thing—if you've got to worry about it, don't do it out loud where the men can hear. They've got enough to worry about."

"Yes sir," said Sherman meekly.

The crewman came back from the lock and put his torch to another section of the wall. Another crewman entered the compartment. His coverall was a mess.

"We got the hydroponics cleaned out," he reported. "The water's still in purification, but the job's done. We dumped everything."

"How much water?" Milburn demanded.

"Thirteen tons and nine hundred pounds, sir. Plus."

"Fine," the Captain said. "Divert it to the drive tank."

"That's doing right now," the crewman reported.

"Get into your suit, then," Milburn ordered. "Report to Staples in the orbitbase. He's going to move some ice over from there, and he can use you."

"Right sir." The crewman started for the suiting room, unfastening his coverall as he went.

"Dump your coverall outside," Milburn called after him. "You won't be needing it again."

"On the know, sir," the man answered.

Roger Sherman was looking down at Earth again, thinking of the menace the all-but-invisible atmosphere was. It could tear a ship to shreds, and melt the shreds to vapor. Even the night side was full of turbulence—great gusts of rampant air that could suck a ship down before its pilot had a chance to pull away—drag it down into air too thick for its hurtling shape to stand against—it would be like hitting a wall.

And the *Jove* wasn't built to pass through atmosphere. Its builders had never meant for it to feel even the touch of air.

12

"Thirteen tons," the Captain repeated, smiling confidently. "And nine hundred pounds. How does it sound now?"

"A little better," Sherman admitted half-heartedly. "But I won't know anything for sure until we're on our way."

Milburn frowned. "How do you figure that?"

"That's when I'll find out how the ship handles," Sherman explained. "We're taking a lot of weight out, and we can't more than rough-guess how much. I've no idea how off-balance we'll be. And I'll be running the reactor wide open. There's a lot of things we can't be sure of until I put the shove under us."

"Umm." Milburn looked thoughtful. "And then it's too late to turn back."

Sherman nodded. "Sink or swim," he said grimly. "Still want to go through with it?"

Milburn looked him blackly in the eyes. "Yes. God-dammit. Yes."

Later, they toured the *Jove* together. Scott Riemer, the ship's engineer, made the tour with them.

All through the ship, men armed with wrenches and cutting torches were tearing out sections of wall and banks of lockers and pieces of equipment which had been ruled expendable. The *Jove* was being trimmed to a few picked bones.

"The hell of it is," Scott Riemer said as they watched the work proceed, "they built this ship with as little waste weight as they could—and now we've got to cut it down."

"Everything that's not absolutely necessary has to go," Sherman insisted. "Everything. A few pounds too much and we'll never make it."

"We'll make it," the Captain said stubbornly.

They came to the galley. It hadn't been touched.

"Dayton! Joe Dayton!" Milburn bawled.

Joe Dayton, the galley master, came out of the fresh food locker with a sack of hydroponic vegetables. He looked startled.

"Why's this stuff still here?" the Captain demanded. His gesture swept the compartment.

"We still have to eat," the galley master explained innocently.

"Like hell we do," Milburn snapped. "Issue a pint of soup to each man—double strength. And a quarter pound of sugar and a quart of water. And then clean this junk out of here."

"All of it?"

"Down to the last tin can," Milburn ordered. "Food and everything. There's plenty of food where we're going, but we've got to get there. Snap to it."

"Yes sir," Dayton gulped.

As they left the galley, Joe Dayton was making soup.

"I've been thinking about that shield we've got between us and the reactor," Scott Riemer said. "It's a lot of dead weight to be carrying around."

"Get a crew and peel it as thin as you dare," Milburn said.

"No," Sherman objected flatly.

Milburn swung on him. "Why not?" he demanded.

"Listen sir," Sherman said. "We won't have enough water, no matter what way you look at it, so I'm going to do the next best thing. I'm going to run the reactor pile hotter than it's ever been before. I'll have to. We're going to need every inch of that shielding. And wish there was more."

Milburn scowled. He turned to the engineer. "What's the shield's safety factor?"

"Two," Riemer said. He knew what was coming.

"And the reactor's overload rating?"

"Three point five," Scott Riemer admitted. "With the understanding that anything over one point five would be of short duration and only in extreme emergency."

"We're doing something this ship wasn't built for," Sherman said. "We're too heavy, and the wrong shape, and the wrong controls—and we don't have enough water to do it. If that's not an emergency, there's no such thing."

"He's right," Milburn told the engineer. "The shield stays."

"It's your decision, sir."

They came to where the men were tearing out the crew's private lockers. The men looked like they didn't like what they were doing, but they were doing it any-

14

way. The walls were already gone from the compartment. This part of the ship was a maze of naked girders, like a scaffold inside a globe.

Sherman saw something small and brown moving out there among the beams. Captain Milburn must have seen it too, because he kicked off toward it and pursued it.

The monkey moved fast. They had a hard time catching up with it. They found it, finally, near the air lock.

Men were towing large sacks of vegetables up from the galley and dumping them in the lock. But one man had stopped and was feeding the monkey a bit of carrot. He was talking to the monkey—senseless things, but said in a friendly voice. He roughed its short fur.

It ate the carrot greedily.

"Galbraith," Milburn said.

The man looked up guiltily. "Sorry sir. I'll get right to work, sir." And as if it explained everything, "He was begging."

The monkey got away from him. It perched on a nearby beam and munched its carrot in small, squirrel-like nibbles.

"Bulkhead has to go," Milburn said.

The Captain could have stuck a knife in him and not brought such a painful look to Galbraith's face.

"He doesn't weigh much," the crewman said, trembling a little.

Milburn didn't argue with him. "He's got to go," he said.

"No! I won't let you," Galbraith cried. He let go of his vegetable sack, he pushed off and drifted away from Milburn. "Here, Bulkhead," he called anxiously. "C'mere, kid." He clapped his hands enticingly and went on calling.

Still nibbling carrot, Bulkhead perched on his beam and goggled at Galbraith innocently. He gathered himself for a leap.

"Bulkhead," Milburn commanded. "Come here."

"No, Bulkhead," Galbraith protested. "*Here*. Here, kid. He'll hurt you. He'll hurt you."

Milburn pulled a carrot out of the sack. He held it so Bulkhead could see it. "Here, Bulkhead," he invited.

Bulkhead sprang toward the Captain.

"No!" Galbraith cried. "No, Bulkhead! No!"

Floating in the air, the monkey twisted and looked back at Galbraith, a look of total innocence. Then, with a flick of his tail he turned around and reached for the carrot.

Milburn caught the monkey's feet and bashed its head against a beam. Galbraith screamed. The monkey's body jerked once like a galvanized frog, and something like a chicken's gizzard bulged from the smashed skull.

The Captain looked at the monkey—made sure it was dead—and tossed it into the air lock. "Space him," he said to the man inside.

Galbraith flung himself at the Captain. His face was twisted with pain and his eyes were frantic with angry tears. "Why did you do that for?" he cried. "He wasn't hurting anybody. He wasn't hurting anybody. Why'd you do that for?"

His fists flailed uselessly on Milburn's chest and shoulders.

Milburn fended him off. "Shut up, God damn you," he growled.

He turned to go away—turned so no one could see his face. "I loved that monk," he murmured bitterly. "As much as you did."

Then the ship was ready. The crew had finished coating its skin with a two inch sheath of the black plaster. It would burn away when the *Jove* hit atmosphere, but the ship itself would be protected from the awful heat of friction with the air. Time after time, the *Jove* would have to skim through the thin upper fringes of the atmosphere and coast out again into space to cool its glowing skin—until finally its terrible plunge was slowed and it would be safe to venture farther down—toward home.

But after each passage, as soon as the ship had cooled, a fresh coat of black plaster would have to be put on. The supply from the orbitbase wouldn't last long. Sherman wondered if it was enough. Cold figures said it was —his private fears said no.

Inside the *Jove*, there was very little left between the reactor's shield and the forward radars. It was like a

16

great cave, its spherical walls braced and counterbraced by thick, stiff beams.

The men wore their spacesuits. The air had been let out of the ship, and of the air lock only the outer door remained. The astrodome cover was down, and the transparent dome itself had been removed. Whatever observations Sherman had to make, he would make them from the air lock door.

And it was dark, and full of deep, thick shadows. The power generator had been jettisoned, and most of the lighting fixtures and circuits. Only the auxiliary generator carried on. It was enough to power the controls and instruments and the necessary forward radar.

It was going to be a long, fearful ride. The atmosphere —so placid in appearance, and so sweet in recollections of warm nights under the stars—was full of terrors. Its turbulence was as unpredictable and savage as disaster. It could suck a ship to its doom in an instant.

Sherman remembered, as if it was only a moment ago, the training officer who had said to him: "Hit the night side when you can and the day side when you have to. The twilight zones are suicide. But however you hit the air, don't forget to pray."

Sherman hadn't thought much about prayers for a long time. He was thinking of them now.

The Captain's voice sounded crisply in his helmet from the speaker at the back of his neck. "Ready, Roger?"

It was like the voice of his conscience, speaking behind him, where he couldn't see . . .

"As ready as I'll ever be," Sherman said without eagerness. He hesitated. "Still want to go through with it?"

"Dammit! We *are* going through with it," Milburn declared.

"All right," Sherman said. "We're going through with it. That was your last chance to say no."

"I didn't say it."

"I didn't try, that other time. This time, I'm going to try."

"Forget about the other time."

Somewhere behind him, the Captain and the men waited, their backs against the bare lead shielding of the

17

reactor—waiting for him to feed the water into the reactor and drive the ship down from its orbit, toward death or toward home.

The instrument dials glowed softly. He read them again. Skin temperature low. Reactor hot—far over in the red. He couldn't help that. It had to be hot.

. . . acceleration zero. Pumps zero. Line of flight steady. Radarscreen blank. Time passing . . .

The controls—pumps, reactor, gyro, jet vanes— glowing each with its own distinct color, all equally in reach of his fingertips. He held himself stiffly, resisting the urge to go ahead and get it over with.

"What're you waiting for?" Milburn rapped impatiently.

"Five minutes." He almost twisted to give the answer back over his shoulder, forgetting the Captain spoke through his suit radio. He glanced back at the time. "Four and a half," he said.

It was good to have the controls in front of him again. There was a feeling of power in it, terrible in its responsibility—but exciting, just the same. The Pacific made a big, wide target. He'd hit it all right—if they didn't burn up in the atmosphere.

The minutes counted off, and then the seconds. Sherman held his hands steady and forced his eyes to watch the time turn around the clock. The seconds were gallingly slow.

He started the pumps, and when they were going and the last few seconds flicked into the past, he fed the water to them. The *Jove* slammed at his back, and drove hard. His sight blurred.

When he could see, he watched the acceleration and the time, and abruptly he choked the pumps. The *Jove* lurched inert.

"How does it look?" Milburn's voice barked out of the radio speaker.

"I'll have to figure," Sherman said. He opened the instrument panel and tore out the graph, wondering why a man in a suit automatically raised his voice. But then he was too busy to think about it.

He read the graph quickly. His practiced eye approximated it, leveled it, squeezed it dry of meaning. He turned it over and scratched figures on the back.

18

He went down to the air lock door and took observations. He went back and checked his figures.

"We need more weight in the five o'clock position," he reported. "Move all the men you can. We're way off balance."

"Right," Milburn said gruffly. And to the men: "You heard what he said. Move."

Looking back, Sherman saw the shadowy movements of spacesuited men in the dark. He touched the controls, shifting the gyro to a new setting. The *Jove* wobbled and then held steady.

"Weight redistributed," Milburn reported.

"Thanks," Sherman said. "Stand by for course correction." He fired a brief blast. The *Jove* drove forward horribly. Then abruptly it was all weightless again.

He went down and took more star sights. "On orbit, Captain," he reported finally. It wasn't perfect, but good enough. With a little luck and a lot of skill, he'd do all right.

PART TWO

IN THE NATIONAL—and only—office of Space Flight Associates, ignoring the dust that filmed his desktop, Joe Webber read *The Washington-Baltimore Post-Sun-Tribune*'s article about American preparations for the international government conference at Canberra.

He hadn't anything else to do.

Once in a while, he glanced out through the one-way glass partition to the outer office. His receptionist—a gray-haired, tired looking woman—seemed always to be manicuring her fingernails.

Or knitting.

Maybe he should try the Sunday supplements again. A piece there would reach a lot of people. But the editors hadn't been in—to him—the last time he made the rounds. It was no use thinking they'd be any more eager if he tried again.

But maybe if he emphasized the adventure, the excitement, the *achievement* of space flight—there were people he could win with a piece like that. The young and star-eyed, the seeking and imagining, the restless ones for whom a colorless, earthbound life held no attraction.

It wasn't as if space flight was irretrievably dead. It would come back. It *had* to come back.

Even if he had to build the rockets with his own bare hands. Even if he had to snatch men off the streets, and seal them in the rockets, and shoot them off at the high, cold stars.

It had been a fine beginning. The ships had gone out —to the moon first, and then to Mars, Venus, and Mercury. And Murchison ventured into the asteroids, and Quintero dared the sun's flaming atmosphere.

Men—all heroes—ranged the new frontier.

But then the politicians killed it. They slashed it out of the budgets. They voted to scrap the fine ships, and to pay off the men who had flown them. They brought the spacemen home as if they were truants and set their feet on the earth.

And America let the politicians do it. The people, the sheep-stupid, foolish people. There had been talk of a tax cut, and the fumble-wits fell for it.

They dragged home the venturous ones—the ones who dared—the only ones who still possessed the qualities that made men men. Robbed them of the only life worthwhile, and took away from them Man's most challenging frontier.

There wasn't any tax cut, of course. Instead, there was a lot of public works construction all over America. A little something for everybody.

You couldn't tell the People they'd been fools. You couldn't tell them they were suckered—that their votes had been bought with a cheapskate promise, and a broken one at that—that in letting themselves be bought they had betrayed the human race.

You couldn't even hint they'd made a small mistake.

You had to forget what they'd done. You had to start over, as if nothing had happened. As if space flight had never happened.

And you had to *sell* them. You had to make them believe in space flight the way they believed in the right to worship as they pleased, and maybe even as they believed in their gods.

You had to make them think of space flight as Man's unalterable destiny. You had to make them send their sons, and maybe even their daughters, and to wish they could go themselves.

But first you had to make them listen.

And nobody listened to Joe Webber, of Space Flight Associates.

Nobody had.

For years . . .

When the mail came, Mrs. Crowder brought it in. There were only three pieces. Two of them were bills. The third bore the letterhead of Brent & Perrault Biologicals.

21

Webber dropped the bills unopened in the waste-basket. He opened the letter. He recognized Andrew Perrault's sprawling scrawl at once.

Dear Joe—
  The missus is plotting a fish fry, and the brat is beginning to wonder what came of her Uncle Joe. So if you're not too busy, you're welcome.

Drew

Webber got out a sheet of Space Flight Associates stationery.

Drew—
  Can't make it to the fish fry, whenever it is. My foot's in the door of something big. Can't leave it for a minute. May be our last chance.
  And send money. Cash running out fast.

He signed it. Then, reconsidering, he added a postscript.

Tell the girl I'm on a trip to Mars. Maybe she'll believe it.

An amber light gleamed suddenly from the panel of his desk. Mrs. Crowder was on the phone.

Webber snapped the listen-in switch.

"—sorry," Mrs. Crowder was saying. "Captain Webber has a visitor. He can't be disturbed."

Mrs. Crowder was following orders perfectly. Joe Webber smiled.

"When can I talk to him?" the man at the other end of the wire persisted.

"He has a very full schedule," Mrs. Crowder apologized. "I might have him call you when he has a minute."

"I'd rather call him."

"He might have a few minutes free at four this afternoon," Mrs. Crowder suggested. "You might . . ."

"Not till then?" the man's anguish was real. "I've got to get him before then. There's a big story breaking, and we've got a deadline to meet. You're sure I can't get him sooner than that?"

"Well . . ."

Joe Webber pressed the I'll-talk-to-him button.

Mrs. Crowder took the signal smoothly. "Just a minute," she said sweetly. "You're a very lucky man. Captain Webber's guest is leaving, and his next appointment isn't here yet. If you can wait a minute, I'll see if he can talk to you."

"Please," the man said urgently.

After a pause, Webber opened his phone. The man in the screen touched his temple.

Joe Webber gestured to his brow in reply.

"I'm George Seeback, with Transocean Press," the man introduced himself quickly. He had slick black hair, crowfooted eyes, and a small brush mustache. "We've got a story breaking down here, and we need some background."

"What kind of background?" Webber narrowed his green-gray eyes and leaned his compact, small-boned body forward. It was the first time in years a newsman had come to him. They'd all given him up as a source of news long ago.

"We want anything you can tell us about the *Jove*."

For a moment, it didn't mean a thing to him. And then it tumbled out of his memory and it was all there.

"The *Jove*?" He tilted back his chair and repeated it as it came to him.

"That was the ship of the first Jupiter expedition," he said. "The only one. Bill Milburn was Captain. Rog Sherman was pilot. Crew and survey team altogether— twenty-five men. They left Orbitbase on June 14th of '91 —supposed to get back . . ."

He clapped a hand to his head. *"My Gawd!"*

The clock on his desk said October 29, 1998.

"You mean they're back?" he exploded.

"Well, not exactly," Seeback said inexpertly. "Uh— how do you spell their names?"

"Hell with their names!" Webber shouted. "Whattaya mean, not exactly?"

"They're on their way down from the orbitbase," Seeback explained.

"Orbitbase?" Webber echoed. "But that was abandoned four years . . ."

He tightened. "What are they coming down *in?*"

"The *Jove,*" Seeback said, as if it was obvious. "What else?"

Webber felt a clammy cold hand clutch his guts. "The *Jove*'s not built for atmosphere!" he cried protestingly.

Seeback shrugged. "All I know is what they tell me. What's wrong with coming down in the *Jove?*"

"What's wrong with it?" Webber exclaimed. "It's suicide, that's what! She's a space ship. The real thing. Not one of those streamlined atmosphere jobs like those goddamned intercontinentals. Atmosphere'll burn her like a meteor."

"Then they don't stand much chance of getting down, do they," Seeback deduced.

"The chance of a snowball in hell," Webber snapped. "All because a bunch of porkbarrel politicians melted down all the shuttles into nickles!"

An arch of interest showed on Seeback's brow. "Can we quote you?" he suggested.

Webber caught his breath. "Can you! You'd damn well better!"

But then, remembering the bitter lesson he'd learned, he said hastily, "No. You'd better not. Just say . . ."

He paused and calculated. "Say I think it's unfortunate—there's a damn good word!—unfortunate there wasn't an atmosphere shuttle kept in condition so it could go up and get them."

Seeback looked disappointed, but he didn't say anything. There was a pause while he made notes. Then . . .

"Something I don't see," he said uncertainly. "Why'd they try coming down if they don't have a chance?"

"How the hell do I know?" Webber demanded. He leaned close to the screen. "Listen, mister—you ever been away from home seven years? So far away you don't even know what home's like any more? And when you come back there's nobody expecting you? They don't even remember you? How'd you feel?"

"I don't know," the newsman admitted. "It never happened to me."

"Well—me, I'd want to land on somebody's neck and make damn well sure he knew he'd come back. If I was up there . . . yeah, I'd try the ride down, too. Better than sit up there and put a callus on my butt. That's the kind of men we are!"

"You'd do that even if you didn't have a chance?" Seeback wondered.

Webber shrugged impatiently. "Well, with Rog for a pilot, maybe they do have a chance. Not a big one, but maybe a chance."

But he didn't believe it. Not even Rog Sherman could do a thing like that.

"They figure to crash land somewhere in the Pacific," Seeback said helpfully.

It seemed a long time to Webber, but he finally got rid of the newsman. He buzzed Mrs. Crowder.

"Find out when the next rocket lifts for Tahiti," he said. "Or Hawaii. I'm going to be in it."

Time after time, the *Jove* slashed through the thin upper atmosphere. Each time her hull was glowing red when she passed on again into space, where she cooled, and the men went outside to renew her protective sheath of black plaster.

Each time, they dropped the exhausted oxygen bottles, and just before the *Jove* re-entered the atmosphere they fired off a set of the probe projectiles, whose motions, observed on a radar screen, would gauge the density and turbulence of the air ahead of the *Jove*.

Roger Sherman watched the radar screen and the hull temperature gauge. His life and the life of every man aboard depended on them. One small miscalculation and the *Jove* would turn briefly to flame, and leave only a trace of vapor to mark where it had ceased to be.

He had figured the orbit almost perfectly, but the atmosphere through which the *Jove* passed could not be predicted exactly. Several times the projectiles wavered, or slowed too quickly, or the hull temperature rose too fast. Quickly, then, but not so quickly that everything was not gauged and estimated in his mind, Sherman fed a precious trickle of water to the irreparably overheating

25

drive-reactor; the fierce jet forced the ship up out of the atmosphere to the safety of space.

Sherman prayed they had dropped enough weight; if they hadn't, the water would give out. And there was nothing left now to jettison.

The passages through atmosphere came closer and closer together. Air leaked in through weakened seams. Each brief respite out in space was shorter than the one before. The hot hours passed, and Sherman sweated and chafed in his pressure suit, and doggedly fought the ship down.

Finally, almost with a sigh, he let the ship down into air for the last time. She thundered endlessly through air, her hull burned almost to the brilliance of a star.

Now Sherman turned the gyro and set the *Jove*'s jet against the direction of her flight. He fed water into the reactor, but now not frugally. The *Jove* slammed hard at the sudden force, but her skeleton held, and she slowed.

Slowly, then, she began truly to fall.

He let her fall, while the chronometer ticked around and around, and then he turned the jet toward Earth and—ignoring the lateral motion of the ship—fought against the implacable pull of gravity.

The *Jove* drifted Earthward like a bubble floating on the wind.

He kept tight control on the flow of water to the reactor. He couldn't waste a drop. He watched the acceleration gauge and held the jet to a steady one-grav drive.

If he had figured everything right, the *Jove* was falling slowly—not too slowly, but slowly enough—toward the watery, open spread of the Pacific.

He didn't *know*, though. He couldn't be sure. The *Jove* was sealed, and there was no way of seeing out.

But she *had* to hit water, he didn't care where she hit, so long as she hit water. The *Jove* didn't have the precision control that would make a normal grounding possible. It would be suicide to try bringing her down on land. Only water offered hope. Only water could absorb enough of the shock when the *Jove* hit that it would not be smashed into junk.

Then the tank went dry. The jet surged, faltered, and ceased. The *Jove* fell free.

Sherman braced himself. All bets were off.

He had time to think about the men in the ship with him: twenty-one lives.

They had trusted him to bring them down alive. They had gambled on his ability. But he wasn't good enough. He'd failed.

He wondered what they were thinking—they at the other end of the empty shell, their backs against the thick lead shield of the reactor. He wondered what they were thinking in their last moments of life.

At the last moment, he remembered to relax. You had a better chance if you relaxed.

Then the *Jove* hit.

Joe Webber cooled his heels at the rocket field. His courtesy card had got him a ticket, but the rocket to Tahiti was full up and he couldn't get a berth. Unless there was a cancellation—and that didn't happen often with rockets—he'd have to wait for the Hawaii rocket. And the Hawaii rocket wouldn't lift for another ten hours.

At forty-five minutes to shiplift, Webber checked again at the reservations counter. The girl told him there wouldn't be any cancellations.

"I'm sorry," she said. She was pretty and black-haired, and she looked like she really meant it.

"I've got to be in that rocket," Webber insisted. "Look—I'll take the shiplift on a deckplate. It won't be the first time I've done it. I'll even pay fare if I have to."

"I'm sorry," she said again. "It's against the company's regulations. And there's the matter of weight."

He told her what she could do with company regulations. "Let's see the weight schedule," he demanded.

"I don't have it," she said. She wasn't apologetic now. She was stiff and pale and trembling angrily.

"Get it," Webber snapped.

"Just who do you think you are!" she flared.

"I'm a spaceman," Webber said. He made it sound as if that fact gave him a right to anything he wanted. "I was going to space before you wet your first pair of diapers. Now let's see that schedule."

"There's no place for you in the rocket," she insisted firmly.

Joe Webber stepped back from the counter. "How much do you think I weigh?"

The question was totally unexpected. The girl looked down at the small, profane, blond man. He was shorter than she was, and she was not tall. If it wasn't for the bitter maturity of his face, she might have thought he was a boy.

"A hundred forty pounds?" she hazarded.

"A hundred twenty-five," Webber told her. "And no baggage. You can squeeze that much aboard any ship that can lift."

The girl's mouth turned stubborn-mad. She picked up a hand phone from the narrow ledge behind the counter. It had a hush filter built into it, so Webber couldn't hear what she said, but there was a sharp, barbed quality to the way she said it.

He felt a burn of satisfaction. Maybe now he'd get a little action.

A door in the wall back of the counter opened. A man came out. He wasn't a tall man, but he was taller than the girl.

He wore the uniform of an Intercontinental Rockets pilot. "What's the trouble, Millie?" he asked.

Then he saw Webber. "Why, Joe!" he exclaimed. He came over and stuck out his hand. "Joe, you old bird-man. How are you!"

"You're still with this bunch of thieves?" Webber demanded.

The man decided to take it as a joke. "It's a living I know," he said deprecatingly. "And if you don't think too much about it, it's just like the old days. You even get a look at the stars—I mean, the way they really are. They don't look the same, down here."

"No. They don't," Joe Webber said. He smiled. He was as good as in that rocket now.

Around the world, aircraft traffic monitor stations watched the *Jove*'s descent on their screens. They watched it ellipse through the fringe of atmosphere, loop out into space, come back again. Each time, it was a little deeper, a little less swift, until it hardly left the atmosphere at all. And then it slowed, and it began to fall.

The stations tracked it halfway around the world. It

fell slowly—almost balloonlike—on a spiral that would intersect the surface of Earth somewhere west of the Americas. When it passed over the African coast, it was only sixty-five miles up. Singapore reported it at forty miles. Rabaul saw it down to thirty-five. The Christmas Island station lost it below the horizon.

The Trans-Pacific watch-ship failed to pick it up.

It had been very low over Christmas Island. The news went around the world that the *Jove* was down.

Fleets of search planes left Papeete and Hawaii hours before dawn. They were slow, lumbering craft, aptly fit for their purpose. They would arrive in the area where the *Jove* went down not long after sunrise.

Joe Webber had hated Intercontinental Rockets ever since the company got its weather observation contract. He had worked for the company for the several years since his retirement, mandatory at 35, from the Space Service (space flight was a young man's game, they said) but he quit when the contract was signed.

He knew what it meant. Weather observation was one of the functions of Orbitbase—the only one of any Earthbound importance.

It meant the end of space flight.

Less than a year from the day the contract was signed, Orbitbase had been abandoned. The last shuttle was on the scrap heap, and the last man had collected his pay and vanished into history. Space flight was dead.

But just now Webber didn't hate the company, because it got him to Tahiti.

It was shortly after dawn. The air was cool and the sky was pale blue and clear when Webber rode the baggage cart in from the field with the rest of the passengers.

In the terminal building, he paused at the newsstand. Bold headlines boasted their news to him. The *Jove* was down. He snatched up a paper and tossed the attendant the first coin that came to his fingers.

He read as he walked, and he didn't watch where he walked. He let the flow of the crowd carry him along.

As he read, one thought stood out in his mind above everything else. Rog had done it. He had brought the *Jove* down. She hadn't burned up.

29

He read about the search that had started.

When he looked up, he was on the copter platz, on the other side of the terminal building from the rocket field.

He climbed into a cab. The copter lifted. "Where?" the driver asked.

"The Air-Sea Rescue station," Webber snapped. "Where else?"

There would be newsmen there. Lots of them—and nothing on their minds but space flight.

They would listen to him while they waited for the *Jove* to be found. And he would be there when the search planes found the *Jove*.

Handled right, the story of the *Jove* would do everything he had wanted to do for four bleak years.

Because the *Jove* had gone to the limits of the far frontier, and had returned to tell the tale. It had put men's feet on the moons of the monster of planets.

Told right, that story would make people think about space flight again. And he could tell them—and make them believe—that space flight wasn't something dead and finished, but something barely begun—and he would make them realize that the destiny of Man was not only the planets, but the stars.

He could do it—now that the *Jove* had come back, now that America would think about space flight again.

The water lifted him, and let him fall.

And lifted him.

And let him fall.

Miraculously, he was alive.

Buoyed up just enough by the airspace in the helmet and the torso of his pressure suit, he floated with his tight-sheathed limbs trailed downward in the water like sea anchors. The keelweight of the oxy-bottles on his back kept his face turned up to the star-spattered sky.

The night was dark and cloudless, but the stars looked wrong. In space, they would be sharp as pinpricks, hot as rage, and dusted across the heavens like chips of a shattered diamond.

Down here, most of them were blotted out, and the ones you could see were sick little gleams, lifeless, and they flickered like candles about to go out.

He couldn't remember much of what happened when

the *Jove* hit. It had all been too fast. There was shock and tumult, pain and blackness. That was all he remembered. When he came out of it, he was alone in the water.

Above him, the stars moved slowly in their tantalizing, astronomical procession. Hours passed, while softly his helmet radio crashed and whispered.

He had kept his radio when the others jettisoned theirs, in the vague hope it would help searchers find them after they were down. The set didn't have much power, but maybe it was possible.

And the others had to be somewhere nearby.

He hoped they were all right.

His legs twinged faintly, naggingly, each time the water lifted him—each time the water let him fall. They were useless. He couldn't move them. He tried not to wonder what was wrong with them.

For the moment, he was all right.

But, when the air in his oxy-bottles gave out, he would have to take off his helmet to breathe. His suit's weight would sink him like a stone. He would have to get out of it quickly, or drown.

He didn't know if he could peel the pressure sheaths off his useless legs.

So he tried not to think about it. He watched the slow procession of the stars. A wave crested over him. Water sluiced down over his face. It blotted out the sight of the stars.

The water lifted him and let him fall. It was a drowsing rhythm, and he was weary to death. He dozed in the pulse of the sea.

The bloody sun inched up from the horizon. Sherman watched.

He hadn't seen the dawn for seven years.

The sea spread smooth as far as he could see. There was no sign of the others. No sign of the *Jove*—not even a scrap of wreckage. And no sign of land. He was alone.

He wondered what had happened to the others. He wondered why he couldn't see them. He hoped they were all right.

He wondered where they were.

"Hello, the *Jove!*"

31

His radio spoke.

"Hello, the *Jove*," the voice repeated exactly. "Do you receive us?"

"Who's that?" His throat was thick with thirst, and his voice was a croak. "I hear you."

"Hello, the *Jove*," the voice said maddeningly. "We understand your radio is set to this frequency. We are listening for your signals. Do you receive us?"

"I hear you plain," Sherman managed, nettled. "What's the matter? Can't you hear me?"

". . . This is the search plane *Hula Fanny*, International Air-Sea Rescue Service. We are listening for your signals. Do you receive us? Hello, the *Jove*. Hello, the *Jove* . . ."

Sherman searched the sky. It was almost cloudless—a high, thin cirrus misted the stratosphere. He searched up and down, all around the horizon, but saw nothing. Once he thought he saw the plane, but when he looked again it was only a bird.

The plane would have to come nearer, he decided, before his small transmitter could reach it.

His oxygen meter said he had three and a half hours' oxygen.

He watched his helmet's small time-dial. Every two minutes, he spoke into the voice-automatic transmitter. He couldn't know if the search plane would come close enough to get his signals, but if it did he wanted to be sure it heard him.

It seemed a long time—though the time-dial said it wasn't—before the search plane's message changed.

"We are receiving you," the voice said suddenly. "We are receiving you. Keep transmitting. We receive you."

Then it hesitated. "You *are* the *Jove*, aren't you?"

"Roger Sherman, pilot of the *Jove*," Sherman said. It was getting easier to talk, though it hurt his dry throat. "I'm in the water. My ship broke up when she hit."

"You're what we're looking for," the voice decided. "Where are you? Can you see us?"

Sherman searched the sky again. It was empty. "I don't see you," he said.

"All right—hold on and we'll put a radio fix on you. Keep transmitting."

"Have you picked up any of the others?" Sherman wanted to know.

"No. Aren't they with you?"

"I haven't seen them since we hit," Sherman said. "They must be in the water somewhere near me, but I haven't seen them. They don't have radios in their suits —we took them out to cut weight. Look for them, will you?"

"That's what we're paid for," the man in the search plane said. "Don't you worry. If they're afloat, we'll find them. Keep transmitting. We are getting a fix on you."

At the Air-Sea Rescue Station, the copter settled on the gravel in front of the operations building. Webber handed the driver a wad without stopping to count it.

He slipped out, a poised little cat of a man. The copter lifted and windmilled off across the bay.

Webber's feet scattered gravel as he approached the operations building.

Inside, out of the morning's brightness, he had to pause to let his eyes adjust before he could find his way. The halls were deserted, and there were no signs to point the way, but he had no trouble finding the plot room.

It was in the center of the building. It was a large room. One of the long walls was a translucent plotting map of the area the station served.

In the northwest sector, a red line circled the area where the *Jove* had most likely gone down. Imperceptibly slow, a wide-winged formation of green dots approached it. The search had started.

On the floor, facing the map, men wearing radio-monitor helmets sat at consoles. They were silent and engrossed, their minds hundreds of miles away, keeping contact with the search planes.

A balding, plump, part-Oriental man patrolled the room, pausing first at one console and then at another. He smoked a large pipe. He spotted Webber and came over.

"Who are you?" he asked. "What are you doing here?"

"I'm Joe Webber," Webber said. "You're looking for some friends of mine."

The plump man glanced back uncertainly at the plot-map.

"That's right, Jack," Webber said.

"You may wait with the newsmen in the gallery," the plump man decided. "I am sure you do not want to interrupt our work."

Joe Webber nodded agreeably. Getting put with the newsmen was just fine with him.

For the first time in years, people were thinking of space flight again. Maybe they wondered what it was like. Maybe they even felt a little uncomfortable because the *Jove* had crashed, and because it was their elected representatives who had knifed space flight, which was why the *Jove* had crashed.

With a little of the right kind of working on, maybe they'd back space flight again.

And newsmen were the people to start with. Get them in the right mood and feed them the right kind of news and they would do most of the work for you.

They would be like a direct wire from you to the people. And from the people it would go to Congress, and from there . . .

Well, anyway, the planets. Maybe someday the stars.

The gallery was a glassed-in balcony that looked across the room at the plotting map. It was crowded. Every seat had a reporter in it. More reporters sat on the aisle steps, or stood, pressed together, in the space behind the last row of seats.

The place was full of cigarette smoke. For a moment, Joe Webber didn't want to go in. The stink of wasted air rankled his keen spaceman's sense of fitness.

But he took a deep breath and pushed into the mob. He elbowed and burrowed through the mess, and finally got to a place where he could see the map.

The man he was crowded against noticed him for a newcomer. "Who're you with?" he asked, bored.

"Space Flight Associates," Webber said.

The newsman looked puzzled. "What's that?" he wondered.

Webber snapped his eyes up at him. He was young, thin, and droop-shouldered. "Kid," he said, "you're new in this game."

The man on Webber's other side spoke up. "It's an outfit you couldn't help but hear about a few years back," he said. "Very noisy. Never did hear what happened to it. It was an American lobby and publicity outfit to promote space flight—a bunch of old spacemen who got hopping mad when the American Congress voted down the space flight appropriation for the '93-'94 fiscal year."

Someone behind Webber leaned forward. "Say—you're Webber, aren't you," he suspected.

"That's me," Webber said.

He was quick to sniff a bit of news, maybe. "What brings you here?" he asked.

Webber was aware that a lot of hands suddenly had open notebooks in them. He nodded at the operations map. "Those are friends of mine out there."

Faces were turned toward him from all directions. "Care to make a statement?" someone invited.

Webber almost jumped at the chance, but stopped himself. Some inner sense warned him to take it slow. It would be bad to look eager. He had waited a long time for a break like this, and now that it had come he had to use it just right.

He shook his head. "I'm not here on business," he said, watching the operations map. "I just hope they find them, that's all."

On the map, the search planes were going into the critical area. There was no sign of anything happening yet.

"Think there's much chance they lived through it?" someone asked.

"Rog is a good pilot," Webber said uneasily.

"Who?"

"Rog Sherman," Webber said. "He's the boy who jockeyed her down. If anyone could bring them through it, he's the man. But . . ."

He shrugged. "It's a tough assignment," he admitted. "He's already done more than I thought any man could."

Step number one. Give them a hero.

"These death watches bore hell out of me," a grim old veteran muttered, hands in pockets.

35

The plane finally came in sight. It was tiny, far off, and close to the horizon. For a moment, Sherman thought it was a bird.

Then he knew it was a plane. Sun glinted on it. "I can see you," he said.

"What's our bearing?" the man in the plane wanted to know.

But the plane was too far away. It didn't seem to move. The surging water under him made it impossible to be sure.

But, minutes later, it was perceptibly larger, and he could see it move.

"You're coming at me," Sherman said. He watched it with a practiced eye. "Just a couple points off."

"Talk us down," the radio voice said. "We'll pick you up."

"Circle," Sherman said. "Look for the others. I can wait."

"Don't be a fool, man. Talk us down. We can hunt for them after we've got you aboard."

The plane was still coming toward him. It was crabbing into the wind. Sherman estimated the wind and the plane's speed, and ordered a series of course changes that would land the plane into the wind and put the plane near him at the end of its run.

The man on the radio hadn't expected anything so complicated. He boggled.

"Are you sure of those figures?"

"Just do as I say," Sherman said.

After a silence, the man on the radio said, "Let's have those figures again."

The plane had passed the first course change point. Sherman figured a new set of courses and recited them slowly enough for the man in the plane to write them down.

The plane made the first turn. It was exactly right in time and bearing, and the changes to follow checked out. Sherman grinned. It wasn't half as tricky as conning a space ship.

The plane passed over him, a hundred yards to the left. It was big and slow, with high wings and tail. Four massive engines pulled it through the air. Its body had a pontoon bottom. Windows glinted brightly on its flanks.

"We see you," the man in the plane said abruptly. "Or somebody. Have you got some kind of suit on?—red above the waist, and the rest of it blue?"

"Those are my colors," Sherman acknowledged.

"How about that helmet—how can you see through it? It looks like a mirror from here."

"Some light gets through—enough," Sherman said. "If it wasn't made like that, the sun'd broil your brains in about five seconds."

The plane reached the end of the dogleg, rose slightly, and turned. Coming toward him, headed into the wind, it began to settle.

It skimmed the water. Its pontoon body cut through wave crests. It cut a trough in the water and breasted into it. Water foamed around it, and then it was placid among the waves.

It taxied toward him, but it veered off course. "Bear to ten o'clock," Sherman ordered. But the plane didn't turn.

"Don't fret yourself," the radio man said. "We don't want to run you down."

When it was abreast of him, a hundred yards off, it stopped. The engines idled. It settled deeper in the water.

A hatch opened under the wing. A boat was swung out and launched. Men piled into it. It cut the water toward him.

A man stood up in the prow. He hefted a coil of rope, swinging it, ready to throw. Sherman waved, and the man's eyes were right on him.

When the boat was close enough, the man hurled the rope. Sherman watched it uncoil toward him. It dropped in the water a few feet from him, floating. He reached out and grabbed it.

It was hard to hold on to because of the thick gloves of his pressure suit. He wound it around his hand and closed his fist on it.

The man in the boat hauled on the rope. The boat maneuvered broadside to Sherman, and men reached over the side to grab his arms. Their mouths moved—they seemed to be saying something, but through his helmet Sherman couldn't hear.

They hauled him up. When they had him half out of

37

the water, they bent him over the gunwale and began to drag him into the boat. He felt a warning twinge in his legs.

"Hold up a minute!" he shouted. "Stop!"

They didn't hear him. They dragged him into the boat. His legs turned to fire.

He screamed, but still they didn't hear. Somebody grabbed his legs and wrestled them over the gunwale. They tumbled him to the floor of the boat. He screamed and screamed. They didn't hear.

He woke with the drone of engines in his ears. It had been in his ears a long time before he was conscious of it, and his body felt with a spaceman's fine sensitivity the minute dip and lift of a plane in flight.

He opened his eyes. He was lying on his back, flat, and a man stood over him. A middle-aged man with old-fashioned glasses and a long, solemn face.

The light was strong, but it didn't hurt his eyes. The doctor glanced down. "You're awake," he noticed. "Good."

He moved down toward Sherman's feet. Sherman couldn't see his feet: the sheet that was spread over him was propped up like a tent over his legs.

The doctor reached out—did something. "Feel anything?" he asked.

Sherman shook his head. "I don't feel a thing."

His legs felt like wet clay—there was no feeling in them. He tried to push himself up, to see, but a thick strap across his chest held him down.

"It's a local anesthetic," the doctor said. "Just relax. You're going to be all right."

The doctor was still down near his feet, doing something. Sherman couldn't see what. "You're a very lucky man," the doctor said. "Lucky to be alive, I mean."

"What about the others?" Sherman wanted to know. "Have they been picked up yet?"

The doctor shrugged, not pausing at his work. "Don't know," he admitted. "Haven't heard."

He went on doing whatever he was doing.

The plane came levelly down from the sky until it touched the water. It paused then, and turned, and taxied across the smooth bay toward the station.

Impatiently pacing, Joe Webber waited in the cluster of newsmen near the ambulance. He watched the plane come toward them. The bright noon sunlight made him squint.

The announcement had said only that one man had been picked up. No name was given, nor had it been said whether or not he was injured.

As it approached the concrete ramp that sloped up out of the water, the plane slowed. Carefully, it nosed up to a yellow flag that stuck up out of the water. Then it gunned its engines and rolled up the ramp on a dolly that cradled its body.

Slowly, it trundled across the concrete field.

The ambulance spurred out to meet it. The reporters yelped and set out in pursuit. Their shirttails flapped in the air.

Joe Webber tried to keep up with them, but his short legs were a handicap. He lost ground steadily.

The ambulance pulled up under the plane's wing. Its panel side opened and two men bounded out with a basket stretcher. The big hatch in the plane's side opened and they climbed in.

The reporters arrived and surrounded the opening. A man appeared in the opening and blocked the way. They shouted questions at him. He shook his head, refusing to answer.

By the time Webber reached the scene, a squad of watchmen had arrived. They cleared an aisle through the mob of reporters between the plane and the ambulance. They were handing the stretcher through the opening when Webber got there.

He squeezed and elbowed his way through the crowded newsmen to the line held by the watchmen. He watched as the stretcher was carried past.

The newsmen were shouting. "Who is it?" they yelled. "Who is it?"

The men handling the stretcher said nothing. They trudged slowly along the aisle the watchmen had cleared.

The man in the stretcher was almost too big for it, and

he was thickly bundled. Only his face showed. It was a rough-hewn, big-boned and pockmarked face. He was either asleep or unconscious.

Webber ducked under the watchmen's arms and stepped out into the aisle. "It's Rog Sherman," he said loudly.

They all know who Sherman was. He didn't have to say any more.

A tall, solemn man in white climbed down out of the plane. He carried a black satchel. His whites were bloodstained.

"Are you a friend of his?" he asked gravely.

"Yeah," Webber said. "I know him."

"Good," the tall man said. "He will need a friend."

"I can imagine," Webber said. "After the deal he's had."

He was careful to say it loud enough for the newsmen to hear.

"Yes," said the doctor.

The ambulance orderlies loaded Sherman into the ambulance. They climbed in themselves. The doctor joined them.

Webber started to get in, too. The doctor leaned out. "I am sorry," he apologized. "There is no room for you. You will come to the hospital?"

Webber hesitated. "What about the rest of them?"

"His companions?" The doctor cocked his head. "I have not heard. I presume they are still being looked for."

"They haven't been found?"

The doctor looked helpless. "I've heard nothing."

Webber accepted it. He stepped back from the ambulance. The orderlies leaned over and pulled down the panel, and the lower panel rose up to meet it and lock. The ambulance crawled out from under the plane's wing, unfurled its rotors, and lifted. It windmilled out across the bay.

A tractor hooked onto the seaplane's dolly and towed it off toward the hangars. The watchmen climbed into their car and drove away. Webber faced the newsmen alone.

Their first question came quickly. "Are you sure it's Sherman?"

Webber nodded. "The rest were all little guys," he said. "He had a tough time to make spaceman's rating with that hulk of his. You've got to be something special when you're that big. But you've seen the kind of pilot he is. There isn't another man living who could have brought the *Jove* down."

It was all true, and he could see they were impressed.

It was a dirty trick to pull on Rog, though, to make a hero of him. But it had to be done.

He smiled at the newsmen. Mentally, he rubbed his palms together.

He had them all to himself.

When Sherman woke again, he was in bed, in a room with drawn shades on the windows. In a corner, a nurse sat watching him.

He tried to prop up on his elbows. He couldn't make it. The nurse got up quickly and came over to the bed.

"Lie back," she said softly, touching his shoulder with a gentle pressure. "Lie back. Rest. You're going to be all right."

Her words relaxed him. He was very tired.

But then he remembered. "Have they found the others?" he asked.

"Don't try to talk," she told him gently.

"Have they found the others?" he repeated insistently. Again he tried to rise.

She shook her head. "I don't know. There hasn't been anything in the papers yet."

"Will you find out?" he pleaded, slumping back on the pillow. "Will you find out for me?"

"If I can," she said kindly.

"Please. I've got to know."

The nurse crossed over to a small stand against the far wall. She took the lid off an enamel pan—took out a syringe, took out something else, and came back.

Sherman looked at the needle. "What's that for?" he asked.

"Something to make you sleep," the nurse said honestly, face grave. She took his arm and wiped it with an alcohol swab.

Sherman tried to push her hand away—the hand with the needle in it. "I don't want to sleep," he said.

41

"You need rest," she said, gently firm. She drove the needle into the sterilized patch on his arm, and emptied it.

"Get a good sleep, spaceman," she said.

He slept.

Webber didn't get in to see Sherman. They told him Sherman was sleeping, and that he would be able to see no one for at least several days—that as soon as it was possible, he would be notified.

Webber accepted it. He didn't care how long he had to wait, so long as he could talk to Rog before the newsmen got at him. He went back to the Search and Rescue station to wait for news of the others.

He couldn't understand why they hadn't been found.

They should have been in the water near Sherman. They should have been picked up.

But he watched the search planes come in, long after dark. They hadn't found a thing. Another day passed, and still they found nothing.

He heard that ships were also patrolling the area where Sherman was found. But there wasn't a trace of the men who were with him.

He got very little sleep. He didn't shave. He drank coffee and ate sandwiches, and called the hospital every hour.

And he talked to the newsmen. He filled them full of stories of the old days—stories of space flight, and Mars, Mercury, Orbitbase, and the moon.

Stories that made good telling. Stories which, repeated, would stir young blood.

Often as not, the way Joe Webber told them, they were about Rog Sherman.

Finally, news came. But it wasn't news of the men of the *Jove*. It was about the *Jove* herself.

The *Jove* had been found.

It was humiliating to be spoon-fed like a baby, by a girl. But Sherman had to endure it. He hadn't the strength to sit up. He couldn't feed himself.

He lost track of time. He slept a lot, and when he woke he did not know if it was afternoon or morning.

Sometimes it was dark and the hospital sounds were softer. He lost count of the days.

But the day came when they propped him up with pillows and he could look down at himself on the bed.

Under the white sheet, his left leg was a round mound like the burrow of a giant mole, down to the tent-peak of his foot. But his right leg wasn't there.

He lifted the sheet and looked. The half-thigh stump was swathed in bandage. It looked oddly like a head with a bandage on it.

He looked at it, and wondered why he felt no more emotion than he did. But the fact he had lost a leg meant strangely little to him. As if it was someone else's leg that was gone.

He hoped the others were all right. He wished he could find someone who knew something about them.

That night, his stump began hurting. He didn't sleep at all, and he had a bad time of it all the next day.

There was someone to see him, they said. He scratched his itching stump through the bandage and said to let him in. It might be someone who could tell him what had happened to the men who had been in the *Jove* with him.

His visitor was a small man. He had pale blond hair, and he looked like a boy except for the lines and the hardness on his face. At first Sherman didn't recognize him.

"Hi, Rog," he said, and then Sherman knew him. Joe Webber.

"How've you been?" Webber smiled.

"All right," Sherman lied. The pain in his stump had flamed for two days, defying all the drugs the doctors permitted him. Then it faded slowly, leaving him weak and exhausted.

He saw Webber's glance at the flat sheet where his leg should have been.

"Yeah," he said carelessly. He shrugged. "I don't miss it."

Webber wet his lips. Uncomfortable, he hadn't a thing to say.

"Joe," Sherman blurted. "What happened to the boys?"

Webber's face stayed the same. He did not speak.

"Doesn't *anybody* know?" Sherman cried.

Webber went over to the wall and brought back a chair. He straddled it, folded his arms on the backrest, and rested his chin on them.

"They didn't make it," he said, looking at the wall beyond Sherman.

"They're dead?" Sherman murmured unbelievingly.

"All of them, Rog."

"They can't be dead," he protested. He felt wretchedly sick. "*I* got out all right."

Webber shook his head. "You were lucky, Rog. Damn lucky," he said. "I saw the pictures they took of her. She's on the bottom, and she's smashed to hell, and everybody but you was trapped inside."

Doggedly, he had to argue. "They had their suits on. They could breathe," he cried despairingly.

"Rog," Webber said harshly. "They're dead. Don't fight it."

"But . . ." He wanted to cry.

"She's two miles down," Webber said. "The pressure killed them."

A terrible heaviness filled Sherman. "I told them I wasn't good enough," he complained. "I warned them."

"You were good enough," Webber said. "And you had to do it, didn't you?"

"Well, we . . ."

"You could have sat up there and starved to death, if your air didn't give out first," Webber snarled. "Look— you want to know who's really to blame? It's the people who killed space flight. The politicians in Washington. They're the ones who made you do it."

He was right. They were the ones to blame. It burst on Sherman's thoughts like the blaze of the unfiltered sun.

"God damn them," he said angrily. Purpose firmed in him. "They'll hear about it," he promised.

"No, Rog—no," Webber said quickly. "There's something more important than that."

"What's more important than . . . ?"

"Space flight's more important," Webber said quietly.

Sherman was baffled speechless. There wasn't any connection. And anyway, space flight was dead.

"Listen," Webber said. "I've been trying to put us back in business for four whole years."

He told Sherman all about Space Flight Associates, and all he had tried to do.

"I couldn't get people to listen to me," he said. "That's what I want you for."

"What can I do?" Sherman wondered. It sounded hopeless to him. "Sure, I want space flight as bad as you do, only . . ."

"You can tell them the things I tried to tell them," Webber said. "They'll listen to you."

"Why me?" Sherman wondered. He felt horribly inadequate. "I mean, who am I? I . . ."

"You're the perfect picture of a guy who was wronged," Webber said. He smiled wryly. "You got put on the spot and you did everything you could, but the luck was against you. That puts a lot of people on your side. If anyone can talk them into backing space flight again, you're the guy who can do it."

"Joe," Sherman said. "I'm with you. If you think I can swing it, I'll try. But the first thing I'm going to say . . ."

His voice turned angry, and his face turned hard.

"Rog—no." Webber pleaded. "You don't get people on your side if you call them sons of bitches. I found that out. I was mad when they killed space flight. I was damn mad, and I didn't care much how I said it. We're not going to make that mistake again. If I have to cut your throat, we're not going to make that mistake again."

"We were forgotten," Sherman said bitterly. "They left us up there and we had to get down by ourselves. Well, I'm *not* forgetting, and I'm not letting them forget, either."

"Rog—listen to me," Webber begged. "If space flight means anything to you—believe me, I *know*."

Sherman's face looked like something hammered out of stone. "We went out there—farther than anyone went before," he said bitterly. "Do you think we did it for fun? Do you think we did it for ourselves?"

45

"You did it for space flight," Webber said. "It was the way you had to go."

"No," Sherman said, bite-lipped. "We did it for *them*. For *people*. Because it's the way people have to go, and we had to blaze the trail."

His fist tightened on the edge of his sheet. "And then we came home, and they hadn't even cared enough to remember us!"

Whipped, sullen, Webber watched them get Sherman ready for the press conference. They helped Sherman into a robe and lifted him into a wheelchair. He was surly and awkward, learning for the first time how handicapped he was without his leg.

When Sherman was ready, Webber brushed the attendants aside and took charge of the wheelchair himself.

"Rog—will you listen?" he pleaded. "Look—you can't do anything for them. They're dead. But you can do something for what they believed in. That makes sense, doesn't it? *Doesn't* it?"

Sherman did not speak. His big hands gripped the wheelchair's armrests, and he looked stiffly straight ahead.

Webber wheeled the chair slowly along the corridor. The corridor was clean, well lighted, and the walls were glazed white tile. The place smelled of harsh soap.

The one thing he hadn't expected was that Rog might not cooperate. Walking along the corridor, he thought suddenly of men walking to their execution, and he knew he was walking to his—to the death of everything he had believed in and labored for.

The press conference was in the old part of the hospital, in an operating theatre long out of use. As they approached, Webber made a last, desperate appeal.

"Rog," he pleaded. "For the last time . . ."

Sherman's square-shouldered body did not move. Webber might as well have been talking to stone.

"No," Sherman said.

And then they were at the door, and the door swung open to let them through. The newsmen were already there, waiting, sitting in the seats of the steep-tiered gallery, smoking. Webber's nose twitched at the smell of tobacco. Grimly, he hunched his shoulders and went in.

He trundled Sherman into the center of the theatre, turned him to face the reporters, and stepped up beside him.

"Gentlemen," he announced. "Roger Sherman, astrogator-pilot and only survivor of the First Jupiter Expedition. He has just been appointed vice-president of Space Flight Associates, and he will be working closely with me for the advancement of space flight.

"As a memorial to his companions," Webber went on, "when the first ship of the second age of space flight lifts from Earth—that ship will be named the *Jove*."

Then, because he had to—because they didn't care much what he said, only cared about Sherman—Webber stepped aside. He had played his last, futile card. He had done all he could. He couldn't do any more.

"Gentlemen," he said. "Roger Sherman."

In his wheelchair, Sherman straightened his body and squared his shoulders. He gripped the armrests.

"Before you ask any questions," he said, looking up at the gallery with agate-hard eyes, "I've something I want to say."

He had a perfect speaking voice. It was just the right kind of voice to go with his hewn-rock face and bull-muscled body.

"Twenty-one men are dead because there was no atmosphere shuttle to meet us at Orbitbase. They were my friends. I did all I could for them, and I almost made it. But I didn't."

His voice rang to the skylight with superbly controlled rage. "They died because the American Congress forgot us—because Congress killed space flight and sold all the shuttles for junk. That Congress, and every man and woman who voted it into office, is responsible for the death of my friends."

He paused. He looked up at the gallery unflinchingly, like a gladiator damning the mob.

"Any questions?" he asked.

Mask-faced, shiny-eyed, Joe Webber climbed the steep stairs toward the empty seats on the top tier of the gallery. The hero he had made had spoken.

God damn you, Rog, he thought. God damn you. If I have to fight you too I'll fight you too.

Because we're going back. We're going back, I don't-care-how-long-it-takes, we're going back . . . out there . . . next time . . .

Joe Webber, climbing, his small, catlike body tightly controlled, deliberate, his gray-green eyes fixed straight ahead, seeing nothing.

Except—

The stars.

PART THREE

In Washington, D. C., nestled in an airshaft-windowed suite in a building which, in its time, had seen almost everything except its now not very distant condemnation, the office of Space Flight Associates (Jos. Webber, pres.) was a meticulously kept-clean example of proud, honest poverty.

Framed Kodachromes hung on the walls. The flag raising on the moon. The sand-and-blood red dunes of Mars. A Venus dragon, photographed in a moment of repellent savagery.

Relics of a memory—of a time now gone, perhaps forever.

Mrs. Crowder, the thin, gray-haired receptionist, sat at her switchboard-desk combination, mending a shirt. Just inside the door a well-worn leather chair slowly collected its daily ration of dust. Beside it, on a low table, was displayed a dentist's office collection of much-thumbed, outdated magazines.

Most of them, somewhere on their covers, proclaimed their inclusion of articles such as, "American Tragedy: the Death of Space Flight" and, "Should we go back to the Moon?"

And the few that didn't announce them on the covers nevertheless had something inside. They were neatly arranged, like a tray of food set out for a party to which nobody came.

Into this scene strolled Andrew Perrault. He was a longshanked, mournful-faced man with a rambling walk, large hands, and lumpy pockets. He crossed to the door of the inner office with a stiff, high-nosed aplomb, as if it was the way to the men's room.

The short-skirted young redhead tagged close behind

49

him. With quick curiosity, her glance darted into every corner of the room—everywhere except the way she was going.

Mrs. Crowder tried to intercept them. "Do you have an appointment?" she asked nervously. She moved mincingly, like a bird.

"Kindly step out of the way, madame," Perrault intoned. "I have business with Mr. Webber—a very grave matter concerning my daughter's honor."

Shocked wordless, Mrs. Crowder backed up a step. Perrault strode on unhindered.

The redhead, as she marched past Mrs. Crowder, nodded perkily. "Scout's honor," she confided.

Perrault reached for the doorknob to the inner sanctum. But the door slammed open before he touched it, and the small blond man stood in the doorway.

"Drew!" the little man exclaimed gladly. "You sonovabitch!"

Perrault stood half again the small man's height. "Your language," he scolded. "In the presence of ladies!"

"Huh? Oh, she's used to it," Webber said, nodding negligently at Mrs. Crowder.

Perrault drew himself up to full stature. "Sir!" he said gravely, "I was referring to my daughter—I think." He smiled lopsidedly. "Kiss your Uncle Joe, Martha."

The redhead slipped past him with an impish gleam in her eye and complied with enthusiasm.

"I said your *Uncle* Joe," Perrault said severely.

Martha Perrault released Webber for a moment. "Oh, Dad," she complained. "You take all the fun out of things." She kissed Webber again, taking her time about it to be sure she did the job thoroughly.

She let him go, finally. He propelled her into his office with a swat on the bottom which she enjoyed with a delighted squeal. He invited Perrault inside with a more formal gesture.

Then he motioned to his receptionist. "Class A calls only, Mrs. Crowder," he instructed. He closed the door.

He walked back to his desk with his visitors one on either side of him. "Young lady," he scolded with cold self-control. "I was kicking rocks on the moon while you were still in diapers."

"Oh, pooh," she said saucily. "I like experienced men."

Webber sat in his chair with an exasperated sigh. Martha sat on his desk, managing to expose almost all of her legs, and tried to muss his short-cropped hair.

"What are you going to do with her?" Webber asked helplessly.

"I've thought of chaining her to a tree or something," Perrault drawled. "But some damn fool would be sure to come along and turn her loose."

"Quit that, you hellion!" Webber yelled.

Somehow, Martha had contrived to slip off the desk into his lap. She was kissing him again.

She got up with unruffled poise and handed him a handkerchief which she took from somewhere inside her sleeveless blouse. "Here—wipe your mouth."

Webber wadded the handkerchief and wiped his lips vigorously. Martha snatched it back and returned it to its hiding place with a hearty immodesty.

Perrault had dragged over a large armchair and sprawled in it. Martha perched on its arm. Her short skirt hitched up dangerously. She examined the exposure critically, but did not try to rearrange things.

Well, she *was* pretty.

Joe Webber tried to ignore her. It took a lot of effort. "What's with the pill and bandage business?" he asked. "What's behind you coming here—besides that little baggage?"

"I'm taller than you are!" Martha declared.

Perrault ignored her. "Business is good," he admitted clumsily. "People *will* get sick. Or else they just like how our medicines taste. Matter of fact, Doc Brent's sick himself."

"Bad?"

Perrault nodded, suddenly unhappy. Here was a thing he could not jest about. "The docs don't answer questions any more," he said glumly. "They just cuss. It's a sure sign."

"He isn't going to get well," Martha said soberly. But she had a teen-ager's characteristic incomprehension of death. It was too much a thing that happened to other people.

"I just thought—we're in the city—we'd come up and

say hello," Perrault explained awkwardly. "Find out how you're doing."

Joe Webber smiled and settled back in his chair. His green eyes glinted with pleasure. "We'll have a colony on the moon inside of two years," he announced.

"You mean it?" Perrault dared to hope. "Is it really true?"

"I've got a tame Senator," Webber said, pleased with himself. "He hasn't actually said he'll push it—yet—but I've got him sold. He'll push it, all right."

"Joe, it's . . . it's wonderful," Perrault said with feeling. "It's been too long."

"Six years too long," Webber muttered. He fiddled with the arm of his chair and avoided Perrault's eyes. "Uh . . . Drew," he said with a terrible embarrassment, "I've got a rent bill here . . ."

Perrault perked up. "May I . . . ?" he suggested hopefully. He stuck out a hand to receive it.

Webber dug the slip of paper from the bottom drawer of his desk.

It was stamped PAST DUE in ugly, bloody-red ink. Someone had scrawled nastily across the bottom, *Our next notice will be your eviction.* Its date was a week old.

Perrault pursed his lips. "And the treasury?"

"I've been rubbing two nickles together so long they feel like dimes."

Perrault's sad eyes examined him silently. "It's like that?"

Webber nodded abjectly. "Like that," he acknowledged.

Perrault rubbed his lip. He shrugged and rummaged in a pocket. He came out with a checkbook.

He leaned forward and took a pen from the holder on Webber's desk. It was dry. He looked around uncertainly.

Martha handed him a pen from inside her blouse. Perrault arched a critical brow as he accepted it.

"I haven't got pockets," she protested innocently.

Perrault scribbled a check, pausing thoughtfully before he filled in the sum. He handed it across to Webber along with the rent bill.

"Buy some ink with the change," he suggested awkwardly.

Webber held the check in both hands and looked at it. His face displayed neither disappointment nor pleasure.

"Need more?" Perrault offered quickly. He started to get out his checkbook again.

Joe Webber shook his head hastily. "This'll last me a couple of months," he said, savoring the thought as if he was already planning how he would spend it. "Maybe three if I stretch it. I'll stretch it."

He laid the check on his desk, and the rent bill on top of it.

"Joe—I've got plenty," Perrault said, plainly offering all of it. "If you need more, all you got to do is say so. If it'll bring back space flight a day sooner, spend it all in an hour. And if you're short—any time, Joe—just tell me."

"Drew—damn it. I hate to ask for money." He looked down at his soiled, frayed sleeve.

"Come on, Joe. Let's go to lunch. I'll buy."

Webber hesitated only a moment. He smiled. He got up. "What are we waiting for?"

Martha slipped off her perch. She snatched her pen out of her father's hand and returned it to the mysterious interior of her blouse. She went toward Webber with that merry look in her eye.

"Keep your distance, Marty," Webber warned, but with a sly look. "You're carrying too much hardware."

Martha laughed exuberantly and kept on coming.

Max Ryan saw the storm while it was still a long way off. It was coming on fast, borne up from the pole by the savage winds that screamed northward over the snowfields.

It was snow. A lot of it, driven with whiplike force by the wind. But it was still far off, and it looked like gray fog squashed down on the shimmering snowfield by the thick clouds piled on top of it.

Nick Fenwick and the kid, Jim Albion, saw it too. They stopped their work and raised their goggles to look at it. Then Fenwick bent over his post-hole digger again, but the boy came running across the loose top-snow.

He was somewhere just past his middle teens, and slim. But his parka made him look thick and clumsy. Ryan saw him coming, but he did not stand up from the packing box he was sitting on while he got the electro-seismographs ready.

"It's coming!" the boy shouted. "We've got to get out of here."

Ryan looked up momentarily. "I can see," he said. "We'll finish up this set of blasts. It won't get here for another twenty minutes. Maybe not for an hour. Plenty of time."

Ryan didn't stop work while he talked. He had taken off his mittens because he couldn't work with them on. His fingers were getting cold, and in a few minutes they would start to frostbite. It was that kind of country.

"But it's practically on top of us!" the boy protested.

The wind was blowing a constant sift of snow around their ankles. Ryan lifted his goggles and looked at the storm. It was bringing even heavier winds with it.

"It's a good fifteen minutes away," he said. He spindled a reel and started threading the tape through the recording inductors. "Plenty of time."

"At least you can pre-warm the engine," the boy pleaded.

Ryan clipped the tape into the receiving reel. "Change the temperature half a degree for half a second near this hardware, and you start having trouble. We'll shoot the blasts. *Then* we'll go."

Down here, where the temperature was often fifty below or lower, your equipment had to be built for the climate. It made them tricky machines, difficult to handle until you learned their peculiarities. You learned other things, too. You learned not to run home to mama every time a cloud poked up from the south.

Or any other direction.

"Go dig your hole," Ryan said.

The boy stood open-mouthed like a fish out of water. He didn't move. He stared at Ryan, dumbfounded.

"Didn't you hear me?" Ryan demanded. "We've a job to do here. Okay. So we do it. Who do you think's running this show? Us, or the country? Now get out there and dig your hole."

The boy backed off, struck dumb. Ryan rubbed warmth into his hands and settled down to his work again.

After standing there a moment while Ryan ignored him, the boy trudged back out to where he had been digging. Ryan did not watch him go. He put the cover on the recording panel and locked it in place.

Every few steps, the boy looked back over his shoulder at the gathering storm.

Martha contrived their seating so that she faced Webber across the narrow width of the table, with her father sitting at one end. When the waiter had taken their orders and gone, she laced her fingers and rested her chin on them, looking at Webber.

"I've been nice to you for a reason," she confided impishly.

"Yeah?" Webber faced her eye for eye, avoiding nothing.

"Where's Roger Sherman?" she said. "I want to meet him."

"The less I see of him, the better I like it," Webber muttered. "After the way he scuttled things . . . I had everything set just right, and *he* had to open his yap."

Martha looked hurt. "How would you feel if *you'd* been piloting the *Jove* and it was *your* friends that got killed?" she demanded.

"I don't care," Webber snapped harshly. "He should have kept his big yap shut."

Martha gripped the edge of the table in her small hands. "Please, Uncle Joe," she pleaded. "Don't hate him, please."

"I'll hate anybody that gets between me and space flight," Webber said dangerously. "I don't care who it is. What's it to you, anyway?"

"I'm going to marry him," she said simply.

From the corner of his eye, Webber saw Perrault's mouth drop open. He felt a little off keel himself. "I don't suppose he's heard about it yet," he said dryly.

Martha shook her head. "That's why you're going to introduce us," she said. "I can't tell him before I've met him, can I?"

She was dreamily silent a moment. "I think I'll seduce him," she decided.

Perrault folded his hands on the tablecloth. "Martha,

you and I are going to have a long talk," he promised. "Don't think you're too old for a bit of the hairbrush on your bare hindquarters."

She smiled charmingly. "Why Dad," she said sweetly. "Do you know?—I think I might enjoy it."

"Good lord," Perrault murmured, amazed. "I do believe you would!"

"How old are you now?" Webber asked.

"Almost eighteen," she said saucily.

"How old?" he repeated, catching a glance from Perrault.

"Well, seventeen and a half," she admitted, unashamed.

"He's thirty," Webber pointed out. "He's got a leg chopped off above the knee . . ."

"Don't talk him down to me," Martha said proudly. "Please, Uncle Joe. I really mean it."

Her earnestness was so transparent and defenseless Webber smiled. "You silly little wench," he said pityingly. "Listen—right after he came back from Jupiter and the *Jove* crashed and he had his leg chopped off, he got a hundred letters a day from dames that sounded just like you. Nutty adolescent girls that were going to take his mind off his troubles by getting in bed with him."

Martha's face was a stubborn mask. "It's not so!" she cried. "Dad—make him stop!"

"He's telling the truth, Marthie," her father said gently.

"Just listen, Marty," Webber said heartlessly. "You're pretty near a grown-up woman, girl, but you're a long way from used to it yet. You're all full of screwy ideas—most of all, sex. Well, he isn't the man for you, Marty. Not any girl. He'll ruin you. He's a sullen, no-good, self-centered son of a bitch."

"It's not like that at all," Martha protested, close to tears but too angry for tears. "Don't you see?—he's like that because he doesn't have any reason for living. He *wants* you to hate him—because of the *Jove* and . . . and everything that happened. Don't you see he can't go on like that? He's got to have someone he can talk to and . . . and love him, and babies . . ."

She stopped, inarticulate, pleading.

56

"*Yeah,*" Webber said harshly, mocking.

"Uncle Joe, you're . . . you're *filthy!*" she cried.

Webber smiled, as if it was flattery. "Yeah, I guess I am."

The waiter came with their order. As he distributed it in front of them, Martha abruptly stood up and marched off.

Perrault protested. "Martha—where are you going?"

Martha turned. "To the john, if you have to be nosy!" she shouted.

Her shoulders were stiff and square. Her back was proud. They watched her vanish.

"Shall I take her plate back?" the waiter suggested.

Perrault shook his head. "But leave the cover on," he suggested. He smiled awkwardly at Webber. "She doesn't sulk long when there's food on the table," he explained. "Only—please, Joe—don't talk Sherman at her again."

"Hell, Drew," Webber complained. "I thought I was doing you a favor."

"Oh, you were," Perrault admitted. "But you hurt her, Joe. I'd rather you didn't."

He pointed at the plate in front of Webber.

"Eat," he said.

They ate in a strained silence for several minutes. Then, abruptly, Webber spoke.

"Your outfit does a lot of institutional-type advertising, doesn't it?" he said.

"Some," Perrault mumbled. "We don't spend a fortune on it."

"There's something you're going to do for me," Webber told him. "You know what they're saying about space flight? They're saying it was money poured down a hole. Nobody made a dime off it."

"But that isn't true," Perrault argued. "If Doc Brent and me hadn't made the Venus trip, and . . . why, we wouldn't be in business. It was those bacteria cultures were brought back . . . we wouldn't be nothing!"

"Exactly," Webber said, grinning wolfishly. "Now, when that tame Senator I've got starts talking like he's going to, people've got to know that. So you're going to run a batch of ads—not just one ad in a lot of places; a lot of ads everywhere. 'The bugs we collected on Venus keep you healthy—and make millions for Brent & Perrault.' That's what you'll tell 'em."

Perrault smiled. "Sure, Joe," he promised. "We won't be that gauche about saying it—you know what I mean—but we'll tell 'em. We'd do anything to help you, Joe. You know that."

"Knew I could count on you," Webber smiled. "Better start things right away and have things ready, but don't put anything out till I give the word. I want to have my Senator ready, and there's a couple of other angles I'm working on. It's in the bag, but we've got to pull it off right."

"Count on me," Perrault promised.

"Drew," Webber said gratefully, "your help's worth all the money in the world. I mean it."

Perrault shrugged, embarrassed. "It comes out before taxes," he said. "Legitimate business expense. It isn't much."

"It'll bring back space flight," Webber said grimly. "That's a promise."

Martha came back, looking clean and untroubled and cheerful. She stopped behind Webber and kissed him chastely on the forehead. "You mean well," she murmured.

She slipped into her chair gracefully. She uncovered her plate. "I'm sorry I made all that fuss, Dad," she apologized. "I hope you're not mad."

Perrault patted her knee. "No, Marthie. I'm not mad."

She wriggled pleasurably. "You're nice, Dad," she murmured softly. "Maybe you ought to whale me a few every once in a while."

"It'll cost money."

"I've got money."

Roger Sherman limped along the dock. It was a bad, lurching limp; he had learned to get around on his new leg, but he hadn't yet learned to walk easily.

Yeah, he had money. Seven years' accumulated pay. Pilot's pay, at Expedition One rates. Plus the bonus the Congress had voted him. Real generous, he thought bitterly. As if they could buy off their conscience.

The tanned, T-shirted, prematurely gray lean man

walked slowly, matching pace with Sherman. "There's not much to see, down that far," he warned.

"The *Jove*'s down there," Sherman said.

"A wreck?" the tanned man asked doubtfully. "You're not thinking of salvage, are you? I'm not equipped for that kind of work."

Sherman shook his head. "I just want to see it," he said. "With my own eyes."

When Webber got back to his office, the mail capsule had come. Mrs. Crowder had sorted the letters into three small piles—bills, advertising, and letters from people he wanted things from. Their electrosorting stripes glistened blackly.

Webber pushed the bills and the advertising off to one side. He picked up the first of the letters. It bore a congressional frank and the return address of Mike Westerberg, U. S. Senator from Alaska. Webber ripped it open.

My dear Joseph:

It was good to have lunch with you the other day, and to hear of your plans. As you must know, no one is more in sympathy with your goals than myself, and I greatly admire the program you outlined. I deeply wish I could take part in it myself.

However, I cannot publicly come out in support of a moon colony at this time. Much as I myself believe that such a colony would relieve economic and spiritual pressures—much as you have convinced me of the place of such a colony in the future of mankind—much as I am ashamed of my colleagues, first for having turned their backs on space flight, and then for having closed their eyes to its obvious significance—I regret I cannot help you.

You have no idea of the public temper at this time. To the public mind, this is a time for retrenchment, curtailment of expenditures, and reduction of taxes. Nothing else matters.

This is foolish shortsightedness, and I—personally—detest it. But I cannot speak against it. I am no more immune to the pressures of public opinion than other men. In fact, because of my position, I am more vulnerable.

If I were to speak for a renaissance of space flight now, I would accomplish nothing but my own destruction. It is a horrible truth—but no less true for being horrible—that the people do not *care* about space flight—not as you and I do, and your friends.

If, any time, the public becomes interested in space flight again, you may be sure I will do anything in my power to revitalize the pioneer spirit which—it seems—our countrymen today regrettably lack.

With my profound regrets,

Very sincerely yours,

Mike Westerberg

Webber tore the letter apart and let the pieces fly, not caring where they fell. "The son of a bitch," he muttered bitterly. "The bastard."

He punched Mrs. Crowder's button. After a brief pause, her face appeared framed in the phone plate. "Yes, Mr. Webber?"

"Get me the Senate Office Building," Webber ordered. "I want to see Westerberg."

Mrs. Crowder vanished from the screen. The blank screen blinked several times, and then a smartly-uniformed young woman appeared. "Senate Office Building," she said pleasantly.

"Westerberg," Webber snapped.

"Yes, sir," she acknowledged, not quite so pleasantly.

The screen blinked again. A young man came on. Webber recognized him as Westerberg's personal assistant.

"Where's Westerberg?" Webber demanded.

"I'm sorry, Mr. Webber," the young man said. He actually sounded like he meant it. "Mr. Westerberg is out of the city."

"Where is he?" Webber insisted. "How can I get hold of him?"

"I'm afraid it will be impossible to contact him," the young man apologized diplomatically. "He's touring the drought area with the National Resources Committee. We're completely out of touch with him here."

Webber doubted that, but it would do him no good to say it. Instead he asked, "When does he get back?"

"We don't know definitely," the young man said uncomfortably. "His plans are fluid for after the tour. He left instructions to make no appointments until after he has returned."

He paused. "Is there something I could do?" he offered.

"Yeah," Webber said bitterly. "You can tell him what I think of him." He broke the connection with a savage sweep of his hand.

He sat glowering at the blank, cold screen, trembling with frustrated rage. "The son of a bitch," he muttered viciously. "The Goddamned son of a bitch!"

The storm was so near you could reach out and touch it. The wind was rising and the looming clouds towered over them like a black prison wall.

"Can't you hurry?" the boy pleaded.

"Plenty of time," Ryan told him. He made a last check of the equipment. "Now back off," he ordered. "And stay back. This hardware is as touchy as a chairman of the board."

Fenwick nudged the boy's arm and walked off. The boy followed. Twenty paces away, Fenwick stopped. "Now don't go any closer," he advised.

Ryan sat down on the packing box. He plugged in the battery leads from the snow buggy. The red light flashed on. A moment later it faded, and the three green lights brightened. Ryan rapped on each of the three seismograph cases, and the green lights flickered each in turn.

Ryan nodded to himself, satisfied. He took the firing board in his lap.

A strong gust of wind slammed into his back. It moaned across the wind-scoured snowfield. But the green lights held steady, ignoring the blast like unblinking eyes. The storm was very near.

Ryan punched the recorder button. Under the protective cover, he heard the snick of the tape as the reels began to turn. A fourth, brighter green light came on.

Ryan settled the firing board firmly across his thighs. He set his mittened thumb against the first toggle and tripped it over.

The three green lights winked. A hundred yards off, the snow erupted in a spume of shattered ice. One of the green lights flickered, and then another. Then the third.

Ryan waited until all three lights were steady again. Then he snapped the second toggle. The explosion this time was two hundred yards away.

The first bits of snow came, flying long like mote-sized darts. The clouds seemed to spread out over them like a blanket flung out to engulf them. The wind wailed mournfully.

"Hurry!" the boy screamed desperately.

Ryan hunched his back against the wind. The tiny pellets of snow rattled soundlessly off the electroseismographs and the recorder.

"Keep him quiet," Ryan shouted, and Fenwick took hold of the boy's arm.

Ryan fired the third blast. He could not hear the explosion above the shriek and thunder of the wind.

He fired the fourth. The blast was four hundred yards away, and he could hardly see it through the thickening snow. He felt the wind clutch and snatch at him.

He triggered the fifth, the last. Five hundred yards. He watched the green lights. One by one, they flickered, then steadied again.

Ryan stood up. He ripped the detonation wires from the firing board. "Let's get out of here!" he shouted loudly, trying to make himself heard.

Fenwick and the kid were already dashing toward him. They had started when he stood up. They were blurred, shadowlike shapes in the blinding snow.

Ryan jerked a thumb at the snow buggy. "Get the preheater roaring," he shouted. "Nick—help me get this hardware aboard."

The kid veered off toward the snow buggy. Fenwick came on. The snow stabbed painfully at Ryan's face. The wind made a low, weird moan, like the howl of a wolf. The sun was blotted out. It was getting dark fast.

Webber took the shuttle jet to New York, to invade the office of Intercontinental Rockets, Inc. It wasn't by invitation.

He cooled his heels in the anteroom for a long time. That was IR, Inc.'s usual way of handling unwelcome guests. Finally, when he had them convinced he wouldn't go away without having talked to someone, the receptionist told him that Mr. Pat Charnwood would see him.

Webber smiled his most ironic smile. Pat Charnwood was Intercontinental's vice president in charge of saying, "We ain't buying, bub; get lost," as pleasantly as possible.

Well, Mr. Sowbelly Charnwood was in for a shock. Because Joe Webber didn't plan to take no for an answer.

He still knew his way around the high echelon offices. He managed to get a step ahead of the girl who was supposed to guide him, and he managed to stay ahead of her all the way to Charnwood's office.

"Thanks, cutie," Webber said, looking her up and down with a penetrating eye. "That's all—unless they let you out nights."

The girl retreated hastily. Webber chuckled. He walked into Charnwood's office and kicked the door shut.

Pat Charnwood stood up quickly and came out from behind his desk. He was a pleasingly plump man in his late thirties, with a trim-thin mustache on his butterball face.

He was impeccably dressed in gray ski pants, bright orange blouse, and a brown tolex vest. He was also wearing the hearty smile that was his stock in trade.

"So you're Captain Webber," he said pleasantly. He gripped Webber's hand firmly. "I've wanted to meet you for a long time."

He ushered Webber to a chair in front of the desk. It was, Webber noticed grimly, one of the kind that looked comfortable until you sat on it. Just the thing for Charnwood's office.

Charnwood settled back behind his desk, and the desk snuggled up to him. It was broad and swept-wing shaped, as if at any moment it might fly. He made himself comfortable.

He steepled his fingers. "So you're the man who went to Mars," he mused, still with that so-glad-to-see-you look on his face. "Those certainly were exciting days. I wish I'd been old enough, then."

63

"With all your lard, it wouldn't have made any difference," Webber snapped. "They'd never have let you in a ship."

Some of the cordiality melted out of Charnwood's face. He forced a smile and glanced down at his girth. "Yes," he sighed regretfully. "But now the solar system's all explored—it's all done."

"Not all the way out, it isn't," Webber said. "Even Jupiter, all we know is what Sherman remembered—and that's damn little."

Charnwood shrugged. "Yes, well . . ." he said, and let it go at that.

He opened a folder set before him on the desk. "I've been looking over the project outline you submitted," he said, still affable, but a little more businesslike. "It isn't often we see such an ambitious project suggested."

"It's the most important thing can happen to the human race," Webber said. He was dead serious, and that was the way he said it.

Charnwood looked up blankly. "I don't understand," he frowned.

"I didn't think you would," Webber told him. It was an indictment. "Here we've been down here crawling around on this one measly planet like bugs on an apple so long you can't take a step without walking on somebody's dirt. Practically prisoners. And now we've got the power to leave it, and we don't do a thing. Hell! All history is the story of men making themselves independent of things. Well, now we've got a chance to take the big step. It's a challenge! Are we going to take it, or aren't we?"

Joe Webber was a small, blond man with fight in his posture, ice and fire in his gray-green eyes.

"You put it very forcefully," Charnwood said, unmoved. "Apparently, it means a lot more to you than to me. I really don't see that it's so important."

Webber's eyes drilled at him. "I know you wouldn't," he said contemptuously. "You're too young to remember. It wasn't too many years ago we stood a fifty-fifty chance of turning this planet so radioactive hot you couldn't keep a virus alive in a lead box two feet thick. It could still happen."

64

Charnwood tried to laugh off the prospect. "Oh, I doubt that," he belittled. "They're still making progress at Canberra, aren't they?"

Webber snorted. "They've been playing patty cake and ring around the rosy for almost a year, if that's what you mean. Listen—I remember once I met a guy that told me he could build an H-bomb in his basement. And he wasn't kidding. He knew how. How do you like that? A couple dozen of those, and *bang!* No more people."

"Well, we all have to take our chances," Charnwood said lightly.

"Not with a moon colony up there," Webber contended. "I mean, there'd still be people. But you can bet your fat gut they won't be down here."

Charnwood chuckled like an idiot. "Well, of course, this is all suppositious," he said carelessly.

"You think so?" Webber challenged.

Charnwood drew himself erect in his chair. "We seem to have digressed, Mr. Webber," he said unctuously. "As I was saying . . ."

"*Captain* Webber," Webber corrected.

"Uh, yes. Captain," Charnwood echoed, unsettled. "As I was saying, we have discussed this project, and we have come to the conclusion . . ."

He left off speaking and pawed through the papers in the folder. "Yes. Here we are," he muttered to himself. He pulled out a page and set it in front of him. He steepled his fingers again, pressing fingertip to fingertip so that his fingers bent into smooth arcs.

"We have decided," he continued as if there had been no pause, "that, although this project has very definite merits to recommend it, we could not at this time justify such an undertaking to our stockholders." He pushed the paper away from him. "I'm sorry, Captain Webber . . ."

"Hogwash," Webber spat.

Charnwood bridled. "I beg your pardon?" he said sharply.

"I used to work for you," Webber said darkly. "I know how they talk about stockholders in the top office. Anything you can put over on them is a score, and you play the game for all it's worth."

For just a moment, then, Charnwood's face was blank and numb. Joe Webber almost laughed out loud. Charnwood very obviously hadn't expected that kind of reaction. He had thought Joe Webber was just like all his other victims—gentlemen who took their lumps and their disappointments without a word, and clumped out of the office with a sort of crestfallen dignity.

Joe Webber wasn't that kind of guy.

"I really must protest," Charnwood said stiffly.

"Why don't you read the way I had the project set up?" Webber demanded. "Is there anything in it you can't sell them?"

"We have studied it very carefully," Charnwood assured him severely. "We cannot see how sponsoring such a colony could be profitable."

"Profit!" Webber said it like a dirty word. "Is that all you can think of? Dollars and cents? I tell you, this thing is bigger than all the money in the world."

"Profit is the only thing a stockholder can understand."

"Hell! Who cares?" Webber argued. "Once you've sold them on it, they're stuck with it."

"We have a certain responsibility to our stockholders," Charnwood said virtuously. "We could not possibly convince them that rockets can haul ores—or even refined metals—down from the moon. Not profitably. Rocket costs are fantastic. We can only make money with passengers or with freight of high value per unit weight where speed is more important than cost. Anything else, to get the business we would have to quote rates less than cost. We'd lose money, and our stockholders know that."

"Who said anything about hauling down ores?" Webber wanted to know. "My idea was to set up the colony and make your money hauling passengers. What's wrong with that?"

"The investment," Charnwood said judiciously, "would be much greater than is justified by the profit we could reasonably expect. It would be years before we could expect any return at all."

"What about the subsidy you get for weather observation?—the one that cut the legs out from under Orbitbase?"

"That has nothing to do with your proposal for a moon colony."

"You could do a lot better job of it if you had a moon colony to do it from," Webber argued. "You don't do it half as good as Orbitbase. You could get more money for it if you did it from the moon."

"Even so, the increase would not be enough to justify such a venture," Charnwood said. He leaned forward, resting his arms on the desk. "I really am sorry, Captain Webber," he projected with a warm, cold-blooded sincerity. "But until the cost of rocket operation becomes considerably less than it is now, a project such as you have proposed will not be commercially feasible."

Webber's stubborn face broke suddenly into a pleased smile. His eyes narrowed shrewdly. "Suppose I came up with something that cut rocket costs to practically nothing," he said temptingly. "Suppose I brought you one you didn't have to buy fuel for—one that didn't burn anything but hydrogen, and didn't need any more than what it could pick up itself as it went along?"

"Uh?" Charnwood wondered.

"There's enough, out there," Webber told him. "It's spread thin—thin as a dead man's breath, but it's there. How'd you like a rocket that didn't need anything but that? Cheap, huh?"

He watched Charnwood nibble the bait, and saw him swallow it. It was written on the man's face. Charnwood was living through the special torment of an underling afraid he will make a mistake.

Joe Webber chuckled secretly, letting none of it show on his face. Charnwood didn't *dare* slam the door in his face. Not now.

"Well, naturally, that would change the complexion of a great many things," Charnwood said cautiously. "We might have to reconsider many of our basic policies. I hope you haven't misunderstood me, Captain Webber. We are not what you would call a conservative firm. Intercontinental Rockets is always willing to undertake new projects, so long as we can reasonably expect an adequate return on our investment."

Webber stood up. "You haven't seen the last of me," he promised insidiously, and walked out, a cocky spring in his stride.

The bathyscaph sank slowly. Sherman crouched on a stool in front of the window. Behind him sat the tanned man, in turtleneck and dungarees now. The tanned man watched the depth gauge, and he kept his hand wrapped around the deadman's ballast release. Now and then he let up a little. Ballast spewed into the water in front of the window, and the bathyscaph's descent slowed.

Sherman watched the daylight fade to a smoky green, and finally to darkness.

"When did this ship go down?" the bathyscaph man asked.

"About a year ago," Sherman said, not turning. The bathyscaph's lights put an eerie glow in the water. It drew sea creatures. They paraded in front of the window. Sherman stared past them, not interested in them—as if he could see all the way to the bottom.

"Somebody you knew aboard?" the bathyscaph man asked.

Sherman nodded. "Friends. Brave men."

"Dirty luck," the bathyscaph man said. "What kind of ship was she?"

"It was a space ship, God damn you," Sherman said.

"Oh. THAT *Jove*."

"Yes," Sherman said, bitterly mimicking. "That *Jove*."

"Then you're . . ."

"Yeah," Sherman said broodingly. "I brought her down."

Joe Webber checked his pockets for cash on hand. He had enough, so he found a phone office and sat down in a booth. He started making long distance calls.

Before he was done, he was going to have a fat bill to pay. But if his calls paid off, it was worth every penny. If it didn't—well, he wouldn't begrudge them. It was worth a try.

He had to make several calls before he found out who he was looking for. He had to make several more before he found the man.

The man he wanted was Morris Gunderman, who had once worked on a joint research project of the Space Service and the Atomic Energy Commission. Webber finally located him at a small technical school in Ohio, where he was assistant dean in charge of research. It sounded like one of those deals where you could count the research staff on the fingers of one hand and have enough fingers left to play a piano. To Webber, it was a hopeful sign.

Gunderman was a thin, hollow-cheeked man with graying hair and slouched shoulders. He wore a blouse that was too small for him, and he did not wear a vest. "You're Gunderman?" Webber asked.

The lean man nodded. "What can I do?"

"You used to work for the Space Service?"

Gunderman shook his head stiffly. "No," he said precisely. "Actually, I was with the AEC, but one of the projects I directed was instigated by the Space Service." He paused. "Could I have your name, sir?"

"Joe Webber," Webber said. "I'm with Space Flight Associates. What sort of work were you doing?"

"Research work," Gunderman said perversely.

"What kind?" Webber persisted.

"Nuclear," Gunderman answered.

The man was as hard to get anything out of as a bottle of vacuum. "Look," Webber said, trying to control his impatience. "There's a few things I want to check with you. All right?"

"If it won't take too long," Gunderman consented.

"All right," Webber agreed. "The way I have it, you were working on a way for a space ship to drive with nothing but the hydrogen out in space."

"That's a very crude way to put it," Gunderman said acridly. "Actually, I was directing research looking into the possibility of developing a controlled hydrogen fusion process suitable to provide the motive power of a rocket."

"That's what I meant," Webber said. "So, what did you find out?"

"Our funds were cut off before we could make any conclusive findings," Gunderman said.

Webber almost swore. His chilly self-control stopped him. "Well, what do you *think?*"

"All our findings were preliminary," Gunderman hedged. "I'm afraid I don't remember the details. It was more than five years ago, you know."

69

"I know," Webber said, utterly without humor. "I want an *opinion*."

"Are you thinking of sponsoring the research yourself?" Gunderman asked shrewdly. A new look had come into his vinegary face—a look of holy dedication.

"I might be," Webber admitted.

"What are your resources?" Gunderman demanded.

"Pretty good," Webber said confidently. He didn't crack a smile, but he wished he could. He had his fish hooked. "What's your advice?"

"I think it is a possibility well worth looking into," Gunderman said.

"How much money would you need?"

Gunderman backed away a little, expostulating. "Well, you know, don't you, how difficult it is to make up a budget for a research project," he evaded.

"How much?" Webber persisted.

"I *was* making out a preliminary budget when the Space Service was disbanded," Gunderman admitted. "Assuming the facilities were available—if I remember correctly—it would cost about two billion, four hundred million dollars."

Webber felt every muscle in his body tighten. The son of a bitch! He'd probably been muttering it in his sleep all these years.

He said the first printable thing he could think of. "Costs have gone down since then, haven't they?" he challenged.

Gunderman appeared to consider. "Perhaps we could do it for an even two billion," he admitted. "On the other hand, it might cost more."

In the quiet that followed, Gunderman said, like an afterthought, "And five years."

Webber forced the money thoughts out of his mind. He'd raise the cash somehow. "Would you like to do it?" he asked.

He saw the hunger in Gunderman's eyes—a hunger he had not seen in any man's eyes since the death of space flight—a hunger he had thought he would never see again.

"As I said," Gunderman repeated, "it is a possibility well worth investigating."

"I'll let you know," Webber said, and broke the connection.

The electroseismographs were in three cases, and the recorder made a fourth. They were all heavy. Shielding them with his body to keep the snow out, Ryan opened each of the seismograph cases and locked the delicate mechanisms in their protective cradles. Then, lifting them one at a time, he and Fenwick muscled them into the snow buggy's storage compartment.

They climbed into the cab. "How's the engine?" Ryan asked.

The boy was in the driver's seat. He twisted around. "She's too cold."

Fenwick closed the door. The pre-heater was going; it was warm in the cab. Ryan unzipped his parka and shrugged out of it. So did Fenwick.

"She'll warm," Ryan said. "Better get out of that igloo suit before you sweat it." He slung his jacket over the back of a seat.

The boy's hands clutched the steering brakes tightly. He stared at the window. It was blind white, like a sightless eye. The wind traced momentary gray-white patterns on the glass.

"We'll never find the camp," he despaired.

"Nothing to stop us," Ryan said, ignoring the storm outside. He reached forward and unzipped the boy's parka. "I told you get out of it."

He peeled it down the boy's back, not gently. He threw it to the back of the cab.

He looked at the dashboard. "She's warming. Start her up."

The boy would have slipped out of the driver's seat, but Ryan clamped down on his shoulders. "You drive," he ordered.

"Me?" The boy's body froze under Ryan's hands. "But . . ." He looked desperately around the cab—at Fenwick, at Ryan, at the storm outside.

"Just one way you'll ever learn to blizzard drive, boy," Ryan said. "Sink or swim."

Again the boy looked at the snow-blinded window, and listened to the storm raging outside. He trembled.

71

"Start her," Ryan said.

"I . . . I can't," the boy cried.

Ryan reached over the boy's shoulder and pressed the starter. The engine was still cold. It turned over several times before it caught. The snow buggy shook with its power.

"Now drive," Ryan barked.

In the pale light inside the cab, the boy's face was white and tortured. He bent forward, as if to press his face against the dashboard.

"Drive!" Ryan yelled.

Momentarily less fearful of the storm than of Ryan, the boy jerked erect. Compulsively, he unlocked the brakes. He put the engine in gear. The machine lurched forward.

It bounced and rocked on the uneven snow, like a ship bucking strong seas.

"I can't see," the boy cried. He clutched the brakes. He leaned forward, trying to peer through the driving snow.

"You don't have to," Ryan said. "That's what we've got a compass for."

He reached over the boy's shoulder again and tapped the gyrocompass dial. "We are now headed," he lectured sarcastically, "in almost exactly the wrong direction. We're a few points south of northwest from camp."

He twisted the knob under the dial. The steady-on notch rotated around the dial's edge to a point four degrees north of southwest.

"That's the way we want to go," he said. "But hold our nose a few points south of it—we've got a big wind to crab into."

The boy didn't move. He didn't seem to hear. He craned his neck, still trying to see. His hands trembled on the brake handles.

"You hear?" Ryan demanded. "Turn us around."

The boy jerked erect. "Oh. Sure. Sure," he said anxiously. He yanked back on the left steering lever—all the way. The snow buggy lurched violently, slewed, and skidded. The compass reeled drunkenly.

Ryan struck the boy's hand off the brake and released

72

it. The snow buggy staggered, swayed dizzily, and steadied. The engine growled, out of gear.

"Want to turn us over?" Ryan demanded. "Now do it right."

Trancelike, the boy put the engine back in gear. The snow buggy leaped forward.

He reached for the brake.

"Throttle," Ryan snapped.

The boy stiffened. He pulled the throttle back. The snow buggy slowed.

"*Now* turn," Ryan said.

Gingerly, the boy eased the steering brake back. The snow buggy hitched, swayed gently, and swung slowly.

Ryan watched the compass. When the needle was still a few points south of the steady-on notch, he tapped the boy's shoulder. "That's enough. Now straight ahead."

The boy let go of the brake. The snow buggy straightened out. Ryan tapped the compass. "Keep us like that."

The boy nodded numbly. He stared straight ahead. The blizzard beat against the window more fiercely than ever.

"Don't mind the outside," Ryan prodded. "Watch the compass."

"But suppose . . ."

"We can't run into anything—there's nothing to run into," Ryan told him impatiently. "The field's as smooth as floe ice."

Obediently, body rigid, the boy looked at the compass.

Ryan sat down in the seat behind the boy. He leaned forward so his face was only inches from the boy's ear.

"Listen, boy," he said quietly. "I know you're green. You don't know this country. All right—so you'll learn. Maybe. But there's one thing you'd better have or all the learning there is won't help—and if you don't have it you'd better get out of the country while you're still alive. You got to have guts."

Charnwood listened. Webber had known he would. The hydrogen rocket would be a cheap rocket, and any man in Intercontinental would give all twelve toes for the credit of bringing it into the company. Especially a man up a blind alley, like Charnwood.

Charnwood started making notes. Webber turned on the persuasion. He pointed out all the things Intercontinental could do if it had a cheap rocket. It could move common freight, as well as passengers. There was a lot of money in common freight. And the rocket might be adapted to other uses—engines, for example. Practically anything could be made to run on hydrogen. It might even be converted into a basic power source.

If Intercontinental owned the patents, it could make a lot of cash.

Charnwood poised his pencil over the memo pad. "But it has to be developed," he inferred, seeking confirmation.

"That's why I brought it to you," Webber said. "You want to develop it, don't you?"

Charnwood wrote something on his pad. "That depends," he said judiciously. "How much will it cost?"

"Look—this is a research job," Webber argued. "It may cost a dime or ten billion dollars. You don't know till you've done it."

"But . . ." Charnwood made a coaxing, half-humorous gesture. "Surely you have some idea. I don't know how thoroughly you have investigated the matter, but you must know approximately how expensive it will be."

Cautiously, Webber moistened his lips. He couldn't evade any longer. He had to give some sort of answer, even if it was a lie.

"I've got a man who can do it for five hundred million," he said. If he had to, he'd get the rest of the money someplace else. Anyway, he didn't want Intercontinental to own the hydrogen rocket without obligation to him, nor without him having a say in what it was used for.

For one thing, there had to be a colony on the moon.

Idly, Charnwood tapped his palm with the pencil. "You realize that's quite a sizable investment," he remarked.

"It's worth it, isn't it?" Webber argued. "Look what you're getting."

Charnwood looked wary. "How sure would we be of success?"

"They've got the science all worked out," Webber

74

lied. "All they've got to do is the engineering.—Look, it's not like you have to lay out the cash all at once. My man says he'll take something like five years to do it. That's only a hundred million a year. That isn't much when you think what you're getting."

"It's entirely too much," Charnwood said decisively.

"Too much!" Webber exploded. "It's worth ten times that. A hundred. You spend that much a year just for rocket fuel."

"I don't doubt a hydrogen rocket would have all the advantages you've mentioned," Charnwood admitted reasonably. "But we have no assurance it is feasible. Now, naturally, I can't give you a definite answer yes or no—we will have to study the matter before we can make a decision. But I very much doubt we will go into such a project—almost certainly not on the scale you propose. We have almost never sponsored engineering research. That is the business of the manufacturers who build our rockets."

"Maybe it's time you got into that business," Webber said, eyes narrowed. "For an outfit that's in business to make money, you're sure not very eager to make it."

"On the contrary," Charnwood corrected urbanely. "If we definitely knew such a rocket could be developed, we would be very anxious to sponsor its development. But we do not have any such guarantee. We might spend all that money and have nothing for it."

"Don't you think it's worth the gamble?" Webber challenged contemptuously. "Think what you'll get if it pays off—and it will if you're willing to spend enough on it."

"I am thinking," Charnwood said, "that if the project failed, we would lose more money than we can afford to lose."

He laid down his pencil and laid his hands flat on his blotter. Raising his voice as a sign the interview was finished, he said, "I'm sorry, Captain Webber. But that is our policy. Engineering research is too costly and uncertain to justify the rewards."

Webber stood up. He leaned across the desk, putting his face close enough to Charnwood's to see the reptilian scaliness of his skin.

"Mister," he promised venomously, "I'm going to put you out of business."

He turned and walked out, back stiff, teeth clenched, eyes hard.

The sea bottom lifted out of the dark fogginess. It was dark brown, slimy, and barren. The pilot released the deadman's grip and iron shot poured from the hoppers. He stopped it and, looking out, gauged the bathyscaph's rate of descent. He released a little more. Now the bathyscaph held almost steady, floating twenty feet above the bottom.

"The wreck should be within a mile of here," the pilot said.

He turned on the engine. The bottom moved underneath. He clamped a set of phones over his ears. He tilted the joystick. The bathyscaph turned slowly. "She won't be hard to find," he said. "This is flat bottom here."

He reversed the turn, a look of concentration on his face. "I think we've got her," he said.

He held the joystick centered. The bathyscaph drove straight ahead.

"Can you imagine people living down here?" the pilot said.

Sherman looked out at the barren sea floor. They were almost two miles down. "Hadn't thought about it," he admitted. "I don't know why not."

"Well, there's talk of it—has been ever since they built that caisson mine in the Sea of Japan. I don't see it, myself."

"If people want to live down here bad enough, they will," Sherman declared.

"There's too much pressure down here," the pilot objected.

"*We're* down here," Sherman pointed out. "Wherever men can go, they can build a city. We could have built one on the moon—we almost did."

"I heard about that," the pilot said. "I'd have liked to be in on it. Only there's a lot of this planet yet, and it comes first."

In Fort Worth, Airframe Fabrications, Inc. was mildly interested in the hydrogen rocket. But just mildly. It would mean, most likely, the sale of more rockets, but —the friendly man in the office explained—"We don't build rocket motors ourselves—only the airframes. So our engineering work is pretty much limited to structural and aerodynamic considerations. But why don't you take this up with Reaction Industries? They're our largest supplier of motors. I'd be happy to give you a letter of introduction . . ."

"Don't bother," Webber said. "There isn't a door yet I haven't been able to get through."

But his reception in the Los Angeles home office of Reaction Industries was noticeably less than enthusiastic. He was taken in charge by that firm's counterpart of Charnwood—a muscular, mid-thirtyish man named Burton.

Burton listened patiently and made desultory notes on his memo pad, but when it was all over, his answer was no.

"We're a producer of chemical fuel rocket motors," he explained. "All our development work is concerned with fuels and improvement of motor design. We have neither the facilities nor the staff to indulge in such a radical enterprise. In fact, our entire production plant is devoted to conventional rocket motors, which involves a considerable investment on our part. So we would be reluctant—understandably, I think—to see such a rocket developed."

"Suppose someone else does it?" Webber challenged. "Where will that leave you? Making buggy whips?"

Burton smiled and shrugged. "In any event, such a development is years away. If and when it comes, we'll be ready for it."

"Yeah—I'll bet you will," Webber sneered. "Just one thing I want to know. Which hand will you hold the lily in?"

General Nucleonics had built the reactor-powered rockets of the Space Service. With the end of space flight, Nucleonics had retired from the field of rocketry. Its frightfully powerful—and equally expensive—rocket en-

77

gines had no buyers in the commercial realm which was all that remained of that brave, brief age.

Webber went to them now. Here was a company with the men, the facilities, and the cash to build a hydrogen rocket.

He thought.

They kept him in Buffalo for three days, talking with one group of men and then another—executives and engineers. He had come armed with a briefcase of papers out of the Space Service files—files which had found their way, somehow, to the office of Space Flight Associates. Before he was through, he'd laid out all the papers and the men had made notes from them in furious concentration.

A week later, he returned to Buffalo. He was conducted to the office of John Trask. Trask was somewhere in his upper forties, and had put on some weight in the usual place. He shook Webber's hand genially.

"Our engineers have studied your proposal," he said by way of preamble. "They report that a hydrogen rocket might be developed—the chances of it are fairly good. However—" and he paused and looked at Webber sternly.

"However," he repeated, "they estimate that we could not complete the necessary work for eight or ten years, at a cost of approximately a billion and a half. I'm afraid, Mr. Webber, we couldn't indulge in such a venture without one hundred per cent certainty of success, nor without definite assurance of its commercial value. We do not have a guarantee on either point."

"That's all you've got to say?" Webber asked numbly. After the fuss—the obvious interest—he hadn't expected this.

"I'm sorry, Mr. Webber," Trask said politely.

"Well . . . look," Webber said desperately. "Suppose you don't go all out? Suppose you take a little longer and don't spend so much?"

"The overall cost would be the same, no matter how long we took," Trask informed him. "As for a small scale project—we considered that. But for the cost to be bearable on a year-to-year basis, the project would have to be scheduled to run forty years. Up to now, it has not been our policy to undertake a project unless it shows

hope of useful results within ten years. We might undertake such a project on a commission basis, however. We
have done that in the past—all patents deriving from the
work being shared with us, your seventy-five per cent to
our twenty-five. If you can arrange the financing, we will
be glad to do business with you."

Webber stood up. "Mister—I've heard of something
for nothing before, but damned if you don't beat it all.
I'll raise that cash—somehow I'll do it. But damned if
I'll bring it to you."

The wind howled like a beast from an alien world. It
swept over the snowfield making strange, low moans. It
slammed against the snow buggy with a drumlike
booming. The snow buggy shook with its pounding.

The boy drove as if in a trance. He worked the
steering brakes desperately, as if fighting them. The compass needle jiggled nervously.

Ryan slouched in his seat. He watched the boy.

Abruptly, the boy spoke. His voice was a tortured,
blubbering sob. "I can't see!" he cried. "We could drive
right through camp and I'd never see it."

"Don't fret yourself," Ryan said unfeelingly. "We'll
make it. You'll be drinking hot chocolate in half an
hour."

Cold air leaked through cracks and joints in the cab's
frame. It streamed in around the door. It was like icicle
knives. Ryan draped his parka over his shoulders. He
watched the boy drive.

"They'll be cities here, someday," he said, amused by
the thought. "And this'll be as simple as a Sunday stroll.
We'd go nuts if we stay, it'll be so tame. We'll have to
go someplace else."

"Sure, but *where*?" Fenwick wondered. "What'll be
left?"

Ryan shrugged. "Don't know. The moon, maybe."

"If they ever go back to the moon," Fenwick said
dourly.

"They'll go back," Ryan said confidently. "When
we've got this country tamed, they'll *have* to. They've
got to have *some* place to send us."

The storm clawed frantically at the snow buggy. The
wind whipped around it and pounded it. In the glazed

white light that came through the blinded windshield, the boy's face was waxy and dry, and tiny beads of sweat clung up close to his hairline. His teeth were clenched and he seemed not to breathe. His hands gripped the steering brakes bloodlessly. His eyes held a desperate terror like a cornered animal.

Finally, Ryan reached over the boy's shoulder. "Time we had a look around."

He snapped on the red-eye. In a moment, the scope took on a gray, dim glow. Ryan twisted the finder knob slowly, watching the scope. Nothing showed for a long time.

"Maybe it's too cold," the boy suggested fearfully. He was gnawing his lip. He worked the steering brakes not with his arms but with his whole body.

Ryan shook his head. "This hardware was built for this kind of weather. It sees anything that's warmer than what's around it—and the camp's a lot warmer than the rest of this country. The snow may be giving it trouble, though. There's a limit how far it can see through that stuff. It's like a brick wall out there."

But then, as Ryan twisted the knob, a faint light patch moved onto the scope from the side. "There it is," he said. He turned up the contrast—the patch turned brighter.

It had no shape. It wavered and swam like a reflection in water. It was fuzzy at the edges. But it held its position.

Ryan centered it in the scope. He checked the finder knob's setting. "South," he ordered.

Compulsively, the boy hauled back on the right steering brake. The snow buggy hitched and skidded and turned into the wind. Ryan turned the finder knob to keep the patch centered.

"Now straight ahead," Ryan directed.

The boy released the brake. The snow buggy plunged straight ahead. Ryan watched the scope. The wind slashed and screamed. The patch slowly drifted off the scope to the left.

"More south," Ryan ordered.

Gritting his teeth as if in pain, the boy obeyed. The wind was like thunder.

Back in his Washington Office, Joe Webber called Gunderman again. The physicist came to the phone almost at once.

"Hi," Webber said, getting the amenities out of the way as fast as he could. "Anybody been talking to you?"

"About the possibility of a rocket using hydrogen as a nuclear fuel?" Gunderman asked pedantically. "Yes. I have been contacted several times. Three times, to be exact, not counting yourself."

"Well? Anything come of it?" If worse came to worse, he'd be satisfied with the rocket being built, with or without him having a say in how it was used.

"They seemed to think my estimate of costs was high," Gunderman said stiffly. "They thought I was bargaining with them."

"Yeah," Webber said. "Well, look, Doc. Would you like to work on it?"

"I might be interested," Gunderman admitted. "Yes."

"Swell—only, look—I'm having trouble raising the cash."

"I'm not surprised," Gunderman said archly. "Even Washington would be hard put, I think, to obtain the funds."

"What I was thinking," Webber went on, ignoring the sarcasm, "could you do it for less money a year, and take longer doing it? Maybe ten years? Fifteen? If you can, I think I can get the cash."

"It would be a smaller project," Gunderman replied. "It would lack the advantages of having a large contributing staff, and the final cost would be greater—perhaps as much as a billion more. But—if that is the best you can offer, I suppose it can be done that way."

Webber smiled. It was a small triumph, but it was a triumph just the same. "I'll have to talk to my money," he said. "But I think you've got a job."

"There's your ship," the pilot said.

Ahead, still indistinct in the murked gloom, a great shape loomed. As the bathyscaph drove nearer, its outline became clear.

It had been like a duncecapped globe, but now its

flank was bashed and twisted. "Circle it," Sherman ordered.

The pilot slowed the engine. The bathyscaph curved around the hulk. The *Jove* was battered and crumpled, like an old man beaten to death.

They came around the *Jove*'s round, bulbous prow. There, the astrodome which had been welded shut had burst open, and a great gash like a groaning mouth cut across the front of the ship.

"I heard about the guys in that ship," the pilot said. "They were wearing space suits so they wouldn't drown. The pressure killed them. It's an ugly way to get it. I guess they're still inside."

Abruptly, Sherman said, "Take us up."

But still he looked out at the wreck, seeing why he had lived—why the others had not.

The pilot released more ballast. The bathyscaph lifted gently.

"I can't see people living down here," he argued doggedly. "The pressure's enough to make a rag doll out of a man."

"Shut up," said Roger Sherman. "Shut your God damn mouth."

Andrew Perrault's summer home in Aspen was a rocket hop and a copter jump from Washington, and had to. Ignoring bells and knockers, he pounded on the Webber made the layover in Denver no longer than he thick oak door.

The heavy door was an incongruous thing. Except for that, the house looked totally transparent—a strut-propped roof over a floor, and lots of spiky, knees-and-elbows furniture placed around.

A small, round, gray-gone woman came to the door. He hadn't seen her coming, and he was startled when the door abruptly opened.

"Why, Mr. Webber," she said pleasantly.

"Joe," Webber corrected, abashed. "Just old Joe."

She smiled and stepped out of the doorway, and Webber walked inside. He looked around. The place looked a lot different from this side of the door. There were a lot of floor-to-ceiling mirrors, artfully placed to give the illusion of spaciousness.

"I suppose you want to see Andy," the nice woman said.

"Yeah. Drew," Webber said. "Is he here?"

"He's down in the library." She led him to a short flight of stairs. They descended and came out in a large, approximately lens-shaped room whose transparent outer wall looked out down a long slope and on to the towering mountains beyond. The inside wall was lined with bookshelves, and the bookshelves were laden with sturdily bound reference volumes.

Perrault was at the study table, bent over an open book, scrawling notes on a pad. He looked up. He turned.

"Joe!" he exclaimed. "This *is* a surprise!"

Webber crossed the room toward him. "Thanks," he said over his shoulder to the woman.

"Hey—don't go, Alice," Perrault urged. He untangled from his stool and stood up. "Stay with us, Alice," he persuaded.

Alice shook her head pleasantly. "You men have your own talk," she smiled. "I'd be in the way." She climbed the stairs.

Perrault looked after her. "There goes the woman I might have married," he said meditatively.

Webber looked around, startled. "Huh? I thought . . ."

"Oh, I *did*," Perrault smiled his lopsided smile.

He reached out and dragged over a chair. One of the kind you could relax in. He gestured Webber into it and settled into another.

"Drew—" Webber said anxiously, "I need money. A lot of it."

Perrault raised his voice. "Alice—" he called. "Bring my checkbook? There's a good girl!"

"All right, Andy," She answered nicely. Her voice came from nowhere, as if she was right in the room.

"How much do you want?" Perrault offered openly. "Anything to bail out a friend."

"Drew," Webber said uneasily, "this isn't like all the other times. I mean a *lot* of money."

Alice Perrault came down the stairs and handed the checkbook to her husband. Perrault waited until she was gone again. Then he asked, "How much, Joe?"

frowning as if he could not imagine a sum so large he could not spare it.

"Two billion," Webber said, and then said hastily, "I don't need it all right now. I won't need some of it for five or ten years. But I've got to have it. It means a moon colony. It means space flight again."

Perrault nodded dumbly. "Joe—I haven't got that kind of money," he protested weakly. "Nowhere near that kind of money. Joe—the company only clears a few hundred thousand a year."

Webber was silent a long time. "Well, fifteen years, then. Twenty."

Perrault shook his head. "Not in a hundred," he said miserably. "I'd give it to you if we had it. You know that, Joe. But we plain don't have that kind of cash."

He was distressed—unhappy. Webber hardly noticed. "That's it, then," he said flatly, bitterly. "No more space flight."

"Joe—I'm sorry," Perrault protested. "You don't know how sorry I am."

Webber ignored him. "I counted on you—you son of a bitch," he muttered wrathfully. "I counted on Rog, and he bitched me. Now *you've* done it. You and your filthy bank accounts. You wouldn't have that money if it wasn't for space flight. Don't you think you owe it anything?"

He stood up, feisty as a yapping pup. "All right—I'll do it alone. All by myself." He turned to leave.

"Joe—wait," Perrault pleaded frantically. "There must be something we can do."

Webber paused at the stairs. He turned. "Yeah? What?" he demanded.

"I don't know," Perrault admitted helplessly. "Sit down, Joe, please. I can't talk to you like this. Come back and sit down."

Webber hesitated, indecisive, but only a moment. Mouth set in a thin, grim line, he went back to his chair. "All right," he said. "Talk."

Perrault's hands fluttered helplessly. "This . . . this money. What's it for?"

Sullen, hunched in the chair, Webber mumbled about Gunderman and the hydrogen rocket, and all that the hydrogen rocket would mean. "It means space flight again—makes it cheap enough that somebody can make money off it. As soon as we've got it, somebody's sure to get into it."

Perrault nodded. He slouched back in his chair. "Joe . . ." he said slowly. "Do you care much how long it takes—just so you know it will happen?"

"I don't care if it takes a thousand years," Webber said. "But I've got to be sure. And I'll never be sure till I see it."

Perrault steepled his fingers. "Suppose you set things up so it couldn't happen any other way," he proposed uncertainly.

Webber shook his head. "If I'm dead before it's finished, I'll never be sure."

Perrault looked him over candidly. "You look good for another sixty-seventy years. That suit you?"

"Just so I'm alive," Webber said doggedly. "I can't trust it to the kids—they're all off to Antarctica if they've got any stuff in 'em—or gabbing about digging mines under the oceans. God damn it—they ought to be up on the moon! They ought to be *doing* something, instead of fooling around on the same bloody planet everyone else has been wearing ruts in for the last million years."

"I've been thinking, Joe," Perrault said. "Why don't you set up a foundation?"

Webber scowled. "What the hell for?" he wondered.

"Why, to develop the hydrogen rocket," Perrault explained.

"Yeah? What would I do for money?"

"Well . . ." Perrault shifted uncomfortably. "Doc Brent has been sort of talking about one. He . . . he's got even more than I've got, because he worked the market a little more shrewd, and he . . . well, he won't be around much longer. He knows it, and he hasn't got anybody much. Only he isn't right settled what kind of foundation to make it."

Webber's eyes narrowed. "So we put the bite on him?"

Perrault shrugged. "I think he'd sort of go for it," he said earnestly. "We always did feel sort of awkward, him and me, being the only people that ever made money off space flight. We sort of feel we owe something—we do,

Joe. Honest. I'll put a little something in the kitty, too, if we can rig it."

Webber shook his head. "It'll still take too long," he objected. "You can't get around that. These young ones don't care. It doesn't mean a thing to them."

"You'd write it in the charter," Perrault explained. "Even if nobody in the whole world cared, the foundation would *have* to care. And some of the young ones care. There's Martha. It means something to her."

"She's different," Webber objected. "She's been around space bugs all her life. There aren't many like that."

"There's some," Perrault argued. "We don't need many, for a start."

Webber shrugged disgustedly. "Well, if that's the best we can do . . ." But it wasn't victory. It was surrender to hopelessness.

"It's the best I can think of," Perrault admitted. "It'll be a long time, and maybe neither of us will live to see it done. But if you can be sure of anything, Joe, that will do the job. And having it won't stop you from trying other things—different ways—like you've been doing all along."

Webber hadn't thought of that. He nodded, smiling, suddenly liking the idea. His mistake had been to think of it as the only thing left to do. It wasn't. As long as he lived, there were things he could try and, failing, he could try again. But now, even if he died, there was a chance of the job going on.

"You'll talk to Doc?" he asked.

"I'll talk to him," Perrault promised. He slapped the arm of his chair, genuinely pleased with himself. "With me and you for a board of directors—maybe Rog . . ."

"Not him," Webber said flatly.

"Why not?" Perrault argued. "He feels as strong about it as we do. Maybe more. And he's fifteen years younger than either of us. It might turn out important, if it takes a long time."

"Well, all right," Webber agreed grudgingly. "But just because he's young."

But he still didn't feel easy. Already he was thinking ahead to the time when the hydrogen rocket was built. It wouldn't do any good if there wasn't anyone to go up in it. You could build a castle on the moon, but that didn't mean you could get the young ones to go there and live in it.

"Marty around?" he asked.

Perrault was surprised. He hadn't expected that question. "She's somewhere around," he decided.

"Find her," Webber said. "I want to talk to her."

Perrault climbed to his feet. Something in the way Webber spoke made him cock an eyebrow. "Private?" he asked.

Webber hesitated. "Yeah. Private," he decided. "Just the two of us."

Perrault paused, then shrugged and slowly, lankly, climbed the stairs.

Since early times, the light of a campfire had brought men out of storms to its warmth. Now, though all the mechanisms were different, it was the same.

At the last, when they were too near the camp for the red-eye to help any more, Ryan zipped into his parka and opened the door. Barehanded, he clung to the door-frame, squinting tightly against the daggerlike chips of flying snow. He shouted commands to the boy above the screech and booming of the wind. He felt the snow buggy respond. His hands grew numb, but he kept his grip. The furious wind slashed and ripped at his face until it, too, was numb, and he was sure it was streaming with blood.

Then, suddenly, it was all over. The snow buggy crept to a stop in front of the shed—in front of the door to its own stall.

He dropped down, and suddenly he was out of the wind. He staggered up to the sliding doors and rolled them open. He shouted for the boy to drive in.

The snow buggy lunged forward. Ryan pushed the doors shut. Suddenly, he was very tired.

They were the last crew back. Ryan looked up and down the shed. Each snow buggy crouched in its stall, and each stall was filled.

His hands had started to frostbite. He rubbed them together vigorously. He rubbed his face, too. Especially his nose. His skin tingled.

Men came running. He unzipped his parka and stood by the snow buggy waiting for them.

"Think we weren't coming?" he taunted boastfully.

The snow buggy was heavily crusted with wind-packed snow. Now, in the warmth of the shed, it began to drip. Fenwick climbed down from the cab. The boy followed, moving woodenly—stumbling and drained.

Ryan walked toward the tunnel into the living quarters. They followed him, first Fenwick, then the boy. He slipped out of his parka and carried it over his arm.

In the common room, he stopped. "Set out the chocolate," he ordered loudly. One of the messboys jumped to obey.

Ryan slung his parka over the back of a bench. He sat down at the table. He ran his fingers through his hair. He rested his face on his hands.

He heard a sound beside him. He looked up. The boy, still tightly zipped in his parka, stood there.

"Sit down," he invited, friendly now.

The boy sat heavily. Ryan got up. "Here—let's get you out of this."

Gently, he peeled the boy out of his parka. The messboy came and set steaming cups in front of them. Ryan sat down again, beside the boy.

"Well—you made up your mind?" he asked. "You going to stay in this country?"

The boy didn't speak at once. Ryan didn't prod him. He waited.

Finally, the boy found his voice. "You . . . you'll let me?" he stammered. "You won't turn in a bad report on me?"

Ryan looked him in the eye. "You're green yet," he said. "You need a lot of seasoning. But you know what it needs to live in this country now, and I think you have the stuff to do it. If you want to stay, it won't be me that says you can't."

He grinned.

The boy took a deep breath. He swallowed. "Then I'll stay," he said. And after a moment he said again, firmly, "I'm staying."

He met Ryan's glance without blinking.

Ryan lifted his cup. A salute.

"Mister," he said evenly. "Welcome to Xanadu Camp."

Marty came down the stairs, her bare feet padding on the steps. She was naked, and her body glistened with tanning oil.

She didn't come near him. It was just as well.

"Hi, Uncle Joe," she said brightly. "I was taking a sunbath. I . . . I don't always run around like this. I mean, not all the time, anyway. Not that it isn't sort of fun." She smiled.

"Siddown," Webber said.

She curled up in a chair, neither modest nor provocative. Just being herself.

"Did you want to tell me something?" she asked.

"Yeah," Webber said, and suddenly he didn't know how he would get around to saying it. "Marty—I've just found out there isn't going to be space flight again. Not in my time."

"Oh, Uncle Joe," she said, understanding. "That's awful."

"I can stand it," Webber said doggedly. "Just so it's someday. That's where you come in."

"Me?" She looked down at herself, as if just now aware of her nakedness.

Webber nodded. "You," he said. "You talked about Rog Sherman a while back—did you mean it, or was it just talk?"

"I mean it, Uncle Joe," she said soberly. "I'm going to marry him."

"What about kids?"

"Lots of 'em," she said hopefully. She moved very slightly, as if conscious of the power in her body.

Webber squared his shoulders and pressed them against the back of his chair. "Okay," he said. "I'll fix you up. But you'd better make good."

With an excited squeal she wriggled out of her chair and climbed up in his lap. She hugged him and pressed her cheek against his face. "Oh, Uncle Joe," she whispered gladly. "You're wonderful!"

She relaxed and slipped down so her head rested against his shoulder. "Just wonderful," she murmured comfortably.

"Martha," Alice Perrault called invisibly, nicely. "You ought to put some clothes on."

Marty sat up straight. "Oh, Ma!" she complained loudly.

Webber put out a hand to steady her. She tensed. He took the hand back and she snuggled against him again.

"You're nice, Uncle Joe," she murmured gratefully, not moving. Not doing anything.

Now he put his arm around her, and she let him. "If I was a couple years younger," he confided roughly, "I'd say to hell with Rog."

She laughed warmly, stretched up and kissed him chastely on the forehead. Then she stood up.

"I'd better go put something on," she said as if the thought of modesty amused her. "Ma gets all fussed when I run around bare. She'd probably die if I answered the door."

"I think you'd better go put something on," Webber agreed carefully. He smiled wryly. "Unless you want to forget about Rog."

He watched her scamper up the stairs, appreciating the young grace of her body. He chuckled. If Sherman didn't marry her, damn if he wouldn't marry her himself. She'd be sort of nice to have around.

And the young ones had to come from somewhere.

PART FOUR

WHEN YOU LEARNED to do something in free fall, you never forgot how. And that was where Joe Webber learned to use a straight razor—on the way to Mercury.

He was just a kid then—a thin, wiry, gray-eyed kid. That was a long time ago.

He hadn't been to space for years, now, but he'd never changed to any other way of shaving.

He cut boldly—slashed the lather off, and with it his three-day beard. His cold, crowfooted eyes squinted back at him from the mirror.

That morning, he saw the white hairs for the first time.

They must have been there a long time, but his bleached-straw blondness hid them well. Now, all of a sudden, there they were, as if his hair had turned white overnight.

Mechanically, he finished shaving. All he could think of was his white hair, his fifty-seven years, and the implacable passage of time.

(Rain pelted the big window heavily. Water streamed down its face. The whole outside was a wet, misty gray.)

He dressed quickly in the clean clothes he had laid out the night before. He ate a bachelor's breakfast of toast and coffee.

Suddenly, he hated his life—the lost hopes, dead dreams—the plodding succession of days. He should have got himself a wife—a woman to share things with, and to help carry the load. Too late, now. He might have married, once. He'd had a chance. But at the time it hadn't seemed important.

Nothing had been important, then, except space flight.

He rinsed his coffee cup, knife, and spoon in the lavatory sink. He brushed the toast crumbs into the waste-basket. He piled everything on top of the hot plate. He put them back in the file and pushed the drawer into the wall.

He rolled up his bedding and crammed it into the adjoining drawer. The drawer jammed. He got down on his knees and put his weight against it. Reluctantly, it closed.

He looked at his watch. Almost nine. He unplugged his desk and pushed it into a corner, then crossed to the storage alcove across from the files.

The big round table was hoary with dust. He dug a worn shirt from the "L" file—laundry. He dusted the table, then rolled it out into the room, set it up, and plugged it in.

Going back to the alcove, he dusted the chairs. He set them around the table like the four points of a compass. Sneezing, he crammed the shirt back in the drawer with his laundry.

Then it was nine o'clock. He went out into the other room and unlocked the door to the corridor. He went back inside to wait.

At thirteen minutes past nine, watching through the one-way transparent partition of the inner room, Webber saw her come in from the corridor. Rain dripped from her storm-skirt and cape. Droplets gleamed in her hair.

He went to the door to meet her.

"Uncle Joe!" she cried gladly. She rushed across the room and swept him up in her arms. She hugged him warmly, like a small boy.

He endured her attentions silently.

"The men will be here in a minute," she went on, bubbling with talk. "Rog is parking the copter. I came on down."

"Glad you came," Webber said, reserved. "Swell seeing you, Marty."

She laughed, pleased. Stepping back, she looked around. "Gosh—every time we come it looks dirtier and older and more like the Sahara."

She was right. He knew it. The room looked desolate —hollow. And it wasn't quite clean, in spite of all he could do.

But he said, stiffly, vainly, "It's your imagination, Marty. It hasn't changed."

"Oh, I know that," she admitted hastily, backing up a little more. "It's just me." She gave him an infectious, wrinkle-nosed smile.

She looked around again—saw the empty receptionist's desk.

"Where's that woman you had?" she wondered.

"Mrs. Bates?" He shrugged. "Had to let her go. Needed the money for something else."

Marty nodded understandingly. "Would you like me for the job?" she offered. "I'm cheap."

Webber gave her a slow, unmistakable look. "I don't think I could stand it," he said.

She stepped up to him and messed his hair. "You're fun, Uncle Joe," she laughed, flattered.

"Yeah," Webber grumbled. He nodded back at the doorway to the inner office. "Let's go inside."

He led the way. Inside, she unsnapped her cape, hesitated, then slipped out of her vest and storm-skirt.

"Think it's warm enough in here?" he wondered.

"Oh, pooh," she replied. "You sound like Rog." She draped the clothes over the desk and sat on them. She leaned forward. "Like me, Uncle Joe?"

"Sometimes," he admitted distantly. He sat down at the table, facing her across it.

"I'm glad you came ahead," he said. "There's a thing or two I want to know."

She perked up willingly. "Sure," she agreed.

Webber rubbed his lip. "How long have you been keeping house with that lummox?"

She looked at the ceiling, thinking. "Nine years," she figured, then bristled. "And he's not a lummox."

"Happy with him?"

"Uh-huh."

Webber went on digging. "No fights or anything?"

She smiled, delighted. "Oh sure. We've had some real wowsers. Why?"

Webber avoided her eyes. He looked off to the window. Heavy rain beat against the glass. "You were going to have kids," he said carefully. "Why didn't you?"

She sobered. "We wanted to," she admitted. "We'd

have them if we could. Lots. But—well, the . . . the doctor says Rog can't. He was out in space too long."

Webber thought about that for a while. "But there's nothing the matter with you," he said finally.

"Not that we know of," she admitted.

Webber nodded. Under the table, where she couldn't see, he doubled a fist. "You've got to have kids," he told her stubbornly. "I don't care how, but you've got to have them."

She frowned. A bit of the vigor went out of her posture. "Why, Uncle Joe? Is it important?"

"You're damn right it's important," Webber said. He leaned hard on the table. "There's got to be someone that wants space flight, Marty. I'm getting old. I was counting on you."

"I'm sorry," she said, small-voiced, holding her body still.

"There's ways you can get them, Marty," Webber said.

She actually looked afraid. "Uncle Joe—please. No," she protested. Spots of color showed on her pale, white face. "It's bad enough—don't make it worse. Rog wanted kids, too."

"I'll talk to him," Webber decided.

"No, Uncle Joe," she said quickly. "Don't. Please."

Webber made an impatient noise. "Ditch him, Marty. He's no good for you."

He wasn't *too* old, yet. At least, he didn't think he was.

Resolute, she shook her head. "Except for that, we've had fun. I don't want to change."

"You're just in the habit of living with him," Webber told her. He knew he couldn't pry her loose all at once, but he had planted the idea. That was all he could hope to do now. It would be a shame to see her go to waste.

"I've said all I'm going to," she told him calmly. She looked up. "Here come the men."

For a moment, Webber thought she'd said it to divert his attention. But he looked. Roger Sherman and Andrew Perrault were coming through the door from the corridor—Perrault with a loose-jointed stroll, Sherman limping.

94

They struggled out of their rain clothes. Perrault laid his over the receptionist's desk. Sherman tossed his on a chair.

Perrault tried to smile. As usual, the result was grotesque. "Joe! How are you?" he crowed.

"Six months older," Webber said grimly. He looked up at the old doctor. "You could do with some hair dye yourself."

Perrault gave him a droll look. "I could do with some *hair*."

Sherman nudged past Perrault and picked Webber up by his belt. "How's things?"

"Put me down," Webber snapped.

Sherman grinned, lifted him a little higher, and let go. Webber dropped. He landed on his feet like a cat—crouched, face twisted in a snarl.

He straightened up, ruffled. He nodded to the doorway behind him. "Let's get inside."

They trooped in after him. Martha had dropped down off the desk and was slipping into her vest. Sherman went over to her. "So here's where you got to."

She got the vest the rest of the way on. "Uh-huh," she said, little-girl-like. "Don't you trust me?"

"Should I?"

"You might as well," she said guilelessly. "You'll have to."

"Wait till I get you home," he threatened. He squeezed her shoulder until it was white, and shook her. But he was smiling, and so was she. She leaned back against him.

"Will you beat me?" she asked hopefully.

"Within an inch of your life," he promised, grinning.

Webber crossed to the table. "Come on," he urged. "Let's get this silly business over with."

Sherman walked Martha over to the table. He glanced at the way the chairs were placed. Firmly, he moved two of them together. He held one for Martha. Then he sat down on the other. Martha wiggled herself comfortable.

Perrault took one of the remaining chairs. "I guess we're ready, youngster."

Webber sat down. He reached under the table and found the switch. He snapped it over. A tiny, amber fleck appeared in the round table's center. Webber opened the folder in front of him.

"March 12, 2009," he said, talking fast, formally. "This is the twenty-first semi-annual meeting of the board of directors of the Dr. Howard R. Brent Foundation for Extraterrestrial Development—a non-profit corporation under the laws of the United States and the Canberra Charter. Chairman and president Joe Webber speaking. Others present—"

He glanced a cue at Perrault.

"Andrew Perrault," the doctor drawled. "Vice-president, secretary-treasurer, and member of the board. Very bored." He smiled clumsily.

"Roger Sherman; field representative and member of the board," Sherman said.

"Martha Sherman," Marty contributed. "Member of the board." She smiled at Webber coquettishly. "Uncle Joe, can't I be something else?"

"We like you like you are," Webber told her. He rapped his fist on the table. "All members present."

He took several blank sheets of paper from the folder and passed one to each of the others. "Minutes of the last meeting have been distributed to the members for signature," he recited. He took another paper from the folder, this one with writing on it. He passed it to Perrault.

"Our secretary-treasurer will read the financial report."

Reluctantly, Perrault glanced at the paper. "You might let me see it before I'm supposed to read it," he complained wryly.

Webber gave him a black look that silenced him. Perrault shrugged and bent to read.

The report was brief and simple. For the most part, the Foundation's money came from Brent & Perrault Biologicals, Inc., of which it owned a two-thirds interest. Nine hundred forty thousand, this half-year. In addition, by methods best left to the imagination, Webber had collected another hundred twenty thousand from unspecified sources.

Better than a million dollars. Good, hard, Canberra-Confederate dollars. But it still didn't add up to much.

Since work had been started on the hydrogen rocket engine, the project had gobbled almost fourteen million. Before it was done, it was going to cost a lot more.

But worth it, Webber told himself. Worth it.

During the last six months, the report went on, the Foundation had spent a couple thousand for office rent, and another thousand five hundred had enabled Webber to keep soul and body together. All the rest had been spent on the engine. Every last plaque of it.

Cash on hand: zero, as usual.

A million Confederate fishskins nearer, Webber thought wretchedly. At the present rate, the engine would be finished in eighty-five years.

Sullenly, he thought about his graying hair, Perrault's bald age, and Sherman's forty years. And Marty's barrenness.

No. It couldn't go on like this.

But all he said was, "President's report."

It was the usual guff. Actually, he couldn't add much to the financial report. The work on the engine was going ahead at the usual snail's crawl. Morris Gunderman even claimed it was a bit ahead of schedule. It was hard to tell. It was a long way from done.

A few technical papers had been placed in the science journals. There was always the hope they might stimulate thought in minds not on the Foundation's payroll, and for whose thinking, therefore, the Foundation would not have to pay.

And it might bring the engine sooner, too.

It was a weak sounding thing, though: the claim that progress was made. It sat very poorly with Webber.

They voted mechanically to continue the existing slate of officers, and, again, to maintain the existing policies and lines of action. There was no other business. Webber ended the meeting by rapping his fist on the table. He reached under the table to kill the recorder.

But he didn't get up. He leaned forward, his weight on his forearms.

"That ought to keep the lawyers happy," he said. "Now we can get down to business."

That surprised them. Usually, when the board meeting ended, the talk turned to other things—to old times, and what was new. Perrault with the gossip from B & P Bio; and Sherman training pilots for Intercon Rockets, the only work he knew well.

Small talk.

The reunions lasted through lunch. Perrault would buy, and afterwards they would go home, leaving him—Webber—to direct the Brent Foundation as he pleased.

So they were surprised, but he gave them no time to ask questions. He bracketed Perrault with his eyes. "Drew—we've got to have more money."

Perrault looked apprehensive. He frowned. "What's the matter, Joe?"

"We're getting old," Webber said. "And we aren't getting anywhere. Not fast enough."

"But Joe," Perrault argued. "The whole idea of the Foundation was so in case something happened to us, the work would get done all the same."

"Do you think it will, if I'm not here to run things?" Webber demanded.

"I don't see why not," Perrault said doubtfully.

"Well, it won't," Webber said. "And the way things are going, it'll take a hundred years to get it done. It might as well be forever."

Perrault shrugged soberly. "I'd like to see it myself," he admitted. "But there's plain no way to do it faster. We don't have the cash."

"We've got to," Webber insisted. "Toss out that kid you've got running the company. Put someone in charge that can make it pay off."

"The company's making as much as it can," Perrault protested. His hand made embarrassed, awkward gestures.

Marty backed him up. "It's true," she said fiercely. "If Mr. Shelby could turn another plaque, he'd do it. The company's doubled its business since he took over."

"It hasn't doubled the payoff," Webber snapped.

"Well, there's been a lot of expenses, building it up," Perrault explained. "In a couple of years, we'll be taking in three times what we were."

"I'll believe it when I see the dividend check," Webber said skeptically. "I've been looking at the stockholders' report. There's a lot of spending you can quit. You're throwing money away."

"But Joe," Perrault argued. "It's investment. That money's going to pay off."

"Yeah? When?" Webber wanted to know. "All I can see is that Shelby pouring cash down the drain. Like what you're putting in research—I mean, you *were*. You're going to stop. Right now."

"Is that an order?" Perrault wondered. He had a hard time believing it.

"If that's how it's got to be, that's it," Webber said inflexibly. "We need the money here, and to hell with the pills."

But Perrault shook his head. "No, Joe," he said painfully. "Joe—in the medicine business, it's research that pays off. It means a lot of money, in the long run."

"I'm not talking about the long run," Webber said. "I'm talking about *now*. And space flight. What's more important than that?"

Perrault made a frantic, hopeless gesture. "That research is *important*, Joe."

Webber wasn't impressed. "Get this," he said. "We need cash. A lot of it. And I don't care too much how we get it. But the company's the place we get it from. You can put it together any way you like, but from here on I want five million every dividend."

A strained, incredulous look came over Perrault's face. "Joe—you can't," he protested.

"Why not?" Webber demanded.

Marty spoke up. "Let him be," she scolded. "Let him have his research. Can't you see it's important to him?"

"Space flight's important," Webber retorted. "That comes first."

She nodded scornfully. "Yes—with you it does. With me . . ." She glanced meaningly at Sherman. "With Dad, it's his research. Don't take it away from him."

"You heard me, Marty. Everything that isn't necessary has to go."

"Necessary to who?" Marty demanded fiercely. "Dad—maybe you'd better tell him about it."

Perrault had crumpled the minutes sheet. Now he began to tear bits off it. "It's a cancer, Joe," he explained reticently. "Not one of the big kinds—they've beat those. This is the kind that comes out of scar tissue —cells that went wrong in the healing."

"I thought they'd beat that kind, too," Webber said.

"Oh no, Joe," Perrault said quickly. "They found a way to prevent it, sure, but that doesn't do any good for the guy that has it already, or the guy they don't prevent it in. That's the guy I want to help. We need an honest to golly cure."

"It doesn't sound important to me," Webber said.

"Ma has it," Marty spoke up soberly. "I guess that makes it important enough."

"She won't be the first to die for space flight," Webber said carelessly.

"I don't know if I want space flight now," Marty said willfully. "After what it's done to Rog. I don't know that I'd want it to happen to others—other women's husbands . . ."

Sherman put a hand on her arm. "Hold up, redhead," he told her. He turned to Webber, eyes calm. "I might better have something clear. She wasn't talking about my leg, was she."

He glanced back at Marty—saw the guilt on her face.

"You've been talking again," he said warningly.

"I'm sorry, Rog," she admitted contritely.

He patted her gently. He smiled. "That's okay, redhead," he said.

He turned back to Webber. "All right. So she told you. All right. It was going to Jupiter that did it—seven solid years out there. But I don't blame anyone. I'm sorry it happened, that's all. And I wish it hadn't. If I'd known it'd happen, maybe I wouldn't have gone. I don't know. But I *didn't* know, and I went. And damn—I'm glad I went. Not glad for some of the things that happened, but —well, that's the game. I'm glad I went."

"All right," Webber sneered. "So you're glad you went. So what?"

Sherman looked grim. "There's one thing more," he said. He shifted in his chair, and leaned forward, his weight on the table. The table creaked.

"When you say you want space flight," he said deliberately, "I'm with you all the way. I want it as bad as you. But I'm not in so much of a hurry I start yelling before I think. I made that mistake once—you taught me yourself—and I learned my lesson."

100

He shook his head, frowning, eyes steady on Webber. "Joe—Doc's company can't support a fast job, even if you bleed it white. Even if you sell off everything including the good will. And you don't have to do it that way. Believe me, Joe—space flight'll come back, if we help it or if we don't. All it needs is some patience."

Webber shook his head, resisting the argument blindly. "You're younger," he said. "I'm too old to be patient."

Sherman slapped his hands flat on the table. "Look, Joe," he said impatiently. "I'm no biologist, but on the way out to Jupiter I had plenty of time to talk with one. And Mike knew his stuff. So you know one thing he told me? He told me, any environment a living thing can adapt itself to live in, if there's nothing already there to stop it—it goes in and makes itself to home. And it lives there. Like once, there wasn't anything on the land—and then the plants came up out of the ocean, and then the animals came up, and now there's even some moving up into the air: birds. And us—we're going out into space. Because we can live out there. And because there's nothing to stop us."

"It's got to make money," Webber muttered fiercely. "Taxpayers won't pay for it. It's got to be business."

Sherman shrugged. "The engine'll fix that," he said. "And you don't have to worry about that, either. It'll get built some day, whether you pay for it or not. I remember that, too. When it's possible to make an invention—when the pieces are around and waiting to get put together, sure enough, some guy comes along and does it. Maybe not the same as somebody else might do it—but the thing works by the same principles and it does the same job. So—Joe, you don't have to worry. We'll go back into space. You can bet on it."

But Webber shook his head. "I've got to be sure," he said tenaciously. "I've got to see it myself."

Sherman banged the table. "Okay," he said. "But lay off Doc. You can't get that cash from the company, no matter what you do."

"I can get more than I'm getting," Webber said stubbornly. "All I want to know, do I get it, or do I come in and get it myself?"

101

Perrault made helpless motions with his hands. "The company won't stand for it," he protested. "It isn't worth enough."

"Look, Drew," Webber said. "Up to now, I've let you run it any way you pleased. I can change that if you make me."

Perrault's face crumpled. His mouth moved and no words came out. "Joe—can't you see?" he pleaded. "I . . . I've got to have that research. Alice . . . not much time, and then you can have it all. And a . . . a couple, three years, we'll be paying it out every dividend anyhow. We'll be big enough, then."

Webber wasn't persuaded. His face was implacable. "I can't wait that long," he said. "How long am I good for? Twenty years? Thirty? We've got to start now."

"People are living longer all the time," Perrault stammered desperately. He dithered his hands. "You'll live to see it, Joe. I promise."

"I'm not people," Webber said, ice cold. "I'm me. Just answer yes or no—do I get it, or do I vote the Foundation's shares and get it anyway?"

Perrault looked close to tears. "You can't," he repeated raggedly. "You can't."

And then, amazingly, he laughed. "By George," he chortled, "you *can't!*"

Webber boggled. "Huh? Are you nuts? What's to stop me?"

Perrault was almost helpless with laughter. "The Foundation," he cried triumphantly. "The Foundation!"

"Hold it," Webber said viciously. "The Foundation's what I say it is. And it does like I say."

"No it doesn't," Perrault laughed crazily. "It's what that silly board meeting says. And we voted like we always did—and now you're trying to switch things around. You can't do it, Joe. You plain can't do it. Not without a meeting of the board."

"Who says so?" Webber demanded.

Perrault spread his hands apologetically. "We'll take it to court if you make us," he said mildly. "We'd win."

Webber said nothing. He pressed his lips together and thought about it. Damn! Drew had him, dead center.

"All right," he decided. "We'll have another meeting of the board." He reached under the table.

"I don't think we will," Sherman said. His deep, deliberate voice commanded the room. "Unless you want to get kicked out as president. We're not your trained seals any more, Joe."

Webber stammered. They had him in a corner. He looked around the table. All he saw was Sherman's grim mouth, Perrault's almost jovial, glistening eyes, and Marty's bowed head.

"Marty?" he asked, searchingly.

She looked up tensely. "I'm sorry, Uncle Joe," she said in a small, embarrassed voice. She clung to Sherman's arm as if for protection.

Webber stood up. He kicked his chair back. "All right," he snarled. "Get out."

For a moment, no one moved. Then they rose, slowly. Marty gathered her clothes from the desk. They walked, disorganized, irresolute, to the door.

Perrault stopped. He turned. "Joe—" he offered, putting out a hand, half hoping.

"Get out, you bastard," Webber rasped.

Perrault backed away as if physically struck. Wordless, unhappy, he turned and nodded to the others. They trooped out. Webber sat there, still stunned by the things that had happened. He watched them go.

Then he just sat there.

Suddenly, he rushed to the door—out into the corridor. He looked both ways.

No one.

He shouted. "Drew! Marty! Rog!"

Silence.

He shouted again, no longer hoping—calling anyway. *"Marty!"*

No one answered. No one came.

He kicked the wall. "Damn!" he muttered. "Sonnovabitch!"

Scuffing his feet, he trudged back inside. He paced around the table, slowly, one step at a time. Rain rattled on the window. He thought he saw a copter windmill off into the low clouds.

He hadn't had much of a breakfast. He'd been counting on the lunch Drew would buy. But now Drew was gone. And Marty. There wouldn't be any lunch—or anything—any more.

And he was hungry.

He searched through his pockets. Just Confederate cash—three plaques and a wedge. He stood there looking at the four flat bits of plastic—three rectangles and a pie-slice triangle. He hadn't realized he was down that far.

Of course, he still had his spaceman's dollar. Some places still took the old American money. But he'd never spend that. He'd starve first.

He wondered how long he could go with just three Confederate dollars and twenty. Not long, that was sure. He shrugged stoically. He'd just have to *make* them last. Somehow.

After Martha and Roger left to catch the Melbourne rocket, Andrew Perrault boarded a sono jet for Denver. He was in good shape, but he'd reached the age now when rocket stewards watched him nervously. Besides, he wanted to think, and that was something you couldn't do in a rocket.

The jet climbed fast through the rain clouds and burst into bright day. It climbed until the clouds looked like cotton spread out on a board.

They cracked the barrier ten minutes after takeoff. Perrault unclasped his safety belt and slouched down. He stretched out his legs. Some of the passengers were filing down into the salon. Not him. The transparent bottom always gave him the willies.

Besides, for the first time in several weeks, he could sit back undisturbed and think hard about his research. Space flight or no space flight, the research came first.

It was Alice's doctor who had started him. When they knew that the cancer was beyond the point where surgery was any use, he said, plainly, "You can do more now than I can."

It was a frightening, cryptic thing to say. Perrault fumbled and mumbled, not understanding.

"You're the best medical biochemist I know of," the younger man explained earnestly. "If anyone can devise a successful treatment, you're the man."

It was flattering, but it was terrible, too. But later,

104

when the shock wore off, his mind began worming its way through the mazes and switchbacks and half-recognized contradictions that characterized modern knowledge of life chemistry, genetic chemistry, and the chemistry of cells, both normal and cancerous.

Two days later, for the first time in months, he coptered out to the plant. He requested lab space, equipment, supplies, and assistants. And he was in business.

It wasn't a simple problem. If it was, it would have been solved years ago. And it was very definitely *his* problem, as he learned very quickly.

He had forgotten, in his years away from large scale, organized research, how narrow was the mind and the talent of the average lab worker. Each of his assistants was, of course, extremely proficient in his specialty, but not one of them was equipped, educationally, temperamentally, or intellectually, to oversee the problem in its myriad aspects and feel a way through to solution. That, he soon realized, would be his job—his exclusively.

And it was a tough one. It required, first of all, an understanding of the healing process. He had to know why scar cells differed from the cells they replaced, and exactly *how* they differed. He had to know why they were different even though cells in the embryo reproduced almost endlessly with no such variation, and why, in spite of the endless process by which, in time, every cell of a man's body was replaced—he had to know why a man's body did not change into scar tissue.

Or did it, he wondered, thinking of the translucent flesh of the very old.

He had to know these things before he could learn the precise nature of the cancer—of which scar tissue was, apparently, a halfway state. Until he understood the cancer, he could not devise a way to fight it.

Because he had to fight it *in Alice*—had to devise a way to destroy the cancerous cells of her body, but a way which would not harm the ordinary, normal cells.

He couldn't imagine how it could be done. Not enough was known yet about genetics, or cell reproduction, or the manifold functions of body and flesh that might have bearing on the matter. Time was short, and the job was big. Perrault didn't know if he could do it, nor could he even guess if he could do it in time. He did

105

not let the uncertainty bother him. The thing was to work as hard as he could. It was the only hope.

He didn't have his notes with him. It didn't matter. He had always prided himself on his faultless memory of complicated detail. Not that he expected a careful thinking-through of the problem and the present state of his knowledge to evoke a sudden brilliant insight. He knew from wry experience that such moments came unbidden, often under incongruous conditions.

But sometimes the mind could be primed to produce such a moment, and that was what he hoped to do.

Only memory of the thing that had happened with Joe disturbed his thinking, as the plane slashed smoothly westward at a thousand miles an hour.

Perrault's home lay northwest of Denver, south of Boulder, in the shadow of the first massive upthrust of the Rocky Mountains.

Alice was sitting in a chair when he came in. She sat in chairs a lot, these days, when she wasn't lying down. It used to be she was always moving around, spritelike and cheerful, watering the plants or dusting imaginary dust off the furniture, or checking up after the cleaning robots. Or puttering in the garden.

There wouldn't be any garden this year.

She had always been small, but now she was thin and her eyes were sunk deep in her skull. Her once honeycolor hair was now white and stringy. There were coarse, ugly lines on her neck.

Perfunctorily, he went over and kissed her. She looked up listlessly. "Did you have a good time, Andy?" she asked.

He shook his head glumly. "Not very," he admitted. He slouched in a chair and began unhappily to tell her about it.

That afternoon, Joe Webber headed west in his copter. The Pittsburgh traffic slowed him down, and it was night before Traffic Control brought him in over the Cuyahoga Valley. He broke from control and landed illegally in an open field. Killing the engine, he settled down to get what sleep he could.

In the morning, he flew into the town for coffee and a

106

doughnut. Then he lifted out to the Foundation's sprawling research establishment on the heights above the river.

Morris Gunderman had an office overlooking the valley. It was a sunny place, well kept, with bamboo curtains to soften the light and—except for the airscreen—it was open to the outside.

Webber had yelped when he saw the luxurious plans, but somehow he hadn't seen them until after the work had gone so far it would cost more to change them than to let them go through. He had never quite forgiven Gunderman for that.

But Gunderman was automatically cordial when Webber walked in, unannounced.

"I wasn't told to expect you," he said, unloading a stack of scientific journals from a chair. He turned it around to face the sumptuous, V-shape desk. "Sit down," he invited. "Sit down."

Webber took the chair, twirled it around, and straddled it. He folded his hands on the back and rested his chin on his knuckles. "Doc," he said. "I want some action."

Gunderman scowled nervously. "Exactly what do you mean?" he hedged.

"I mean you've been making progress—you say—for ten whole years, and you don't look a whittle closer than when you started."

Gunderman fitted a cigarette into a sleek, long filter—the kind that took everything out of the smoke but air. He lit up and exhaled a faint cloud.

"I can see how it might look that way," he admitted. "To a layman, that is." He regarded Webber negligently.

"Yeah?" Webber prodded, eyes intent.

"Why, yes," Gunderman said smoothly. "You see, at this stage of development, the problem is entirely a matter of fundamental knowledge." He made a careless, summing-up gesture, as if it was obvious.

"I don't see it," Webber said.

Gunderman arched his brows. "I mean to say," he pronounced, "it is not a mere matter of engineering. If it was, we could complete the work in one or two years, on a fraction of our budget."

"Well, why can't you?" Webber wanted to know.

Gunderman shrugged glibly. "We do not have all the information we need," he explained. "Before we can design the engine, we will have to define the principles by which it will operate."

"You don't know how it'll work?" Webber demanded, appalled.

"That is a crude way of putting it," Gunderman said smugly. "Actually, we know it is possible. Anything is possible—it is merely a question of applying scientific laws to the problem. I am speaking of ends, not means, mind you. Of course, you cannot violate a law of nature."

"Okay. Stop right there," Webber said. "We'd better get a few things straight. We should have a long time ago."

"Certainly," Gunderman agreed. He made an I-have-nothing-to-hide gesture.

"You don't know how to make it," Webber said. "Right?"

"Not *precisely*," Gunderman emphasized. "We are working to find that out."

"Hmm," Webber muttered skeptically. "How?"

Gunderman folded his hands. "We are conducting research along several lines," he recited. "Several dozen lines, I should say. Basically, we are investigating the behavior of light nuclei and of particles—sometimes heavier nuclei where we can draw inferences. We are inquiring into the precise nature of the various characteristics—stability, credibility, wholeness, morbidity, transcience—in short, Mr. Webber, you might say the entire range of nuclear and subnuclear knowledge."

"All this just to build the engine," Webber said. It wasn't a question.

"All of it is necessary," Gunderman stated. "After all, at this point we do not know what are the principles we will use in the design of the engine. Undoubtedly, we have discovered some of them, but until we know them all—and until we have fitted them into a coherent pattern—it cannot look particularly promising to a layman such as yourself."

"So you haven't as much as a guess how the engine works," Webber inferred grimly.

"Suppose we consider the problem in detail," Gunderman suggested persuasively. He ticked the points off on his fingers. "The fuel must be hydrogen. We have settled that. Very well. But even if the ship is moving quite swiftly, and even if the intake is quite large, the hydrogen would be very rarefied—practically a vacuum. Very well. Thirdly, it must be a chain reaction. Of course, it would be terribly difficult to maintain such a reaction under near-vacuum conditions, but that is the only efficient means of producing energy. Moreover, it must be a reaction we can rigidly control. Now—we know of several reactions which involve hydrogen. However, none even approaches our specifications. That, Mr. Webber, is the problem we must solve."

"Tough, huh?" Webber concluded.

Gunderman nodded. He knocked ash off his cigarette. "It is very difficult," he said primly. "It will probably require a discovery on the order of the Yang-Lee assymmetry rule. Such discoveries are not an everyday occurrence. If they come once in a generation, we are very fortunate."

"So that's what I've been paying for," Webber grumbled. He smouldered. "Well, we'll change that. Starting right now, anything that doesn't go into the engine doesn't go on the bill."

"You can't be serious," Gunderman protested, shocked profoundly. "Mr. Webber—it is impossible at this point to divide the useful knowledge from the useless. So we must discover both. It is the only way."

Webber rapped his knuckles on the chair's back. "You've been using that excuse for everything you felt like doing," he accused. "It's going to stop."

Gunderman drew himself up. "Mr. Webber. Unless I am permitted to approve whatever research I think promising, I will be compelled to resign."

"Then quit," Webber told him. "I'll find somebody that can get more results and less talk."

Something very like fright touched Gunderman's features. "I am not accustomed to be spoken to this way," he said stiffly. "I have dealt as best I could with a very refractory problem. I tell you—there is no other way to do it."

Webber considered. He couldn't be sure if Gunderman's splutter came from a scientist or a con man. But he'd used up a lot of money and a lot of time, and couldn't show much for either.

"Suppose I keep you," Webber proposed. "What will I get?"

Gunderman made a helpless gesture. "I have been doing all that is possible," he said weakly. "What more could I promise?"

It had the ring of truth—or a very shrewd lie. "I'll talk to some people," Webber said at last. "They'd better agree with you."

Then he was silent again, mulling. "Suppose I get more money?" he suggested.

Gunderman didn't *look* hungry. "Perhaps we could accelerate things," he shrugged. "There are several questions that look interesting."

"Interesting?" Webber echoed critically.

Gunderman corrected himself. "Promising, I should say," he said. "And we might retain a few more consultants—some of our most important steps forward have been contributed by consultants."

"I'll keep it in mind, then," Webber said. "Another thing—this talk about seventy or eighty years. That's out. I want it finished in ten."

Gunderman looked doubtful. "We might do it, if we have the funds," he said cautiously. "But I cannot promise. In work of this nature, there are limits to how fast it can be done."

"You didn't talk like that ten years ago," Webber accused. "You said give you the money and you'd have it done in five."

Gunderman made a that-was-ten-years-ago shrug. "I must have been enthusiastic," he explained uncomfortably. "I had not examined the problem in detail."

Well, that was all he could get, Webber figured. But he remembered too vividly how Perrault had walked out of his office. Better to make peace.

"Hell," he muttered viciously. "Do what you can."

At least he had put the fear of God in him. Maybe it would do some good.

When he got back to Washington, late in the day, he checked the phone. There weren't any calls. Half a dozen capsules lay in the mail chute. He lined them up on the desk and tore them open one by one.

Two of them were crank stuff. One ranted that God had never intended for men to go into space. The other claimed that a shipload of Martians had grounded in a Himalayan valley. It asked for two million dollars, Confederate (none of that worthless pre-Canberra trash, please) to finance establishing contact with them. Webber smiled grimly. He'd been to Mars—second expedition—and there weren't any Martians.

Three of the letters were routine Foundation business. Two whopping bills and a research grant request. Webber put them aside.

The last one was different. Webber knew it as soon as he tore off the cap and dumped the pack of papers on his desk. He broke the string.

It was quite an assortment: four thousand shares of General Nucleonics, twenty-two hundred of Intercontinental Rockets, and a couple thousand each of Transocean Cargoes and Lindner Enterprises. They were made out to him, Joseph R. Webber, and there was a small white card.

Marty, it said.

He'd known she had money. Perrault had given her a big piece of B & P Bio when she married, and she must have reinvested the income off that. Even so, he hadn't thought she had enough to toss blue chips at his feet like wastepaper, but it was the kind of thing you could expect her to do.

Webber hardly thought about it, though. She'd done it, and that was enough for him.

God damn! Now there was a woman you could fall in love with three times a day, and six on weekends. Too bad she was married.

The nucleus of Mayflower Dome had been built on shore and towed out over the Atlantic Ridge, and sunk. That was five years ago. Since then, half a dozen sea domes had been started. Now this one, the first, was almost done.

Joe Webber disembarked onto the service barge under a lead gray, rain-wracked sky. The cargo ship began to unload the machines. Webber walked around the barge, keeping catlike balance as the deck rolled sluggishly and wallowed in the waves. Finally, he got the attention of the man who, shouting orders, was directing the barge side of the unloading.

"Hey, Jack," Webber shouted into the wind. "How do I get down from here?"

The foreman looked him over. "You got business here?"

"Sure I got business here," Webber yelled. "You think I'm here for two weeks' vacation?"

The foreman turned away. He shouted at the unloading crew. "Hey—not there! You want to bust our bottom open? Over *there!*" He turned back to Webber. "Who you want to see?"

"Fred Bendix," Webber told him, turning his face out of the wind.

"Who're you? What kind of business?"

"I'm Joe Webber, and it's between me and him."

The foreman stumped over to a shack in one corner of the barge. Webber waited where he was. After a short wait, the foreman came back.

"You can ride down in the next ferry," he said. "It'll be a couple of hours. He says you can wait in the shack."

Webber nodded. "I'll wait out here." He turned his face into the wind. Spray chipped at his face. The barge rolled under his feet. He kept his balance. He smiled.

The massive steel girders seemed to groan under the weight of the seas. Joe Webber looked around, edgy, making the cramped place familiar in his mind.

It wasn't much different from a space ship—the same crowded feel of the quarters and the smells of metal. But never had there been the overpowering awareness of the megatons of water pressing down.

"How can you stand it down here?" Webber grumbled.

Fred Bendix grinned. He leaned back against a beam and looked up at the low ceiling. He was a short, block-stocky man with abundant black hair and a dark complexion. His face was a collection of knobby prominences.

"You get used to it," he said carelessly. "Still chasing the moon, are you?"

"You're damn right," Webber said.

Bendix chuckled. "Good old Joe," he said. "Why don't you give it up? I could use a man like you down here."

"I wouldn't give it up for anything," Webber told him fiercely. "Everybody else deserted, but not me. Somebody's got to stay with it."

Bendix ambled down the corridor. "Don't worry about it," he jollied. "When the time comes, so many of 'em'll head for the moon they'll weigh it down. It'll crash in the Pacific Ocean, just like the *Jove*."

"They'd better," Webber promised. "I'll make them."

Bendix grinned. "When the time comes, better take advantage of your big head start, or you'll get tromped in the rush. Look—when they pulled Orbitbase out from under me, they put me on the ground with nothing but a lot of money in my pocket. My legs were so weak I practically had to have a wheelchair. So I got into the water, and I bought myself a bathyscaph. You know what I found?"

"Fish," Webber sneered.

Bendix tapped Webber's chest with a stiff, hard finger. "This planet's got more water than land," he said. "And it's as different from land as the moon. This down here's as much our country as space. And it's easier to get at. We're going to settle it. That's what I've started, right here."

"You're about as far from space as you can get," Webber said bitingly. "What do you call that?"

Bendix chuckled mockingly. "Joe—this is wild country down here. Now. But it won't be always. We'll tame it down to nothing. We'll settle it like Canada."

"So what?" Webber demanded. "That won't put people on the moon."

"Yeah, Joe. Sure," Bendix admitted amiably. "But someday there won't be any more ocean bottom to settle. Then what's going to happen to the guys that don't want to settle down with a door-to-door salesman for a next-door neighbor?"

Webber shook his head. "You're asking. You answer."

"They'll go to the moon, Joe," Bendix told him. "And after that, Mars. And Venus. Maybe—hell, if we can set up shop down here, we can put up on Jupiter. What's to stop us?"

"Money," Webber said flatly. "A lot of cheapjack businessmen. They won't pay out for it unless they see a profit. So I've got to rig it for them—the bastards."

He put himself in front of Bendix to block the man's pacing. He grabbed Fred's shoulders. "Look, Fred. I need money. A lot of it. Right now."

Bendix backed off. "Don't look at me, boy," he advised. "I'm living off broken promises now."

Webber went after him. "I'm not kidding, Fred. Look —you've been making payments on the moon-base plans I dug out for you. Okay. Why not pay up the rest of it now?"

Bendix gave him an empty-pocket shrug. "Why are you in such an all of a sudden hurry?" he wondered. "You used to talk like all the time in the world."

"I'm getting old," Webber said grimly. "And I'm not getting anywhere."

"Where's there to get?" Bendix argued. "I tell you once, I tell you half a million times—when the time comes they'll be standing room only in your rockets. It's just the time ain't right."

"I'm going to *make* it right," Webber said intently. "I've *got* to."

Bendix made a none-of-my-affair flap of the hands. "Your ulcer, Joe. Not mine. Me—sure, I'd help out if I could. But all I got's tied up in this overgrowed terrarium. Give me a couple-three years, I'll be in business, but right now I ain't got the price of a two-dollar wristwatch wholesale."

"That's your last word?" Webber asked stonily.

"Sorry, Joe. That's it."

Webber turned away. "How do I get out of this rabbit hole?" He started walking.

"Joe—wait up," Bendix spoke abruptly.

Webber stopped. He turned, but he stayed where he was. He waited, coldly.

114

"I thought of something," Bendix said hopefully. He approached.

Webber listened suspiciously, saying nothing.

Bendix came closer. "Look—the mine's going to be in production three months from now. Our stock'll jump its market a mile. We haven't been letting it out, on account of if we had a setback it wouldn't do our stock any good. You're the only guy I'm tipping. If you buy us on the market now, you'll wind up with pockets so full you'll have to use your shoulderblades to walk with."

"You aren't conning, are you?" Webber asked suspiciously. "You're not trying to sell me a bale of paper."

"Why'd I do a thing like that for?" Bendix wondered. "Hell, we're sold out of our issue for years. It won't make me a paper palinquin. I'm just doing this for you, boy. Get your feet out of the mud."

"Well, it better go up," Webber threatened. "It better."

The trip south from McMurdo Sound was a long one, and it was hard on the nerves. The small electric car screamed through the ice tunnel hour after hour, shunting from one track to the other and back again to avoid the ponderous ore trains which, during this brief shipping season, were coming down from Southern Cross one right after the other.

Joe Webber sweated the whole time for fear the block controls would blow a transistor and smash him head on into one of the trains. Several times, it was close, but the big brain knew what it was doing. Nothing happened.

When he got to Southern Cross—a city built on the crags of a mountain and hollowed out of the rock—they told him Seldon Trask was down in the diggings.

Joe Webber had come four hundred miles in five hours, and he was beat out as hell. But he just dropped his travel bag where he stood and told them to lead the way. After a bit of argument, he was given over to a coveralled boy who did just that.

Southern Cross Mining Corp. had been a nickel and a dime per share back in the old pre-Union America, but that was before the discovery of the Deep Froze Lode, which all by itself had doubled the world's known copper reserves.

The boy took Webber down in a slope-shaft elevator to the mine-head which jutted out onto the glacier, then down a flight of steps into the glacier itself. Surprisingly, it was warm inside the concrete-plastic walls.

They came out in a tunnel. It was full of the rumble of ore trains. The big cars rolled massively past—going on up to the marshalling tunnels where the trains were made up for the long journey down to McMurdo.

They climbed onto one of the eight-seat cars that sat on a spur near their entrance. The boy started the motor; the car rolled slowly along the track, then abruptly accelerated. It jogged over onto the main line, meshing in between two trains of clanking, empty ore cars.

Somewhere, the concrete walls changed to rock. Webber didn't notice exactly where. The small, open car dodged from track to track, in among the thundering, clanging, metal-screeching trains. It was even worse than the trip up from McMurdo, where the clearances had been on the order of tenth-miles. Here it was feet. Sometimes inches.

Seldon Trask was deep in the mine. The place was not well lighted; normally, it was inhabited only by the ravenous machines that ripped ore from the surrounding rock. At first, he wasn't visible in the small group of men clustered up to the silent monster, but when his name was called he crawled out of an access in the machine's flank and stood up.

He was stripped to a tight pair of shorts. He was well-muscled, swart, and almost exactly five feet tall. He looked to be in his mid-late thirties. His blond hair was a tangled mess, and his body was liberally smudged with grime.

He saw Webber and strode over. "Why didn't you say you were coming?" he demanded, grinning warmly. He pointed his wrench at the boy. "Hi, Tim. You bring him down?"

The boy nodded. "He wants to see you."

"Okay," Trask said. "While he's seeing me, you can keep the job going on."

The boy peeled out of his coverall, kicked off his

shoes, and took the wrench. Bare as a babe, he squeezed into the machine.

Trask stuck his feet in the boy's castoff shoes. He started to trudge back along the tunnel, nodding Webber to come with him.

"Trouble with machines," he complained, "they break down right when you want them most. And the engineers that dream them up—they must think people are made like snakes. Him and me are about the only people around here that can get in that particular hole. Even us, we can't hardly wear our skins or we get hung up."

He stopped and turned to Webber. "So what's on your mind?"

"I need money," Webber said, and told him why.

Trask listened, and mulled. "You put me in a spot," he confessed. "You're doing a thing that's got to be done. I mean, space flight shouldn't ought to be a tax-payer's job. It ought to pay its own way. It won't ever be here to stay—not for sure—till it can. Now me, I'm happy here. I'm doing the job I'd've done on the moon if they hadn't quit things. But I like what you're doing. I'd help out if I could. Only I can't."

"What's to stop you?" Webber challenged.

Trask made an embarrassed, helpless kind of shrug. "Sure," he admitted. "I was the guy behind this mine— I got this whole business started. This country's full of guys that started things they couldn't finish. I was lucky, or something—I'm at work I like in a country I like. But I don't run the company and I don't have a say in how it *is* run. I can't dip into the cash box. I have to wait for them to hand it over—and don't think they don't ask real careful what I want it for."

He kicked a bit of rock. It clattered off into the darkness. "Sorry, Joe. Don't mean to disappoint you. But that's how it is."

Webber scuffed his feet. "So you quit me, too," he muttered bitterly.

"Joe—I'd go with you if I could," Trask protested. "Only—"

"I don't want excuses," Webber snapped. "I want money. I'm going to get it."

"I don't got it," Trask repeated. "But—"

Webber stalked away. "Then I'll get it someplace else," he announced over his shoulder.

Trask came after him, spun him around, and pinned him against the rock wall of the tunnel. "You God damned muck head," he muttered, rubbing his fist against the tip of Webber's nose. "You're as dumb as you ever was. You'd rather fight than get what you want. If you give me a chance, I'll tell you something that might help."

Webber pushed the man back. He stood free of the wall, breathing harshly. "I'm listening," he challenged, cat-poised.

"Okay. Listen," Trask told him. He looked around warily, but they were alone. "Our stock's gone too high," he said. "It's going to come down."

"That's going to get me money?" Webber demanded.

"Let me finish," Trask urged. "Our shipping season's too short. We can't ship as much as we ought to justify the price our stock is getting. It's going to be specially bad this year, because the Sound stayed froze a whole month longer than it's supposed to. When the how-much we shipped this season gets totalled, it won't take any numbers monkey to figure Southern Cross stock is pulling down too much price tag. She'll drop eight-ten-a dozen points on the market."

"So what do I do?" Webber demanded. "Buy up and lose my shirt? I *want* money. I don't want to give it away."

"I'm not saying buy stock," Trask said impatiently. "I'm saying sell us short."

"Huh?" Webber frowned suspiciously. "How does that go?"

"You get yourself a sucker," Trask explained. "And you make him a deal to deliver such and such number of shares on such and such a date at such and such a rate under the going price. He thinks he's getting a sharp deal, so he takes it. Then, when the stock goes down under the price you set, you buy up and deliver and he shells out—and you've got yourself the difference between what you pay and what *he* has to pay you."

"What if it doesn't go down?" Webber objected.

"Then you still have to deliver, and you *do* lose your

shirt," Trask admitted. "But I tell you, Joe. It's going down. Hell—I'm doing it myself."

Webber scratched an itch. "You're sure?" he demanded.

"You bet I'm sure," Trask grinned. "I'm going to get this outfit back." He nudged Webber. "I better get back."

They walked back to the machine. "Remember," Trask repeated absolutely. "Down eight points at least come the first of July."

Perrault had a tough job, and he hadn't time to do it right. He had to cross his fingers, guess, and go on. But he had to guess right. A bad guess would wipe out all the time he saved.

And Alice, slowly, was getting worse.

A lot of nights, he didn't sleep much. Days, he drowsed at his desk, mindless.

Time passed.

Which day it was, precisely, Perrault never afterwards remembered. But one day he discovered one of his assistants had blundered.

Tripod was one of the experimental white rats. He was a particularly ugly specimen and, early in his career, he had made himself considerably uglier. He had caught his left hind leg in the wire-screen floor of his cage so inextricably that, to get loose, he gnawed the leg off. He was busily eating the leg when he was found.

Something about the incident gave Perrault a macabre amusement. He made a pet of the creature, and let it be known that henceforth the three-legged rat would take part in experiments only as a control—that Tripod himself would never be experimented on.

In time, Tripod aged. His sleek fur turned scraggly; his snout lost its rattish pointedness. Perrault put him on pension: to be fed, and his cage kept clean. Otherwise, he was to be left alone.

Every now and then, Perrault took him out of his cage and petted him.

So one day, when he did it, he discovered the metal band on Tripod's remaining hind leg. He checked the number on the charts. Mildly annoyed, he hunted up Will Piston.

Will Piston was a young man—not quite thirty—with short cropped hair and mild eyes and a lean, athletic build. He was tremendously competent and painstaking, so long as he was given a complete understanding of what was wanted. If he was allowed any latitude, though, he was sure to mess things up good.

So Perrault found Will Piston and brought him back to the room where the animals were kept, and he showed the young man the band on Tripod's leg and showed him the chart where Tripod's number was listed.

"I don't understand," Will Piston frowned worriedly. "Have . . . have I done something wrong?"

Perrault shrugged. It was nothing worth making a fuss about. "Only checking, boy," he drawled. "That's right?—what it says here?"

Will Piston looked at the chart. "Yes sir," he said, still uncomfortable. "I remember because he's the one with only three legs. Yes—he's getting the series."

Perrault worked his mouth into a thoughtful shape. Anyway, one that looked thoughtful. "Gone very far with it?" he asked.

The younger man shook his head. "Two of the five injections," he said. "And the additive in the food— about a week and a half. Should I take him off?"

Perrault considered. "I don't suppose," he decided. His too-large mouth twisted in a solemn smile. "Be interesting to see what the stuff does to a decrepit old rodent like him."

"Yes sir," Will Piston responded. "Anything else?"

Perrault shook his head. "I don't suppose," he said again.

It was a sort of guess and by gosh experiment—or maybe a latter day witch's brew. After months of studying the chemistry of genetics and cell reproduction, he had decided that the trouble was that when a cell reproduced, the new cell's genes were not quite perfect. They were infinitesimal mutations. The gradual change from one generation to the next was negligible, but over a man's life-span there came a slow, cumulative degeneration. Sometimes the end mutation was cancerous. More often it was not malign, but the new cells did not have the vigor of the cells they replaced.

120

This was called age, and the final extreme was senility.

Sometimes, as when a wound healed, cells had to reproduce more quickly than usual. So, instead of forming healthy flesh and tissue, scars would form—sub-standard cells grown hastily to close the gap. Because of the speed with which it happened, cancerous cells were more likely than in the more usual circumstances.

Scar tissue was necessary, or even tiny wounds might be deadly. But, Perrault wondered, did scar tissue have to remain? Did it have to be scar from the moment of wound until the person died? It did not, he resolved, and plunged into his desperate search.

While Alice weakened—slowly, gamely—he experimented. Hormones—especially those of the thymus—were tested, and their consequence defined and measured. He devised new, hormone-like compounds, and tried them—seeing as his goal some stimulant that would persuade a body's healthy cells to take some notice of the cells adjoining, and to attack and destroy any cells lacking vigor or full usefulness—or which were too markedly dissimilar from their parent cells.

It shouldn't be *too* hard. Already, the body had a tendency in that direction. Interpersonal surgical transplants were almost impossible because of it, and even blood transfusions sometimes caused violent reactions. If he could simply intensify and channel this natural tendency—if he could do it in time . . .

He tried his pseudo-hormones in rats, mice, cats, dogs, guinea pigs and monkeys. Some died. Some showed no change. And some became monstrosities.

Tripod was only an incident. The work continued.

And Alice got worse.

And time marched on.

Fred Bendix sent word when the first sub-freighter sailed from Mayflower Dome. It gave Joe Webber a couple of days to move north to the New York-Philly-New Haven metropolitan district. He located a man who had served under him on the Mars expedition; he was living in suburban south Jersey. Without much in the way of amenities, Webber moved in with him.

In the morning, he rode the underground up to Manhattan and began his vigil at the brokerage office of Fischman, Powell, Walsh & Lorraine.

He sat in the auditorium along with hundreds of other investors, watching the big screen. It was a perfect, no time-lag duplicate of the master board of the Exchange, half the island away. He watched the quotation on Neptune Mines. It rose only a quarter point between the opening at ten and the closing at three.

It would go up twice that every ten minutes when the ore ship entered the St. Lawrence.

Southern Cross held steady at 147.2.

He had sold the shares Marty gave him. The money he got bought nineteen thousand shares of Neptune Mines. And he made contracts to deliver a total of twenty-three thousand shares of Southern Cross on July 10th—three weeks away, now—at a price of 145.

On the strength of the contracts, he got credit with the brokerage house up to the sum he would get for the shares. So he was able to put all he had into Neptune Mines.

But Mr. Walsh was less than enthusiastic about the whole business—had been from the beginning. Right at the start, he advised against selling Marty's shares. They were good, dependable investments.

"It's very unusual for a dedicated foundation such as you are acting for," he said, "to engage in speculative activities. The correct policy is to hold shares and bonds in stable, long-proven corporations, and derive your income from the dividends paid on those shares. This playing the market—I can't say I approve."

"Where's the law says I can't?" Webber challenged.

"Well, I wouldn't go so far as to say it's illegal," Walsh admitted. "But I'd advise against it. I think it's unwise."

"It's lily livered bastards like you that let space flight die," Webber accused. "You couldn't see a profit in it, so you wouldn't pay for it. Well, I'm going to fix it for you. I'm going to make it pay off. But I got to have a lot of cash to do it. Fast."

"I can't say I appreciate your attitude," Walsh said, the perfect model of unruffled diplomacy. "As the responsible officer of a foundation, you should realize haste and recklessness are never good policy."

"I've been a goddamn rabbit ten whole years," Webber answered. "It didn't get me a thing. I'm still where I started. Just tell me one thing—do you want the business, or do I take it someplace else?'

A businessman is, first and last, a businessman.

The year's production figures for the Southern Cross mine were published in the morning faxsheet, the news having been released late the previous afternoon. As soon as the market opened, Southern Cross began to slip. By noon it was down to 138.4.

Meanwhile, Neptune moved up another point to 33.6. Three months ago, when Webber bought his shares, it had been 26.3, and he had got five hundred shares for as low as 24.2.

Already he had a tidy profit on the books, and the sub-freighter was still half a day out from the St. Lawrence.

The sub-freighter, filmed from a copter, was on the 'vision next morning. Neptune was up to 44 by noon. And Southern Cross dropped to 129.

At one-thirty, Neptune paused at 53.4. Southern Cross slid to 123.

Mr. Walsh slipped into the seat beside him. He nodded at the Southern Cross quotation. "You'd better start buying," he advised.

"Why?" Webber wanted to know. "It's still going down."

"It's levelling off," Walsh warned. "You've got to pick up a lot of shares. You can get them cheaper on a falling market."

"I'll get 'em when it hits bottom," Webber said.

Walsh shrugged. "What about Neptune? Want to take your profit?"

"I'll stick," Webber said.

The Southern Cross quotation changed: 123.2.

"That may have been bottom," Walsh said calmly.

"It'll drop," Webber said tightly.

The quotation changed again: 123.3.

"It's going down," Webber insisted grimly.

The quotation blinked. 123.5. It was rising.

"Shall we buy?" Walsh asked.

"No," Webber told him. "She'll be going down again. She's got to go down."

"The market doesn't answer to any man's will," Walsh advised. "You'd better buy. There's still a good profit to be made, but I don't think it will fall this low again."

His glance shifted. "And you might better think about your Neptune shares." He pointed at the screen. Neptune was down to 50.3. "The profit takers have moved in," he said.

It was a dark and ugly hour and a half. When the market shut down at three, Southern Cross was up to 130, and Neptune had slipped back to 47.2.

Webber held on grimly. He refused to sell. Or buy.

That was the weekend. On Saturday, he walked along the bank of a tidewater creek and threw stones at the fiddler crabs. They were quick little devils. He never hit one of them.

Sunday, he lay naked in the sun, tanning and sweating, and now and then thinking of Marty.

He thought some of the market, too, but he was grimly satisfied with the way he was doing things. Southern Cross would drop again, and then he'd buy. And Neptune would go up, and he'd sell.

But Marty—damn if there wasn't a woman! She'd be hard to pry loose from Sherman, but she was worth it. And a woman like her, childless, wouldn't stick forever with a sterile man. She just wasn't built for it. He'd work on her.

He grinned at the hot sun, his eyes blind behind his opaque contact lenses. They'd make a pair, him and Marty. He imagined her here in the sun, beside him, drowsing on the blanket after love.

Monday morning, Southern Cross edged up to 135, and then the bulls climbed on and rode it up to 140. When it edged up to 142.7, Webber heard a rustle beside him. Walsh settled down in the seat.

"I think you'd better start buying," he advised.

Webber gave him one black glance. He looked up at the screen again. Southern Cross jumped to 143, and then 143.1.

He nibbled his lip. There was still a little profit left. Damn little. And it melted away as he watched.

He clenched his teeth. He felt something twisting inside him. He clutched the armrests until his fingernails hurt.

"God damn," he muttered, like an evil prayer. "God damn. God damn."

"Well?" Mr. Walsh prompted expectantly.

"The goddamn bastards," Webber muttered. "Yeah. They've got me. Damn them. Yeah. Go buy. The goddamn bastards . . ."

Walsh picked up a microphone—spoke softly into it.

The screen was like a battleground. Joe Webber watched it, twisting in his seat as if with pain. Southern Cross moved up. It crossed 145 and kept on going, wiping out his profit. When it hit 146.3, he snatched the mike. "Quit buying," he screamed. "For Chrissake quit buying!"

"Your account, please?" a polite female voice inquired.

Webber cursed her.

Southern Cross slipped to 144. He started buying again. The price went up and he quit. This time it didn't go down. Desperately, he bought more, and the price edged up to 147.5.

Then it was three, and the market shut down.

Before he staggered out, Webber checked the Neptune reading. It had held firm near 46 all day. It was still there.

Next day, he held off buying until a half hour before the market closed. Southern Cross slumped to 143.7, and he picked up a couple thousand shares. At three, the market closed with Southern Cross at 144.6.

That gave him eighteen thousand shares. He had to get five thousand more.

He got them the next day, but he had to go up to 146.6 to get them. The way it came out, he had spent almost as much for the twenty-three thousand shares as he would get for them.

And Neptune went down a little, to 44.6.

If he had taken Walsh's advice, he'd have been well ahead of the game. But he'd waited too long. As it stood, he'd break even on the Southern Cross deal, and he still had a profit in the Neptune shares.

Not as big a profit as it might have been, if he'd sold when it was high, but it was sure to go up again—the company was just getting started.

So he didn't sell.

By Friday, Southern Cross was down to 130.

Webber stormed into Walsh's office. Walsh stayed calm.

"Apparently, it was your buying that held the market up," he explained.

"Damn you. You told me to buy."

Walsh shrugged. "There was no way of knowing," he said. "It seemed good advice at the time. Actually, you're lucky to have come out with a whole skin. Perhaps now you'd like to think about an investment portfolio more suitable to your purposes."

Webber told him three impossible things he could do with his portfolio.

On July 10th, he delivered on the short-sale contracts. By the time broker's fees were subtracted, and the credit he'd used to buy the shares was returned, all he got was a check for a hundred and thirty-four dollars.

It wasn't much profit. He sat down and figured out how much he had in the Neptune shares.

The profit came out to less than four hundred thousand.

Hell, he got more than that every time B & P paid a dividend. It was a far cry from the cash he had to have.

But Neptune stayed where it was, around 45.

And Southern Cross—mocking—stayed down.

At Perrault's home, in the shadow of the mountains, Marty answered the door. Webber hadn't thought she'd be there.

She was wearing a seamless black leotard that sheathed her flawlessly from throat to ankles, leaving only her white hands and feet bare. She was an exciting woman any time; in this garment . . . it was not a modest garment.

Webber wondered where Rog was.

She got over her surprise. "Uncle Joe—oh, I'm glad you're here."

She said it in a tight, tense voice.

"What're you here for?" Webber wanted to know.

She looked back over her shoulder. "It's Ma," she said, as if that was enough. It was.

"Rog?" Webber quizzed, warily hoping.

"He had to stay in Melbourne," she said.

So she was still with him. Webber put the matter out of his thoughts.

"Did you get the shares I sent you?" Marty asked. "I never heard a word . . ."

Webber cut her off. "Yeah. I got 'em," he said. "Thanks. Where's your old man?"

"He's at the plant," she answered. "He's desperate. Ma's pretty bad."

Webber turned and headed back along the flagstone path, head down like a charging bull.

"Aren't you coming in?" Marty called after him.

Webber stopped—looked back at her. Damn, he thought. If he could just get her loose.

"I've got to see your dad," he said.

"Is it important?" she wondered.

"You're damn right it's important," Webber shouted. He climbed into the copter. He throttled up. He lifted.

Looking down, he saw her still framed in the doorway. She waved, but he couldn't see the look on her face. He was too far away.

At the plant, he had to fight, curse, browbeat, and cajole his way through the roadblocks set up to discourage the unwelcome rubberneck. But he got through.

He prowled through the research division. It was a lot of corridors and rooms, and Perrault wasn't in any of them. Finally, Webber turned an unfamiliar corner and saw the old man far down toward the other end, ambling slackly away from him.

"Hey, Drew!" he yelled.

Perrault turned woodenly. Stoop-shouldered, he peered back along the corridor, as if his eyes were bad.

"Drew!" Webber yelled, walking fast down the corridor. "Hey. It's me. Joe."

Perrault's bones seemed to loosen. He shuffled forward.

"Joe," he nodded, courtly but reserved.

They met. "Look, Drew," Webber said. "I got a lot to apologize for." He wasn't really sorry about anything, except that he'd been whipped. But he was here with his hat in his hands, and a little crow-eating ought to make things simpler.

Perrault waited voicelessly. He was gaunt and glum, and his color was bad. He looked haunted.

Webber stuck out his hand. "Are we quits?"

Perrault shrugged slackly. "I suppose." He turned and trudged along the corridor. "Come along, Joe," he mumbled. "Make yourself at home."

Webber walked with him. "I've been thinking, Drew," he said. "What d'you say we make a deal?"

"Deal?" Perrault echoed wonderingly. "What on?"

"You know what I mean," Webber said. "I need money, and you want the business built up. Okay. We'll trade."

"How, Joe?"

The corridor turned into another wing of the building. "Suppose I don't take as much for a couple of years," Webber proposed. "You build up, and then you pay out some real cash. How about it?"

"If you want it that way," Perrault agreed glumly, his thoughts clearly on something else. "It don't make much difference."

"Okay. We'll do it," Webber decided. "How big can you make it?"

Perrault shrugged. "Don't know," he mumbled. "Can't build up too awful fast. Let Shelby figure it out."

"Okay, Drew. That suits." It was the only way left open to him. Poor as it was, he had to take it.

But he didn't like it.

Perrault wandered into a room. It smelled like a zoo, and the wall was lined tier on tier with cubbyhole cages. Glum-faced, Perrault opened one of the cages and lifted the rat out by its scruff. Cradling it in his broad, long-fingered hand, he stroked its sleek white fur. He might have been looking at something miles away.

The rat accepted the attention placidly. Then it struggled, as if uncomfortable.

Perrault looked down. "Why, you're not Tripod," he murmured. He upended the rat to look at the band on its leg.

His mouth dropped open in a breathless O. No words came out. He gawked flatfootedly, his eyes full of wonder.

"Joe—look at him," he whispered unbelievingly. He held the rat out, bottom up, for Webber to see.

"What about him?" Webber demanded, not even looking.

"It's growing back," Perrault exclaimed. "His leg's grown back."

Webber looked. The left hind leg had an embryonic, unfinished glossiness. "Yeah?" he scowled.

"Do you see it, Joe? Do you see it?" he pleaded.

Webber nodded. "Yeah. So what?"

"He's grew it back," Perrault insisted excitedly. "And he . . . he's gone young. He . . . he used to be a beat-up old critter. He's got young again."

"Nice trick," Webber said. He narrowed his eyes, abruptly thoughtful.

"Don't you see?—Don't you see, Joe?" Perrault cried happily. "It's . . . It's . . ."

With a hand suddenly fumbling like an empty glove, he chucked the rat back in its cage. He bolted to the counter on the other side of the room. He tore wildly through a pile of papers. His trembling, clumsy fingers scattered them on the floor.

Then he stopped. Stopped dead, and snatched up a scratch pad and scribbled on it, and opened a cabinet and pulled out bottles of fluid and powders, tumbling other bottles to the floor where they smashed unnoticed.

He piled them into his pockets. Then he stumbled hurriedly, clumsily to the door.

"Joe! Are you coming?"

"Yeah," Webber said over his shoulder. "In a minute."

But Perrault was already gone.

Webber opened the cage and dragged the rat out. It was a fat, healthy specimen. With one vicious twist he wrung its neck. He didn't even give it time to squeak.

Holding the dead thing in his hands, he looked around. There wasn't any place to hide it. He tore the band off its leg. Crossing to the window, he threw it out with all his strength. Then he crumpled the band to a pellet and swallowed it.

It all took less than fifteen seconds. Then he went after Drew.

Perrault took the company's copter—the one used for emergency shipments. It was fast and he flew it manual. The make-way transmitter cleared traffic ahead of them.

As soon as they were airborne, Webber started asking questions.

"Suppose you used this junk on me and you," he said. "It'd turn us younger. Right?"

"I . . . I guess so," Perrault stammered. The big copter's engine screamed powerfully. The red flashers threw their off-on, eerie light on them.

"Is it permanent?" Webber asked.

"I don't know," Perrault said gleefully. "I don't care."

"Anybody know about this besides me and you?" Webber asked more carefully.

"No, Joe. Just us," Perrault answered.

"What about your assistants?"

"They don't know the whole of it. All they know is this and that. They didn't know what they were doing half the time."

"But they've got hints."

"Oh, sure, Joe. Sure. But . . . Joe, I didn't think it'd be anything like this. I hadn't any idea . . ."

"Okay. Swell," Webber said. "Drew—you and me, we're going to keep this to ourselves."

"What? Joe, we can't!"

"Why the hell not?" Webber demanded. He watched the hogback line of mountains loom nearer and nearer. "First of all, all those guys you had working—you're going to keep 'em working for you, and you'll give 'em enough that they can't do any thinking on their own. And you're going to keep your mouth shut."

"But why, Joe? Why?"

"It's an advantage," Webber said. "You don't give advantages up."

"An advantage?" Perrault repeated dumbly. "How?"

"How the hell do I know?" Webber demanded. "I'll think of something. But we're keeping it to ourselves. Understand?"

"Sure, Joe. Sure," Perrault said absently. The mountains were close. He started the copter down.

Perrault put the copter down on the lawn, close to the house. He scrambled out while the rotors still wheeled free. He ran clumsily across the grass, the bottles in his pockets clacking.

"Marthie!" he hollered. "Marthie!"

Webber went after him. As they were coming down, he had seen the other copter down by the garage. A doctor or somebody, he thought. That could wreck everything.

Perrault's legs were longer, but Webber was in better shape. He stayed right behind the old doctor all the way to the house.

Marty showed in the doorway just in time to get almost knocked down. She was still wearing black. Perrault hugged her.

"Marthie, girl. I've got it," he laughed.

Maybe she didn't hear. Her face had a remote, stilled look. "I tried to call you, Dad," she said. Her voice was small, frightened. "Nobody knew where you were."

Perrault started past her. "It happened awful sudden," Marty said.

Perrault stopped. He turned slowly. His face was apprehensive, blank, and numb.

"You're too late, Dad," she said, as kindly as she could.

Perrault turned away. He stumbled to a chair and slumped down. He shook his head. "Marthie, girl—I was *that* close," he said haggardly, and burrowed his face in his hands.

Webber had stayed back out of the way. Now he came forward. "It's something for you, too," he told Marty. He jerked a thumb at Perrault. "That stuff he's got is damn good. I'm betting it'll fix Rog up. You'll have kids, Marty."

She looked at him gravely. "Honest?"

"It grew a rat's leg back," Webber told her. "I figure

it can grow back your boyfriend's. If it can do that, it can fix up the rest of him, too."

Marty bent down and kissed him fervently. "I hope you're right, Uncle Joe," she breathed.

Then she went over and squeezed into the chair with her father. She put an arm around him. "You're going to be a grandfather, Dad."

He looked up slowly. "You mean it, Marthie?"

She nodded. "Uh-huh," she said brightly. "I hope."

Then the three sober-suited, professionally blank-faced men came out wheeling the shrouded stretcher. They paused, seeing people they hadn't seen when they came in.

Webber jerked a thumb at the door. "Just keep moving," he ordered.

They went.

Joe Webber felt good. Perrault's whatchamacallit was just the thing he needed, and Alice's death would help cover up. It would explain to the assistants why Perrault lost interest in the business.

But the big thing—it would turn him young. And it would *keep* him young.

Sure, he wouldn't get Marty, now. The nesting instinct was strong in her, and she'd be satisfied with Rog now that he could make her pregnant. Well, he'd never had more than a halfway chance of getting her, anyway.

But he had time, now. He would see that engine built —see space flight pay its way. There would be time—and time to colonize the moon, and Mars, and time for whatever came after that.

He would see the job done. All the way to the end.

And maybe—maybe—one of Marty's babies would turn out to be a girl that looked a little like her. That was something worth waiting a long time for.

And he *could* wait, now. He could be patient.

. . . Now.

PART FIVE

USING TANK HYDROGEN—that being more dependable for low-speed maneuvers than the stuff picked up along the way—Roger Sherman eased the rocket down on the moon. It touched at exactly zero speed. Sherman starved the fireball until it died. Then he shut down the board.

His engineer, Phil Brembeck—a new man for Sherman, and a young one—wasn't expecting that soft a grounding. "That was a real neat put-down, Mr. Sherman," he said respectfully as he unstrapped from the power-assist articulating frame.

Rog Sherman smiled. In the old days, the spacemen called it a real neat put-down if you could still find the body. Or part of it. Brembeck was too young to know that. A hundred years too young.

"Call me Don," Sherman said gruffly. "Thanks."

Brembeck undogged the hatchway and went down. He didn't bother with the ladder rungs—just held loosely to the upright and dropped. You could do things like that in moon gravity.

Sherman followed.

They had to wait in the baggage section. Just below, the newsmen were crowding out onto the stairs. The stewards hadn't opened the lock yet, so they hadn't any place to go. They stood where they were, all of them, blocking the way.

"That's the trouble with a load of rubbernecks," Sherman grumbled matter-of-factly. He sat on an empty baggage rack and began to write up his flight report.

"Does it take much practice to make put-downs like that?" Brembeck wondered.

Sherman nodded. "Some," he admitted, grinning.

"Guess I've had it. Been with Moon Flights since the start. And Intercon Rockets before that."

"Honest?" Brembeck echoed. "But that's twelve years. You don't hardly look old enough."

Sherman grinned devilishly. "How old do you think I am?"

He was a big man, as muscular as a bull, and his face was like something hacked out of granite. He could have been twenty or forty, and you couldn't tell the difference.

Brembeck hesitated, obviously upping his estimate. "Twenty-eight?" he hazarded.

"Thirty-four," Sherman told him. The lie, so long a habit, came easy to his lips. "And I started young. I was a big kid, and I lied about my age."

"You really wanted to fly the rockets, huh?"

"Yeah," Sherman nodded. "Phil, it's like . . . like coming alive when you've been dead. I . . ." He grinned. "I guess it runs in the family. Rog Sherman was my great-grandfather."

That lie, too, came easy. Well, he couldn't say out loud he was the original Rog Sherman. Not without rousing a lot of questions he couldn't answer just yet.

"The man that crashed his ship in the Pacific?" Brembeck asked.

Sherman chuckled to himself. Always, whenever his ego was getting too big, someone said something like that. They always remembered how he'd crashed the *Jove* and how he was the only man to come out alive. No one ever remembered *why* he'd crashed.

Outwardly, he only nodded. "That's him," he acknowledged.

"Gosh," Brembeck marvelled. He looked at Sherman with even greater respect. "I'll bet you know a lot about the old days."

Sherman shook his head. "Not any more than anyone else. He died a long time before I was born. Copter crash."

Brembeck looked disappointed, but he didn't give up. "Well, at least you know some things about Sherman, don't you?"

"Oh, some," Sherman admitted.

"Well, look—was it really true, that story they tell?

About how he didn't have a leg, but he got to be a spaceman anyway?"

Sherman shook his head. "Not exactly. He lost it when the *Jove* crashed. You got that out of Kellermann's book, didn't you?"

"I read it somewhere," Brembeck admitted. "I don't remember who wrote it."

"It was Kellermann," Sherman said. Kellermann hadn't got hardly anything right, but kids had been gobbling it up from his book for almost twenty years now.

"Actually, it isn't hard to get around without a leg," Sherman went on. "It didn't keep him from getting married and raising a crop of kids."

"He must have been quite a man," Brembeck said. He was still thinking about the book, Sherman decided.

"Oh, he got around all right," Sherman admitted. "Steel leg and all." Inside his soft spaceman's boots, Sherman wiggled his toes, remembering how it had been to be without them.

The young man looked expectant, but Sherman had finished. "Well, anyway, I'll bet it was real exciting back then," he said, disappointed. "I mean, everywhere they went, they were going there for the first time."

Sherman shrugged. "There's that," he admitted. "But there were a lot of milk runs, too. And even on the big ones, they were cooped in their ships for months at a time. Sometimes years."

The young man nodded. "Yeah. I guess so," he said, not caring for Sherman's too-realistic view. "It's too bad they didn't have the hydrogen rocket back then. They could of gone a lot faster."

"And maybe they'd of had today a hundred years ago," Sherman pointed out. "We wouldn't of been here to see it, then. Look at it that way, son. Now's the time to be alive. The space flight they had back then—nothing came of it. *Now* we've got a colony on the moon. Not just a couple of shacks, either. It's a city—a whole damn countryside. And starting tomorrow it pays its own bills. All of them. We're seeing history made."

"I guess you're right," Phil Brembeck admitted grudgingly, still lost in his daydream of adventurous yesterdays and might-have-beens.

Two women and a man came up the stairs. They looked to be all of an age—their early twenties: Sherman's wife, their daughter, and his father-in-law.

Andrew Perrault came first, squeezing through the crowded newsmen, mumbling apologies. He was lank, tall, hollow cheeked, and had a too-broad mouth and solemn eyes. Then Martha—Marty—Mrs. Sherman—red-haired, small, shiny-nosed, and quick. And then Sandra, looking much like her mother in the face, but taller and more solidly built, black-haired and not so happy. She looked a little older than her mother.

They came up the ladder to the baggage compartment. "Hi, people," Sherman said, getting up.

Andrew Perrault stopped, clicked his heels, and bowed from the waist. He didn't crack a smile.

Sherman nodded to Brembeck. "My engineer, Phil Brembeck," he introduced. "Phil—this is Bruce Wylde." He indicated Perrault.

Perrault made another slight bow. "And may I present," he told Sherman, still deadpan, "your wife, the former Joan Masters. And her sister, Melissa Grant."

"I think we've been introduced," Marty smirked. She got her arms around Sherman's neck and pulled his head down to kiss him. He straightened up, grinning. She squealed delightedly, her feet a dozen inches off the deck.

"Seems to me . . ." Perrault mumbled, wry-mouthed. She dropped back, giggling soundlessly. "Now I *know* we have!"

"I promise not to breathe a word," Perrault assured solemnly.

Sherman nodded absently, still grinning. "Yeah," he said. "What's the bottleneck down below?"

"The usual," Marty shrugged lightly. "Waiting for the bus." She strolled around him, looking him up and down like a cattle buyer pleased with a bargain.

Perrault took a small, aimless step. "Hit the moon in half of no time," he grumbled. "Wait an hour for the bus."

"Not if . . ." Sandra started to say, but she glanced at Brembeck and stopped. "Not if Les wants to keep those men down there happy, he won't. He'll get it here faster than that. He's real good at getting things done when he wants them."

Her voice had a bitterness in it.

"Easy, baby," Sherman gentled. He swatted her bottom. She turned up to him and smiled nicely—something like worship in her eyes.

With a puzzled brow, Phil Brembeck looked from Sandra to Sherman to Marty. Marty didn't look the least bit disturbed. Helplessly, he looked at Perrault. Perrault shrugged and gave him a sad-clown smile.

The mutter of talk down below changed its rhythm and tone. Sherman went to the hatchway and looked down.

"Guess you were right," he decided. "They've got the lock open."

The passenger section of the bus was raised up on high stilts and its rear was sealed to the rocket's lock.

They were the last ones into the bus, but a lot of seats were unoccupied. The newsmen were crowded down at the front end, the ones on the fringe of the mob standing on seats or on tiptoe, craning their necks to see over the men in front of them.

The steward slammed the door and tested the seal, then spun the big wheel that unlocked the bus from the rocket. The bus began to settle down on its chassis.

From the middle of the crowded newsmen, a sharp voice spoke loudly. "Okay, you guys," it said. "Let's break it up. Lots of time for yammer later. Right now, let's get into town."

Reluctantly, the crowd broke up. The newsmen filed back along the aisles and slipped into the seats. They looked out the dark-tinted windows at the harsh, sun-blasted moonscape. The inhospitable plain was dotted with small structures—here and there a pressure dome—but mostly things were out in the open.

Rockets jutted at the black sky—the hard glitter of stars—like silver monoliths. They were narrow and tall, those ships, and they looked like spindles wrapped in tightly cinched scrolls. It was a design virtually forced by their space-breathing hydrogen engines—by their need for gaping intakes fore and aft. But they were sweet ships, almost as cheap to fly as hitch-hiking.

Sherman and the others took the rearmost seats. They

didn't look out, except casually. They had seen it all a hundred times.

The bus lurched forward.

The man who had been in the middle of the crowd walked down the aisle. He was small, pale blond, green-gray eyed, and determined. He looked like a boy in his middle teens.

Joe Webber.

One of the newsmen tried to stop him midway along the aisle. Webber brushed past. "Later," he said curtly.

He walked all the way to the rear of the bus. He stood in front of Sherman, fists on hips, balancing his body against the jostling of the bus.

"How was the ride?"

Sherman acknowledged. "No trouble," he said.

Webber's eyes moved to Marty, and Sandra and Andrew Perrault. "What're you here for?" he demanded.

"We want to see the colony go off subsidy," Marty said calmly. "Don offered the ride . . . here we are."

"We'd like to talk a bit, Les," Perrault mumbled embarrassedly.

"Not here," Webber told him. It was like a warning.

"Well, no," Perrault admitted. "It's only what we came for."

Webber looked dangerous. "You funning me?" he asked with narrowed eyes.

"Only answering," Perrault drawled. "You want I should call you by your right name?"

Webber turned away. "See me later," he snapped. He walked off.

Phil Brembeck watched Webber's retreating back. "Was that who I think it was?" he asked.

Sherman had almost forgotten the boy. He nodded. "Yeah. Les Grant. Head of the Brent Foundation."

"You know him?" Brembeck wondered, awed.

"He's an old friend," Sherman said, in a tone which did not imply much in the way of friendship.

"Why, if it wasn't for him, we wouldn't even have the hydrogen rocket," Brembeck exclaimed. "He almost built this place."

"Yeah," Sherman muttered. "All by his self."

Sandra, sitting beside him, turned to him fiercely.

"Don," she said. "It's true. We couldn't have done it without him."

"Yeah, baby," Sherman admitted, as if weary of the argument. "Yeah. I know. Only . . ."

He let his voice trail off. "What is it, baby? Are you fixing to move in with him again?"

Sandra tossed her head. "Maybe. I don't know."

"Baby—it's no good. You know what he's like."

"I *don't* know," she insisted. "I keep hoping—this time it might be different—now . . . now that he's finally done. Maybe this time it would be all right."

Sherman ran his big hand through her short hair, roughing the back of her head. "Baby, he won't quit now," he warned. "There's Mars . . . and Venus. . ."

"I know. I know." Sandra looked at her feet. "But it doesn't have to be *him,* does it?"

"He thinks it does," Sherman muttered. "Baby—he's made a mess of your life. Why don't you give him up? He won't change."

"I can't," Sandra protested, shaking her head. "I don't *want* to give him up. When it gets so I can't stand him, I move out. And . . . and after a while, it doesn't look as bad as it did, and I . . . I want to live with him again. So I go back. I can't help myself."

Sherman put his arm around her. Let Brembeck think whatever he wanted. A father had responsibilities to his daughter.

"Look," he said understandingly. "You're mixed up, and anything I tried to say, I'd upset you. I think you'd better have a talk with your ma. I don't know if she can help, but . . . well, sometimes it's sort of good to talk things out with her."

"Sure, D . . . Don," she nodded, still looking down at her feet. "Only—I'm grown up, now. I've been grown up a long time, and I know what I'm doing. Sometimes I don't think you see that."

Sherman slipped his arm out from around her. He looked at his hand, not sure what to do with it. "Yeah, baby. Yeah. Maybe you've got something there."

The bus approached a sheer, shard-faced cliff, then abruptly plunged into a tunnel. Vast doors parted to admit it, and clamped shut behind. Ahead, other doors opened. A booming thunder roared through the tunnel. The sound came of tires on pavement.

The bus emerged into an arch-roofed cavern, brightly lighted, with docks along both the long walls. The bus backed up to one of them. The steward opened the door.

Joe Webber walked down the aisle. "End of the line, boys," he announced loudly. "You got rooms at the Craters Hotel—first on your right off the concourse. Pick up the keys at the desk. Hour and a half for lunch, and we'll meet in the lobby for a tour of the city."

The newsmen started struggling out of their seats. Webber came up to Sherman.

"Why'd you bring 'em?" he demanded, nodding around at Martha and Perrault and Sandra.

"When can we see you?" Sherman countered.

"Why'd you bring 'em?" Webber insisted dangerously.

"They wanted to see you," Sherman said. He stood up, towering over the small, boy-sized man. "So do I."

"God damn it, not *now*," Webber protested. "Of all the bastard times, you got to make it now? Right now—God damn it, Don—I *can't*."

"Why not?" Sherman asked, his voice as hard as his rocklike face. "What's wrong with now? It's the most logical time I can think of."

"I ain't got time," Webber argued. "I got to nurse-maid these interview boys halfway around the moon and tell 'em what the other half looks like. After I've got rid of 'em, and I've wrapped up the Foundation business here . . ."

"No begging off, Les," Sherman warned. "Bruce here—" he nodded at Perrault "—he's too soft to put it plain. But we mean business, this time. Set a time, Les. We'll be there. You'd better be there, too."

Joe Webber made a helpless, exasperated gesture. "Gimmie a week. A couple of weeks, and you can have me all you want."

"That's a long way off," Sherman criticized.

"There's all kinds of damn little things to clear up," Webber complained. "I got appointments from here to forever. I'll have to kick some bird out on his duff to make room for you. For godsake, Don. Give me time!"

Sherman glanced at Marty—at Perrault. "Well, all right," he said grudgingly. "We've waited this long. What's another week? But that's all, Les. One more week. You've been warned."

"Warned about what?" Webber demanded.

"You know, Les," Sherman said. "You know."

"All right, you bastard," Webber grumbled. "Now get out of my way."

From nothing, Joe Webber had raised the Brent Foundation to financial power. It had taken a long time, but he'd had that time. A hundred years.

The first rocket to hit the moon in a hundred years was his, and every ship that followed it—in either the Foundation's name or, more recently, in the name of the Foundation-owned Moon Flights, Inc.

And every one of those ships was powered by a hydrogen rocket—the engine he'd paid Foundation money to develop. It was the thing that made commercial space flight possible.

And he'd built Moon City. It had taken a lot of cash—good, hard Confederate dollars—and he'd paid for it from the Foundation's treasury. Just the same, not a single brick or bit of airspace in the city was Foundation property. The city owned everything—even the Foundation's own office. The Foundation paid rent at the standard rate.

Joe Webber told this to the newsmen when they started their tour of the city—how the Foundation had grown since the days of its first director, Joe Webber, who had been his great-grandfather, and how he, Lester Grant, had revived space flight and built Moon City. He told them he was proud of his city, and proud of himself for having given it away.

The tour began in the business district. The walkways were crowded with shoppers. Traffic buzzed in the streets. Lavish shops stood open to them, doorless portals and glassless display islands. Three banks raised massive facades to the high, arched ceiling, which shone with a strong, pearl-like brilliance.

They moved on to the apartment district, where broad, green parks surrounded roof-propping, block-tower buildings. Parks with trees and flowered shrubs

141

and undulant lawns, and sunlight-strong light pouring warm from the sky-like roof. Sunbathers dozed on blankets, their bare bodies browning. In the largest park of all, a sinuous, slow river wound, broadening often into deep, cool pools where naked teenagers splashed and swam.

And he showed them where workmen were cutting new caverns out of ancient rock. Moon City was growing.

The factories were located in the cliff-face that fronted the city. Some extended beyond that wall, to make use of the near-total, inexhaustible vacuum out there. Here an electronics factory built vacuum tubes far superior to any made on Earth. Here chemical firms created compounds impossible on Earth, by processes no atmosphere allowed, and half a dozen ceramics producers made fittings and equipment with strange, rare properties, from minerals found only on the airless, waterless, sun-scorched moon.

And pharmacy suppliers—among them the old firm of Brent & Perrault—sealed total-pure-culture antibiotics in pure-sterile packs.

The procession moved on. Joe Webber told them that Moon City's utilities were more crucially important than in even the biggest metropolis on Earth. And he showed them the air-maintenance plant.

Through a silver-faced window, they looked out on acres of thin, threadlike tubules exposed to the sun—where carbon dioxide forced through them was reduced to its components: black carbon and fresh, good oxygen. He said that the plant reclaimed enough in the long lunar day to last through the long lunar night.

And he showed them the light-studded monitor board of the city's ventilation network, and he demonstrated the stand-by network always ready for emergencies. He explained the fire-quenching system, and the bad-air drill.

The water service also used the sun's hot brilliance. It distilled the city's sewage and recovered the water in it. Not *all* the water—that was not possible—but the loss was more than made up by the water drawn from deep wells—water trapped in the bowels of the moon since geological time began. It was full of mineral salts—undrinkable and even poisonous—but they could be extracted. It was an almost inexhaustible reservoir. Through human ingenuity, the moon was being made a fertile paradise.

Joe Webber showed the newsmen the gardens. There, in giant trays so closely sandwiched one on top of the other that a man could hardly belly-crawl between, plants grew lushly in superenriched earth. Warm lamps glowed on the leaves, forcing growth. Water trickled into the narrow furrows.

They watched the endless harvest move slowly through the vast cavern—the trays removed and the fruit stripped from the plants, and the uprooted plants delivered to the livestock as fodder, or pulverized and added to the soil before it was processed and planted again.

The power for all these functions—for the water pumps, and the blowers for air, the lights without which Moon City would be night-dark caverns, and the force that drove the myriad machines of the factories, homes, and the electric cars that buzzed through the streets—all these took their power from three sources.

The sun, in the moon's long day, supplied its share. So did a pair of nuclear reactors.

But the one largest, most depended-on source was a long row of dynamos turned by the same force as powered the rockets. In fact, the dynamos were simply more efficient models of the generators those ships used to supply their electrical needs. The diffused, all but immeasurable hydrogen of space—collected by great, gulping scoops and changed to jetting fury as ionic helium—was all the fuel needed.

A fuel as inexhaustible—and cheap—as space itself.

The Port Authority was last. Joe Webber took the newsmen through the warehouse-freighthandling district. It was busy and vast. Great masses of cargo trundled in and out—moon-manufactured goods and newly minted metals going down to Earth, and Earth goods—foodstuffs, cloth, tools, seeds, and children's toys—brought up from below.

For a while, they watched. Then, in a pressurized bus, they went outside.

They passed ships loading and unloading. Webber pointed to the towering gantries—each like a scaffold built around its prisoned ship. Some handled vacuum-

143

stable cargoes. Others—like the one unloading a cargo of meat—were equipped to handle cargoes at Earth-normal pressure.

They circled the repair shops, and the traffic control tower with its guide-beam transmitters and flare signals—its whirling search and track antennae.

And he showed them the ships—ships that leaped at the stars with flame in their guts, or came down out of the dark, starry sky with a slow, buoyant steadiness, as if feeling their way.

He was proud of his city. After twelve years of building, it was done.

Moon City and the lesser towns of its financial hegemony had outgrown the need of subsidy from the Brent Foundation, he said. The young, new country was mature enough, now, to take care of itself.

Tomorrow, he told them, they'd attend the independence ceremonies.

He left them to file their stories.

The newsmen were there a full week. They had interviews with the city officials, with the factory managers, and with the moonside director of Moon Flights, Inc. They prowled through the city, seeing it for themselves, finding stories of their own to write about and send back to Earth. They toured the mines whose ores fed the steel mills, and they visited other nearby mines. The moon was rich in strange, rare minerals.

At the week's end, Joe Webber sent them off on a three-day hop-rocket junket to Blankside, with stops at Vacuum and Boiled Rock. To shepherd them around, he sent one of his sons—the loyal one—Bob Webber, who just now was using the name Tom Spilka, and who explained his resemblance to Webber by saying he was Lester Grant's cousin. He stood taller than Webber. He was seventy-eight years old.

When he saw the newsmen off, Joe Webber told them he would hold one final press conference before they went back to Earth. He said that then he'd tell them of the Brent Foundation's future plans.

When they were gone—and off his nerves—he went back to his office. It was a fine, comfortable, roomy place

—spic-span, and polished chrome, and rich, soft carpet. And back of the raised desk was a wall-size window that looked out on the busy rocket field and the sun-scarred moonscape beyond.

He put through a call to the Sherman apartment.

Ten minutes later, the clan began to gather in his waiting room. At the end of half an hour there were almost forty of them. Webber looked them over in his peephole screen.

Almost all of them were there—all of Perrault's eternally youthful changelings as happened to be in the city just then. Among them, he saw four of his own sons and three of his daughters.

Webber seethed. That they should come here with the others—on *their* side! Sandra—damn her—had her finger on them.

And he didn't.

Webber let the Clan wait out there, stewing, for another fifteen minutes. Then he buzzed his receptionist.

"I'll see four," he told her. "The Howards, that Wylde character, and my wife. The rest of 'em can wait out there."

That was the way to do it. Cut 'em off from their moral support. Cut 'em up and wear 'em down.

They came in. Sherman was first, but as soon as he was inside Marty moved ahead of him. She was wearing her mad-and-wanting-something clothes—black slack-suit and scarlet cape. And lipstick the color of flame. Sandra, following her, looked colorless and already defeated.

Behind them, Andre Perrault strolled in, hand in pocket, as if he didn't care—as if he hadn't ever cared, and never would, but had a duty to be done.

They stopped in front of Webber's desk, Marty half a step closer than the rest, chin up. There were chairs, but they didn't sit down. They'd come for something. They were going to get it.

They thought.

Joe Webber chuckled silently.

The door clicked shut. Joe Webber touched the lock-stud on his control board. Now they couldn't get out until he let them out. And no one could get in.

He sat up straight in his chair and, from that height, looked down at them.

145

"Okay," he challenged. "You're calling this dance. What's on your minds?"

"Why can't the rest of us come in?" Marty demanded.

Webber's mouth twisted. "This is an office," he told her. "Not a goddamn stockyard. If I want a bunch of bleating sheep in here, I'll say so. Besides, you're the ones that want to do the talking, ain't you?"

"What if we are?" Marty argued. "It concerns them, too. They have a right to be here."

"They don't have any right if I don't say they do," Webber snapped. "And I don't."

"And I think it's time they found out Dad's treatment is permanent," Marty went on stubbornly. "I think it's time we told them they don't need renewal every two years. That's really why you kept them out, isn't it?"

"Hell—so what if it is?" Webber shrugged. "Damn it, that's how we keep 'em under control. If they wasn't coming back to the tit all the time, they'd spill their guts. We'd have a hell of a muxx. That all you wanted to talk about?"

"No, it isn't," Sherman said. His eyes were level with Webber's. He nodded to Perrault. "It's yours, Doc. Talk for it."

Perrault scuffed a half step forward, glum-mouthed and embarrassed. He held his hands as if he had a hat in them.

"Don't mean to bother you, Joe," he apologized. "Only—well, Marthie and me and the rest of us—we want to tell people about my process. I mean, it's something we shouldn't ought to keep to ourselves."

"You've kept your yap awful shut for the last hundred years," Webber pointed out.

Perrault swallowed. "Well, you wanted us to," he explained lamely. "At least, you always persuaded me off it. Oh, you were sort of right, I guess—I don't argue that none. I mean, it makes sort of sense, if people don't get old and die off, and a man can make love to his wife at a hundred years old, we got to have some place to put all the extra people you get. But we got that now. We got the whole moon. So I don't see much reason to keep shut no longer."

"If we'd known it would take this long," Marty put in willfully, "we'd have gone ahead anyway."

Webber shifted his glance. His fist tightened. "That's fighting dirty," he accused. "If I could of got us here half a day faster, I'd of done it."

He stopped, and his eyes narrowed shrewdly. "You put 'em up to this, didn't you," he charged.

She met his gaze firmly. "I haven't said a thing they didn't already think," she answered defiantly.

Webber nodded, grinning devilishly. "That's what I figured." He shifted back to Perrault. "Doc," he asked pointedly. "You want to turn the moon into an anthill?"

Perrault frowned and backed away. "Why not?" he shrugged. "I mean, it's all the way we can live here. And there's Mars. And Venus. Plenty of room for people, now . . ."

"The wrong kind of people," Webber snapped bitterly.

"Now, Joe . . ." Sandra offered gently.

"Shut up, Sandy," Webber told her carelessly. "Look, you guys. It's always the same way. Men make a place fit to live in, and then a damn bunch of rabbits move in—squeeze 'em out. Doc—you want to do that to every planet there is?"

"Be fair, Joe," Perrault pleaded, his hands flapping uselessly. "Here we are, you and us, young as kids for the rest of our lives, and if anything gets us it won't be old age or half a dozen other things. It's sort of selfish if we don't let other people have it. It's not right."

Webber nodded, like a judge acknowledging an argument but reserving his judgment. "Marty? You're behind this brawl. Let's hear some talk off your own mouth."

Marty let her hand slip from Sherman's arm. "Dad's already said it," she declared, brave-voiced. She tried to stand a little taller than she was. "We've practically had to live like criminals, because you wouldn't let Dad tell. We've had to change our names, and hide, and be afraid to show our faces. . . . It's time we stopped. We should have a long time ago."

"You could of flapped it any time you wanted," Webber snapped. "You all could. A couple of words in the right ears . . . Well, why didn't you?"

Marty's chin came up. "It was Dad's," she flashed. "You made him promise . . ."

She ran out of words. Webber smirked.

Roger Sherman strode forward and leaned his weight on the high desk. His eyes were only inches from Webber's, and steady.

"We stuck with you for a hundred years," the big man said. "We gave you everything you wanted. Because we wanted space flight every bit as bad as you did. Well, you've got it."

Webber didn't flinch. "So?" he challenged.

"So do one decent thing in your life," Sherman told him. "You made Doc a promise once—that you'd turn it loose when we'd finished the job. Well, it's done. So let the poor guy live with himself. You think he likes it—with a secret like that inside his skull?"

"The job's not finished yet," Webber told him evenly, his glacial gray-green eyes like precious beads. "So far—" he gestured disgustedly. "This ain't nothing."

Sherman glanced back at Sandra. She looked self-possessed—independent—looking at nothing.

"I warned you, Sandy," Sherman said, plain-voiced.

She tossed her head airily, not answering.

"Look," Webber said. "We got the moon. That's swell. That's great. But it's just the beginning."

"The job's done, Joe," Sherman told him inflexibly. "It was done when you got the hydrogen rocket built. A business can make a profit off space flight now. You didn't have to do any more."

Webber smiled, with clenched teeth and narrowed eyes. "Look," he said persuasively. "Thanks to Doc here, we got a lot of life ahead of us. I don't know about you, but I'm not going to spend the next thousand years twiddling my thumbs."

Sherman backed off a step. "Go on," he prodded. His big hands were fists at his sides.

"I could of built this city a hell of a lot faster," Webber said. "You know why I didn't? It would of used up the Foundation. I didn't want that. I got a lot of use for the Foundation, yet. I kept it in class A shape."

"I wondered about that," Sherman muttered.

"Shut up," Webber told him calmly. He talked to the four of them. "I got plans, people. Big plans."

"Mars or Venus?" Sherman said.

"Hell!" Webber sneered. "You think that's big. Listen, Rog—all you people—I've seen all I want of this neck of the woods."

He kicked his chair around—turned his back to them and pointed at the big window back of his desk—pointed out at the port, at the black night, and the far, bright stars.

"*That's* where we're going," he said fiercely. "Out there."

He was pointing upward. Not one planet was in sight. Just stars.

"Out there!" Joe Webber said again.

For a moment, no one spoke. Then Sherman objected. "Those stars are a long way off."

Webber turned back slowly. "So what?" he demanded confidently. "We just spent a hundred years getting *this* far. We ought to find a star with decent planets in half that time."

He smiled, real pleased with himself. "I got a ship building," he informed them. "It's been building for a year and a half. A big ship. Big enough to start off with a thousand people and have room enough for all the brats born in the next hundred years. Thanks to Doc, it's no problem at all. All we got to do is sit on our cans till we get there."

Sherman nodded reluctantly. "But why keep Doc's process a secret?" he wondered. "I don't even think you *can*—unless you're mighty quiet at recruiting."

Webber chuckled. "So who's going to tell 'em how long it'll take?" he wanted to know.

Sherman paused amid dead silence. "I don't like the sound of that," he warned.

Webber picked up an ornament on his desk—an ugly, twisted chunk of metal. Sometimes he claimed it was a piece of the old Orbitbase—maybe all that was left. After it was abandoned when the First Age of Space Flight ended, Orbitbase had circled Earth—a thousand miles up—for more than fifty years. Then, thirty-four years ago, it had slipped into Earth's atmosphere and turned into a meteor.

Wherever it came from, the metal chunk was black and massive—though not, here in moon gravity, very heavy. Joe Webber toyed with it, smiling cockily.

"Okay," he admitted carelessly. "So it's a goddamn swindle. How else do I get 'em to sign up?"

"Why not tell them the truth?" Marty wondered. "It wouldn't hurt to tell them how long it might be, if they know they'll still be young and alive when they get there. What's wrong with that?"

"The people we'd get that way, I don't want," Webber told her. "They'd be the kind that crawl into holes and lock the door. Sure—I'd get 'em *in* the ship all right, but when we got out there they'd be no good. They wouldn't go *out*. Dammit—if I wanted slobs like that, I'd fill the whole ship with dirt and take worms. Nuts—the only kind of people worth taking on a trip like this you don't get telling 'em they'll sit on their cans for a hundred years. You got to make 'em think they'll get there about the middle of next week, so they can get right down to work. Any other kind would be no damn good."

The argument had truth in it. A lot of truth. Sherman bent close to Marty. There was hasty consultation. Marty twitched her shoulders. No one else said a word.

Joe Webber hefted his ornament. "Just one thing I want to know," he said tightly. "You want to come with me, or do you like it here?"

Sherman and Marty traded glances. Perrault made a glum, submissive shrug. Sandra just stood there, not seeming to breathe.

"Don't think I like this," Sherman told Webber grudgingly. "I don't. But we'd like to go. Marty and me, that is. I can't speak for the rest of us." He gestured to the door to the waiting room.

"Tell 'em, out there," Webber said. "They'll sign on."

"That's for them to decide," Sherman said.

Webber laughed. He clunked the ornament back on his desk. "Okay," he said. "So I'm a son of a bitch. If you can cook it up better, you can have the whole show and I'll shake your hand. But you won't. My way's the only way."

"Maybe," Sherman admitted, not liking the thought.

"And you'll keep Doc's treatment secret?" Webber insisted.

Sherman looked to Perrault. Perrault looked to Marty. He shrugged half-heartedly.

"If you'll fix things so it's released when we've gone," Sherman bargained.

"Fair enough," Webber judged.

Sherman turned to his companions. "All right," he said finally. He let his breath out and scuffed his feet. "I guess that's it."

They walked to the door. Sherman slipped an arm around Marty. They went out slowly.

Sandra lingered a little behind the others, but she was almost out the door before Joe Webber called her back.

"Sandy . . ."

She turned slowly—stepped back into the room—felt the solid door close at her back.

"Yes?" she responded.

Joe Webber slipped down from behind his desk. He walked over to her. He looked up at her.

"Sandy—look," he said, and he was not the same man he had been a few moments before. "Maybe now's a good time to talk about it. I'm three kinds of bastard, but—well, we got a long ride ahead. What do you say we try and raise another crop of kids? It'll help pass the time."

Maybe she trembled inside. She didn't show it. She remained as still as pure white stone.

"Well, one kid, anyhow," Webber said, more anxiously. "Space 'em out, like the others do it. One at a time. I guess that's the best way, actually, for the kid. No sense to be in a hurry. We got time."

His eyes bored into her, watchful, wary—a little desperate.

"Sandy—how about it?" he pleaded.

"All right," she answered calmly.

All he ever had to do was ask.

Most of the newsmen were feature writers, knowing only the art of reducing elaborate facts to a garbled simplicity. But a few were science and technology men, and when Webber announced his interstellar project they pounced like a pack of wolves.

They stood up—half a dozen of them—looking up at him, impatient with questions. Webber looked from one to another, slowly, and deliberately chose Hayes Planchette, a good bet to be the most dangerous of all—a paunchy, gray-looking man with a prow-like nose, a retreating hairline, and an oratorical bearing.

"Mr. Grant," he declared. "First of all, let me state that I greatly admire the ambitiousness of this project. However, you seem to contradict a number of facts I have always believed to be true. Scientific facts. Is it possible my knowledge is outdated?"

"Why not?" Webber wanted to know. He volunteered nothing.

Planchette made a curt, annoyed gesture. "May I check these facts with you?" he requested. "And will you correct my errors?"

"Sure," Webber told him jauntily. "But I'm weak on the science. Don't look for too much."

Planchette set his thick-fingered hands on the back of the chair in front of him. He leaned his weight on them. "It was my understanding that the nearest star is approximately four light years away."

Webber nodded. "Yeah?"

"I believe a light year is defined as the distance a particle of light will travel in a year."

"Schoolbook stuff," Webber said contemptuously. "What's the point?"

"I have been told," Planchette went on implacably, "that no material body can exceed—or even match—the speed of light."

"I guess that's right," Webber hedged. "Like I say, I'm weak on a lot of this stuff."

"Then I would like to know," Planchette demanded logically, "how long do you expect to be on this voyage?"

Webber appeared to consider. "That's a tough one to answer," he said. "Maybe we'll have to try a couple dozen stars before we find one with a planet fit to live on."

Planchette looked nettled. "Perhaps if I rephrased the question," he specified. "Assuming that the first star you

152

visit has a suitable planet, approximately how long will it take you to get there?"

"I don't have the figures," Webber told him. "There aren't any figures—we haven't decided where to head for first. But the way our science boys talk, I'd figure it about two weeks or a month."

Drawing to his full height, Planchette arched his brows. It was quite a performance. "May I say," he intoned, "I find this difficult to believe?"

"Say anything you damn please," Webber told him carelessly. "The trouble with you, you don't look at it right."

Planchette turned pink. "Explain," he demanded.

Webber made a whipping gesture. "Look," he said. "I told you I'm weak on the science. I don't know the details. But our science boys say they can get us there. So okay. I'm not asking a bunch of bonehead questions I wouldn't know the answers to if I had 'em tattooed on my eyelids."

"But the velocity of light . . ." Planchette argued.

Webber snorted disgustedly. "Hell with the speed of light," he spat. "That's the same as saying men can't fly because they don't have feathers."

"But the velocity of light is . . ."

"Can it," Webber snapped impatiently. "Look. There's a lot of rules about how this universe is put together. You can't bust 'em. Okay. But suppose you want to do a thing and it looks like the rules say you can't. Looks like you're stuck, don't it. That's when some ape starts yapping about how it's impossible, just because he doesn't know how to do it. And a bunch of dumb yokels believe him."

"You have not yet explained," Planchette insisted.

"I don't talk the language," Webber said. "All I can talk is the right way to think. Look—it's a funny thing about the universe. It won't give a damn what you do if you don't break the rules. And if you look at the rules real careful, it's just like a tax lawyer reading the laws. You can do damn near anything you want. All you got to do is figure out a way. That's what engineers are for."

"I'm afraid your answer does not satisfy me," Planchette stated.

"Well, it's all the answer I know," Webber said.

Planchette bobbed a chill apology. "Excuse me. I did not mean to imply you had not done your best. Now perhaps you could tell us the men who developed this . . . shall I say miraculous? . . . evasion of the rules—and we shall ask them."

Webber shook his head. "Sorry. That's out."

"May I ask why?" Planchette demanded.

"Sure," Webber said cheerfully. "It's not like we don't *want* to give 'em credit. Those boys did a damn good job. But there's a few other things that come with it besides putting a ship all the way from one star to the next in a couple of days. Things I don't think you'd want just anybody to have. So we're keeping the lid on."

"I see," Planchette said frigidly. "Don't you think that, by doing this, you are taking upon yourself a decision which is by right the duty of the Secretary of Confederate Nations?"

"If we left it to him, we'd have to turn it loose, first," Webber said. "That'd make it too late. There's been too many things turned loose before people were ready for 'em. It made a mess every time. Well, it won't happen this time. Not till the world's been got ready for it."

"Well, at least you might tell us their names," Planchette said stiffly.

"Sorry," Webber shook his head. "Just their names'd be a pretty big hint how it works. They're just about the only guys that could of done it. And they're keeping shut. They know how it's stacked."

Planchette tapped his notebook on the chair in front of him. "I presume that is the reason I have not seen any mention in scientific literature."

"That's part of it," Webber nodded. "But how come you're so sure you haven't?"

Planchette sat down, rage-faced. Others clamored for attention.

"How can a thing like that be used for a weapon?" one of them asked.

"I didn't say it was a weapon," Webber said.

"Then how is it dangerous?" the newsman persisted.

"I can't tell you that," Webber said. "It's a dead giveaway."

It went on like that for a while—the newsmen trying

154

to pry hints from Webber, Webber fending them off. Then a feature writer who had somehow managed to stay up with things stood up with his ballpoint poised over his book.

"You said, did you not," he said, "that you yourself will go on this expedition?"

"You'd have a hell of a time to make me stay behind," Webber said.

"And the plan—I think you said—is to establish a colony without returning to Earth."

"That's right," Webber said. "It's a one-way trip. Anybody that signs on, signs on for keeps."

The man perked up at that. "Are you suggesting people might regret going with you?"

"I'm suggesting," Webber answered firmly, "that people that just want to go for the ride better think twice. Building a colony up from scratch won't be a maypole dance. This is going to be the biggest thing people ever did, and there's some of it that's going to be tough. Damn tough. We don't want lily-livers."

"Well," the newsman said, a bit uncomfortable now, "I was wondering—even if this invention is something dangerous in the wrong hands, aren't you making some provision to leave it behind? I mean, you won't simply go off with it, will you?"

Webber leaned his elbows on the speaker's stand. "Look," he said. "Just because I'm going doesn't mean the Brent Foundation's closing up. It just means they'll be somebody else taking over. It'll be his job to sit on the lid. And keep the work going on."

Some of the other feature writers were getting the drift again. "Has your successor been chosen?" one of them asked.

"Not yet," Webber said. "The ship won't be done for a couple of years. Lots of time to hunt up the right man."

"You spoke of the work going on," another spoke up. "What other projects do you have in mind?"

"I don't," Webber answered. "Our cash is going into the ship—all of it. When it's built—well, the guy that comes after me can have his pick of jobs. There's still Mars and Venus, and it's about time we sent out another expedition to Jupiter—especially because all we have from the first expedition is what Roger Sherman remembered. Or he can build another ship. If I had any say in it, that's what I'd say. Mars and Venus can take care of themselves. So can Jupiter. But these starships—they're something more than any business can pay for, just on speculation. That makes it our job."

"Then you don't see much commercial value in interstellar colonization," someone inferred.

Webber nodded. "Not right now. Not with the moon just getting opened up. And Mars and Venus right next door. When they're played out—a couple thousand years from now—*then* it's important. But we've got to start now, so when the time comes we'll be spread out all over this part of the galaxy. How's *that* sound, boys? An empire in the stars!"

It sounded good. To his own ears, *very* good.

"So it's a goddamn lie," Webber argued. "So what? I couldn't tell 'em the truth, could I? And I had to say something."

Marty, Roger Sherman, and Perrault had been in the back of the room all the time. "You were all ready to tell them," Marty accused. "You knew you were going to say it."

"Well, hell," Webber protested. "Sure I did. You don't think I'd of got up there without being ready if they asked me. You think I'm screwy?"

"We don't like it, Joe," Sherman said. He towered over Webber massively. "Letting people think it is one thing. Lying is something else."

"Yeah?" Webber sneered. "Are *you* doing anything? Are you gonna get us out there? Who got us this far, will ya tell me?"

Roger Sherman turned stone silent.

"No, Joe," Perrault complained. "There's plenty of folks know you can't move a ship only so fast. They'll peel the skin off you."

Webber chuckled. "Nuts, Doc. We got the edge."

Perrault arched a quizzical brow. "Uh?" he uttered.

"It's simple," Webber explained jauntily. "I've said we can do it. All they can say is they don't know how. They can't prove a damn thing."

He chuckled. "Hell, I bet they fall all over us, just to

try and find out. They'll be the biggest suckers of the lot. Hey—you know?—some guy might even get nosy enough to go out and invent it himself. How's that for a laugh?"

"It's not possible, Joe," Sherman said. "I've studied it."

"Yeah? When?"

"The last time I went through college," Sherman said.

"So you got five diplomas," Webber sneered. "So what? Look—I bet we get half a hundred top brains signing on just to be curious."

"Uncle Joe," Marty said. "What happens when they find out?"

"I don't get you," Webber scowled. "Who says they're gonna find out?"

"Suppose you get away with it," Marty explained thoughtfully. "Suppose you get them into the ship and we start out. A whole thousand of them. You'll have to tell them the truth, then."

"Not before I have to, I won't," Webber snapped.

"But you'll have to eventually," Marty pointed out. "What happens then?"

Webber shrugged. He didn't care. "How the hell should I know? Hell—forget it. I'll think of something. Have I ever slipped yet?"

"They'll kill you, Uncle Joe," Marty said. "They'll kill you when they find out how you've tricked them. Maybe all of us."

"Who the hell cares?" Webber snarled. "Ain't it worth getting killed for?"

Bob Webber was at dinner when his phone chimed. He went into the other room to answer it. His wife went on eating, and his small twin boys played with their food.

He came back. "It was Dad," he said. "He wants me. I'd better go."

"But you just got back," Cheryl protested. "You haven't even finished eating."

"He said right away," Bob said. "I'd better go."

It was not an even fight. "Oh, go ahead," she told

him with a flash of temper. She turned to the boys. "Eat your dinners."

Bob was at the Brent Foundation office in ten minutes. No one stopped him. He paused in Webber's waiting room.

"He said you should go right in, Mr. Spilka," the receptionist told him.

"What does he want?" Bob asked worriedly.

"How should I know?" she shrugged prettily.

Bob shrugged too. Slowly, he approached the door to the sanctum. To the lion's den.

The receptionist's box clacked noisily. "Hasn't he got here yet?" it demanded.

"He's on his way in, Mr. Grant," the receptionist answered. Bob opened the door and went in.

He hesitated just inside. Joe Webber came down from behind the high desk and crossed the carpet toward him. "Hi, Son."

"Did you want me?" Bob asked.

"Yeah," Joe Webber said. He took his son's elbow and steered him toward the social alcove. He nodded at the couch. "Sit," he said, and perched up on the back of a chair.

"Son," he announced. "You're going to disappear."

Disappearing was a thing they all had to do now and then—all who had gotten Perrault's almost magical treatment—whenever their permanent youth became embarrassing. Sometimes it was simple—a mere matter of dropping out of sight. Sometimes it was not so simple, and the disappearance had to be arranged so that death was presumed—a copter lost over a lake in a storm. A mountain climb in wild country. A vacation to the bandit country of Afghanistan. And once Andrew Perrault—then serving as the Brent Foundation's treasurer—had absconded with a satchel of money.

"Do I have to?" Bob asked. "Nobody's said a thing about my age."

"You'll have to get a new face, too," Joe Webber went on, as if Bob hadn't spoken. "You've shown it around too much, and you look too much like me."

For one stunned moment, Bob said nothing. Then, "If

you think it's necessary, Dad. What sort of disguise do you want?"

"I mean surgery," Webber said.

Bob frowned. He'd lived all his seventy-eight years with the same face. In that time, he'd disappeared twice —changed his name and assumed a fictional past. But his face was a personal thing. He had always considered it inviolate. Maybe because it was his father's face. Or maybe just because of one of the peculiar consequences of Perrault's discovery.

"But Dad," he argued sensibly. "Plastic surgery isn't any good with us. Two months after the scars heal, we're back with the same face we started."

Webber smiled, foxlike. "Yeah. I know," he said. "But one thing we didn't try. Suppose we stuck chunks of plastic up next to the bones? It'd change all the lines. Suppose we nailed 'em to the bones with rivets, so they don't get pushed out? How does that sound?"

"I only wanted to know how we'd do it," Bob said submissively.

"Swell," Webber smiled. "We'll put another inch in your legs, too."

Again the stunned pause. "Is it necessary?" Bob wondered.

Webber dropped down off the chair. "You're damn right it's necessary," he snapped. "Or we wouldn't be doing it. Listen—you're going to run the Foundation when I go. It's big now. We can't have you look anything like me."

Bob Webber had taken titular control of the Foundation twice, when Webber had to disappear. Rog Sherman and Perrault had filled in, too, under various names. But always Joe Webber had been there, behind the scenes, still running the show. Being put on his permanent own was a new thought to Bob.

"Do you think I can handle it?" he wondered.

"You'll have to," Webber said. "I can't trust anybody else."

"Well, all right," Bob accepted.

"Great," Webber smiled. "You go to the hospital tomorrow. You'll go in as a cancer-exploratory operation patient, but we'll run you through as an accident case up from one of the mines."

"Am I supposed to die, this time?" Bob wondered.

Webber chuckled. "Yeah. We'll tell 'em the doctors fought bravely but the patient died. It all fits together. You get a new face and legs and get rid of Tom Spilka, all at the same time."

Bob looked down at his feet. "Does it have to be tomorrow?"

"We got to work fast," Webber told him. "We got just time enough to get your face fixed and give you a good solid background before I take off. Not one of those paper and tall story jobs, this time. When you move in here, you'll be coming from someplace. That's the way it's got to be."

"Well, all right," Bob said reluctantly. "Cheryl won't like it, though."

Webber turned around viciously. "Who in hell asked her to like it?" he snapped. "She got herself a good deal —what's she bitching about? If you hadn't married her, she'd be a wrinkled old bag by now."

"Well, we're stuck with her, now," Bob said. "If we don't keep her under control, she could do a lot of damage talking to the wrong people."

"She'll keep her mouth shut," Webber said confidently. "All of 'em will. They know what side the butter's on. Anyway, I'll take most of 'em with me."

"That's good," Bob said thankfully. "I don't know if I could handle them. Someday they're sure to find out the treatment doesn't need renewing. They'll be mad about that—and I wouldn't have any control on them."

He paused thoughtfully. "What about the Foundation? What do you want me to do?"

"Build another ship," Webber said.

"And follow you?"

"No. Send it someplace else. A whole different direction."

Bob frowned. "*Send* it?"

"Yeah. You don't go."

"Why?"

"Because I want you to stay behind."

"Why? What do I do then?"

"You build another ship," Joe Webber said. "You keep on building them."

Hayes Planchette, the science newsman, showed up again a week later.

Joe Webber avoided him as long as he could—even set up a parade of people into and out of his office, all with appointments. Not to be outbluffed, Planchette demonstrated his willingness to wait as long as necessary by setting up camp in the waiting room. There, in full view of the receptionist, he whiled the hours studiously reading science journals from his bulging briefcase.

The tactics paid off. On the morning of the third day, Webber ran out of people. When Planchette showed up to renew the siege, Webber told his receptionist to send the man in.

Planchette entered the sanctum. He moved with a ponderous austerity.

"Hi," Webber said. "You still on the moon? I thought you went down with the rest of 'em."

"That I did," Planchette said, his hands at his sides, his plump front bulging. "I came up again last Monday."

Webber gestured him into a hard chair set close to the front of his cliff-like desk. "Well, what's on your mind?"

Planchette settled into the chair, wheezing. He crossed his legs. He slapped his notebook down on the chair arm. He was a very ugly man.

"Mr. Grant," he began incisively. "I have interviewed three men who are experts on relativity physics. They inform me it is absolutely impossible for a physical object to move faster than light."

"You checked with the wrong guys," Webber told him. "They don't know any better."

Planchette colored. "They are men at the height of their profession," he declared.

"I don't care if they're at the height of a pile of garbage," Webber snapped. "Hell with 'em. *I'm* going to do it, and I don't give a damn if they wipe their noses. Hell—we've done it already, in tests."

"I informed them that you claim you can do it," Planchette stated. "They informed me it is not possible. In those words, Mr. Grant."

"Well, what did you expect 'em to say," Webber wanted to know, "after you backed 'em up into a corner like that?"

Glowering, Planchette gripped the chair arms as if he intended to hurl himself out of the chair. "Mr. Grant," he said, surly. "A scientist is the most honest man in the world. His science obliges him to tell the truth."

"Well, these guys were lying," Webber said. "All they should of said—they don't know how we'll do it. And we'll *do* it, damn you. Damn everybody! We'll do it."

"I have also talked," Planchette said implacably, "to Mr. Amos Savery. I believe he was your director of research. But he told me he knew nothing of any research on this matter. I find this, Mr. Grant, very curious."

"All he was in charge of," Webber said, "was the hydrogen rocket. This other thing—we rigged it up thirty years ago. It's been locked in the vault ever since."

"You seem to have an answer for everything," Planchette said, firm-lipped.

Webber narrowed his gray-green eyes. "Look, Planchette," he said. "If you think I'm lying, why don't you say it out plain?"

"I would not go so far as to make accusations," Planchette said carefully. "I am trying to obtain the facts. However, before I can accept your claims, I must insist that they be proved."

"You don't insist anything," Joe Webber told him. "You can think what you god damn please. *We're* going to do it. What kind of a shakedown are you trying to pull, anyway?"

"You can prove it very easily," Planchette said calmly. "By a demonstration."

Webber squinted down at him hard. "You got six months or a year you're not using?"

Planchette frowned woodenly. "Would a demonstration take that long?" he wondered sarcastically.

"The demonstration wouldn't," Webber told him. "But you'd be that long getting back. When you're going that fast, you get out beyond Pluto in less than five minutes. The astrogation's hell. The first test we did, the guy was four years getting back. He damn near starved."

"But if he could travel so fast . . ." Planchette objected.

"He overshot," Webber said. "Ten times. And he wore the rig out. He had to crawl home."

"I see," Planchette said, biting on the words. "As I said, you seem to have an answer for everything. But do you realize, Mr. Grant, that by refusing to demonstrate— no matter what excuses you give—you create doubt of your truthfulness? That is very poor public relations, Mr. Grant."

"Can I help it if that's how things are?" Webber protested innocently. "Any time you got a year, I'll give you a demonstration that'll freeze your whiskers."

"I seem to recall," Planchette went on deliberately, "you plan to recruit approximately one thousand citizens to make the voyage with you. Don't you think, Mr. Grant, that the Confederate government is interested in the welfare of its citizens? Don't you think it might be wise to convince me that a physical object can be moved faster than light?—prove it to me, in confidence if you insist, instead of to a panel convened by the government? Such a panel, I might warn you, would be far more hostile than myself."

"I'll chance it," Webber said. He wasn't worried.

Planchette scowled. "When you first announced development of the hydrogen rocket," he said thoughtfully, "an article was published which observed that spaceships so equipped could cross the galaxy without refueling. It further suggested that a band of far-seeing, selfless persons could, if they wished, set out in such a ship. And their descendants, a century later, would colonize the planets of another star. I remember that article quite vividly. I wrote it."

"So you know how to write," Webber shrugged, unimpressed. "There's just one thing wrong with a setup like that. Those kids at the end of the line. I'm betting if we tried it that way, they'd be so coddled cozy by the time they got there, they'd stay in the ship. A hell of a colony you'd get that way."

"Hummm, yes," Planchette admitted. "But, if that is the only way possible, it would have to be done that way."

"Well, it isn't," Webber stated.

"So you say," Planchette acknowledged. "However, I believe it is the only possible way. Mind you now, Mr. Grant—I have nothing against such a plan. I think, in fact, quite highly of it. Provided, that is, that those who

163

enlist are completely aware of the terms—that they know they will not themselves live to see their destination. But to entice men and women aboard by fraud and lies . . ."

"It's on the level, Planchette," Webber stated coldly. His gray-green eyes were steady, hard, and out of place in his boylike face. "We'll get there fast," he said. "I'm going to see it."

Planchette considered. "Yes," he mulled grudgingly. "I do not doubt you believe it. You are not the man to embark on a project you cannot see through to completion. But . . . I insist, Mr. Grant, with all respect to you —your claims are incompatible with scientific fact. Established, tested fact. I think—perhaps you have forgotten that the men who—so you tell me—invented this miraculous device—these men might have . . ."

"We tested it," Joe Webber said in a flat voice, permitting no question. "It works."

Planchette rubbed his hawky nose. "Yes. So you say," he said. "Uncritical men have been duped before . . ."

"I'll make you a deal, Planchette."

He said it abruptly, like a conspirator. Planchette drew himself up. "I do not make bargains," he said firmly.

"You'll make this one," Webber said. "Wait till you've heard it."

"Mr. Grant," Planchette insisted virtuously, "I am responsible to my employer and—through him—to his subscribers. I consider it a sacred trust. I will falsify nothing. I will gloss over nothing. I will report the complete facts as I know them to the best of my ability. Always."

"Cut the pulpit stuff," Webber told him. "I was going to say—if you're so goddamn sure it won't work, why don't you come along and see for yourself? And if it doesn't work, I'll turn the ship around and come home."

Planchette arched his brows. "Pardon me?"

"Yeah," Webber persuaded. "Why not? You're so god damn sweaty to find out how it works, you'd boil your grandma in jelly preserves. Well, here's your chance. If I'm wrong, you ain't lost a thing. What's wrong with that?"

164

Planchette considered slowly. "I am a reporter," he pronounced. "When I ask questions, I ask them so I can report the answers. Were I to go with you, I would be cut off from the people to whom I would make my reports."

Webber smirked. "You're betting it don't work," he reminded. "If you're right, you got nothing to lose."

Planchette settled back in the chair, pudgy hands on his thighs. "The challenge is hard to refuse," he admitted judiciously. "However, before I accepted, I would want to thoroughly investigate your Foundation—its history, its policies, its personnel, and its plans. I would expect your help and your complete cooperation—and permission to publish whatever I learned."

"You'd get it," Webber promised. "But there's be some things you won't find out. You'll get some doors slammed in your face."

"Furthermore," Planchette stipulated, "when we have set out, I must have permission to transmit dispatches back to Earth."

"You've got it," Webber said. "But we're not taking too big a set. It won't get through for long."

Planchette made a nod of accepting inevitables. "And, if I am right—and I am confident I am—I'll hold you to your promise. When you have tried—and failed—to travel faster than the speed of light, you will turn the ship back and come home."

Webber twisted his mouth in a satisfied smile. He stuck out his hand. "Planchette," he said, "you've got yourself a deal."

Potemkin, who revised the Russian countryside to please the eye and sensibilities of a touring Catherine the Great, could have learned a few tricks from Joe Webber. With lies and with files of falsified records—the only kind the Foundation had ever kept—he gave Planchette an incorrect but uncontestable portrait of the Brent Foundation.

When Planchette asked to tour the *Pioneer*—the still-unfinished starship—Joe Webber smiled and said that he personally would show him around. Nor could Planchette politely refuse, even if he suspected ulterior motives.

Joe Webber picked Sherman to pilot their ship. He knew too much—Rog did—but he could keep his mouth shut. And he'd keep his mouth shut, too, about the size of the ship under construction. That was the really important thing.

For the first time in months, Sherman's engineer was Phil Brembeck. During the pre-flight and shiplift, they had no time for talk, but after shiplift, after they had closed the tanks and the fireball was burning space, Brembeck said, "You know Lester Grant, don't you?"

Sherman nodded. "I know him."

They were driving up at two gravities. It would be hours before turnover, and more hours, then, before they had to match-in on the *Pioneer*'s orbit around Earth.

"Well, I was wondering," Brembeck said, very conscious that the man was only a few decks below them. "Could you talk to him for me?"

"I can talk to him," Sherman said. "What about? I can't say he'll listen."

"Well, it's . . . it's sort of complicated," the young man explained. "You see—well, I want to get married."

Sherman looked up from his instruments, frowning quizzically. "Has he got a daughter I didn't know about?" he wondered.

"Oh, no," Brembeck said quickly, misunderstood. "It's . . . I told you it was complicated."

"I believe you," Sherman said.

"I . . . well, there's this girl," the young man explained. "Her name's Norma. She doesn't like my job."

"Women don't," Sherman told him, as if speaking from long and wearying experience. "It's new, so they think it's dangerous. Les can't do anything for you there."

"Oh, she doesn't mind me flying rockets," Brembeck explained. "The trouble is, she doesn't think I'd be home enough."

Sherman scowled agreement. "She's right, Phil. With an Earth-moon run, it's a day up and another day down. You've got to lay over. My wife hates it, too. I'd put in for hop-rocket runs around the moon, and set us up permanent in the City—but the moon's not the place to raise kids. They've got to grow up in a gravity, or they're stuck on the moon all their lives. I suppose that's all right, but . . ."

"That's what I thought," Brembeck said earnestly. "I wouldn't want it, either. I mean, I'd want my kids so they could go . . . oh, I don't know—I guess, as far as I've gone. Farther."

"So what do you want me to say to Les Grant?"

"Well," Brembeck made an awkward, effacing gesture. "I figured the thing to do was to sign us up for the ship—the . . . well, you know the one I mean. Norma sort of liked the idea. I mean, she didn't just say okay. She really liked it. So I went and signed us up."

Sherman frowned. "Sounds like your trouble's all over."

"That's what I thought," the young man confessed. "Only . . . well, I got rejected. They said they had enough fireball watchdogs."

Sherman didn't say anything at once. He knew it wasn't true—the *Pioneer*'s roster didn't list but a dozen men trained in the handling of ships and their hydrogen engines—barely enough to staff the control room. Of course, there'd be plenty of time to train rocket crews before they made planetfall, but they were going to need an awful lot of men. The *Pioneer* was going to carry fifty atmosphere shuttles, and during the early phases of putting the colony down, every one of them would be needed.

But he didn't tell Brembeck. He looked at a blank bulkhead, beyond the young man.

"So you want me to talk to Les Grant," Sherman said.

"If you would," Brembeck said awkwardly. He wanted to go—he wanted it badly. But he wouldn't plead.

"I can do it," Sherman said. "I can't say I can get results. He's a hard man to talk to, some ways. But I'll try."

"Would you?" Brembeck asked hopefully.

"Yeah," Sherman said. "I'll try. But be sure of one thing. Be sure she's the right girl. Because, Phil—if she isn't, you'll be stuck with her a hell of a long time."

167

The *Pioneer* lay in its orbit, inert, with neither acceleration nor spin. There was no perceptible gravity. Nothing had weight.

The big ship was being built from the core outwards. Only a few decks had been completed—enough for the construction men to live in while they worked on the rest.

It was into one of these completed, pressurized decks that Webber and Hayes Planchette disembarked. In no-weight, Planchette was ungainly as a man with four left feet. It took the help of a couple of workmen to get him as far as the corridor adjoining the dockyard compartment.

"Ain't you ever airswum before?" Joe Webber asked him cheerily.

Planchette clutched queasily to a pair of the hand grasps that studded the decks and walls.

"I never have," he admitted with unsteady dignity. "Fortunately, I came prepared." He crammed a handful of capsules into his mouth. He found them uncommonly hard to swallow.

"If I had known it would be like this . . ." he confessed, and hiccupped violently.

"I didn't invite you," Webber reminded. "You wanted to come."

Planchette swallowed manfully. He pressed a hand against his bulging paunch. "I am beginning to regret it."

"What the hell," Webber argued jauntily. "It ain't often a guy gets to airswim these days. Write a column about it."

Planchette's innards, numbed by drugs, were coming under control. "At the moment," he said, swallowing, "—at the moment, I am far more interested in this ship. I came here, after all, to see it."

"There ain't much to see, yet," Webber said. He nodded around at their surroundings. They were at the intersection of a long, curving corridor and a straight one that butt-ended into it. The walls were bare metal. They were clinging to the out-ship wall, legs dangling in air, and nothing was either up or down.

In the opposite wall, the in-ship corridor opened. Its long, metallically undecorated length reached deep into

168

the ship. It was like a well, plumbed bottomless to infinity.

"Well, let's go," Webber urged.

"Yes. Of course," Planchette said, without enthusiasm. "Uh . . . how do we . . . ah, move?"

Webber chuckled. "Two ways," he said. "You can jump—like an ape—or you can crawl. You better crawl."

Planchette examined their environment reluctantly. "Yes," he decided. "That might be best."

Joe Webber doubled his legs under him. He pushed off gently. Slowly, he drifted toward the mouth of the corridor. Planchette looked after him, fascinated, for a moment. Then, scrambling madly from hand grasp to hand grasp, he followed.

"Don't get going too fast," Webber warned. "You'll bust your skull or something."

An apprehensive look came onto Planchette's face. He slowed down. He passed himself from one hand grasp to the next at the hitching pace of an inchworm.

"I would have liked," he puffed, "to have studied the architect's plans."

"There's enough to load a dozen rockets," Webber said.

"The master sheets would be enough," Planchette said, heaving himself along.

Joe Webber floated effortlessly ahead of him, looking back. "All they show is where the rest of 'em fit together," Webber said. "You saw 'em."

He didn't mention the other set of master plans, infinitely detailed, which was carefully mis-filed in Webber's locked private office file. It would have shown too many decks—too many fitted for residential use, too many equipped with the facilities which would make the ship livable—too many for only a thousand men and women.

Planchette's breath was coming hard. He sweated like a pig. His face was a blotchy red. "Can we stop?" he wheezed.

"Why not?" Webber agreed. Almost carelessly, he reached out and grabbed a hand grasp as he drifted past it. Instantly, his body swung inward against the wall, but at the last moment he let go his hold and stopped himself with both hands palm-flat against the wall. His knees and feet banged on the metal. He grabbed the hand grasp again, and dangled there.

"You got to be part monkey," he confided, grinning.

For Hayes Planchette, getting stopped wasn't as easy. In spite of his hand-over-hand, humping progress, his body had gathered momentum. His hand pulled free of the hand grasp. Yelping explosively, spinning dizzily head over heels, he floundered for another hold, missed —caught one and slammed into the wall, rebounded, and ballooned toward Webber. Desperately, he flailed his arms and howled. Webber moved out of his way and grabbed his sash as he drifted past.

"You got to watch yourself," he advised.

Planchette clung to the hand grasps with both hands. His breath came in gulping, stentorian heaves. He was suddenly disgustingly sick.

"I think we better go back," Planchette said.

"I thought you wanted to see the ship."

The newsman pressed his forehead against the hard metal wall. His arms trembled. "No," he shuddered. "No!"

Roger Sherman came flying down the corridor toward them. He doubled up into a somersault and quickly stopped with his heel against a hand grasp.

"I've been looking for you, Les," he said. Then he glanced at Planchette. His face turned hard. "What happened?"

"He wants to catch his breath," Webber said.

The floating globules of vomit were unmistakable. Sherman narrowed his eyes. "Did you take him out here without any instruction?" he demanded suspiciously.

"Hell, it takes a couple weeks' practice," Webber complained. "We're here for a couple of hours."

"Six," Sherman corrected. He lowered his voice dangerously. "Are you trying to kill him?"

"Hell, Don," Joe Webber protested loudly. "He can get around all right. He got this far, didn't he?"

"Yeah," Sherman said ironically. "But can he make it back?"

"I think we had better go back," Planchette said carefully, in a hoarse, haggard voice.

"You'll need help," Sherman said. He maneuvered

over beside the newsman and offered the broad expanse of his shoulders. "Ride my back," he directed.

Planchette hesitated. Then, one hand at a time, he grabbed handfuls of Sherman's blouse at the shoulders. He was clumsy and frantic. Sherman maneuvered his body up and backwards, under Planchette and, reaching back, helped the newsman get his legs astride of him. Planchette's knees locked viselike around his middle.

"Hang on tight," Sherman told him. "Now, where do you want to go?"

"Back," the newsman repeated, his dignity tattered. "Back."

"I thought you wanted to see the ship."

"I think we had better go back," Planchette repeated doggedly.

Webber prodded Sherman with a fist. He nodded back along the corridor—back the way they'd come.

Sherman made a helpless gesture. "Might as well," he decided. He pushed off. Planchette uttered a nervous yelp, and his knees clamped Sherman's ribs. "Relax," Sherman advised. "Enjoy the ride."

Joe Webber floated along beside them. He looked like a cat licking cream off its jowls.

"Les," Sherman said, and his voice held a calm rage, "don't ever take a man out in no-weight without instruction. You could kill him."

"Heart failure in no-grav?" Webber wondered mockingly. "You nuts or something?"

Sherman jerked a thumb over his shoulder at Planchette. "This guy wasn't far from it," he said.

"Yeah?" Webber demanded, and changed the subject. "You were looking for me. What for?"

"We'll talk about it later," Sherman said.

Moon City's coaxial television carried progress reports on the starship's construction. Months passed, and in the high fidelity picture screens the *Pioneer* took shape, until finally the hull was intact from end to end.

It floated massively—a quiescent leviathan—in its orbit around earth. Its silver, gleaming flanks were curved and smooth, without a chip of ornament.

It looked like a scroll, tightly cinched, and from the open ends protruded the *Pioneer's* bulk—at one end, the mouthlike orifice of the hydrogen rocket; at the other, the slightly bulbed astrodome with its barely discernable telescope slit.

In the background, occulting most of the black sky and untwinkling stars, Earth bulged gigantically upward. Wrapped in atmosphere, misty, it was green and blue, with the bright white clouds and mottled other colors of deserts and mountains. Round a swelling—straining upward like a seed-pod bursting—that was Earth.

Around the *Pioneer*, the cargo ships nuzzled like minnows surrounding a whale. One by one, endlessly, they disappeared inside the vast, hatched flanks.

With a balloonlike steadiness, the camera advanced toward the ship—advanced until it was an overwhelming mass, big as the world. Then, suddenly, it was inside, and the scene was of workmen and machines, and the disordered order of work going on.

The news talker's voice came on again. It said, "—the largest single structure ever built by men.

"Within the month, the General Nucleonics construction team expects to complete installation of the most powerful hydrogen engine on record, and . . ."

"It's beautiful," Marty breathed.

"You'd better like it," Sherman muttered. "It's going to be home for a good long time."

". . . Foundation has tentatively set the push-off for sometime in March of next year," the talker said. "Meanwhile, in an interview, expedition press officer Hayes Planchette repeated again that he cannot explain how the *Pioneer* can travel faster than light. He admitted that presently accepted theory considers faster than light travel impossible, and that he himself has been without success in his attempts to learn how the *Pioneer* can attain such speeds. The Brent Foundation, he explained, is witholding that information for reasons of public safety—but it has given assurance that unless the *Pioneer* actually performs as claimed, the expedition will be cancelled. However, Planchette said, the only way a man can find out how the starship does it, will be to join the expedition."

"I don't like it," Sherman grumbled.

"The Brent Foundation," the talker went on, "has announced that the *Pioneer*'s roster is nearly complete.

Still needed are men and women with training in ecology, agricultural science, and mining geology. Preference will be given to married couples, and children are encouraged. Director of the Foundation Lester Grant reemphasized that the *Pioneer*'s expedition will not be a commercial venture, but an attempt to set up a self-sufficient human colony on . . ."

Sherman got up and snapped off the set. The picture of the *Pioneer*'s busy interior collapsed shudderingly and dwindled into gray distance. "I don't like it," he repeated.

Marty hadn't moved. Naked, she lay under the sun lamp, bare bottom up and her chin raptly pillowed on her interlaced, small hands. A good tan was the fashion in Moon City, and—like most redheads—she had a hard time keeping hers. She worked on it whenever she got a chance.

Now she hunched her shoulders glumly. "I don't like it either," she admitted reasonably. "But what are we going to do about it?"

Sherman turned and looked down at her. He leaned his shoulders against the wall. "That's the hell of it," he grumbled. "Nothing."

"Why not?" Marty prodded. She rolled over and sat up effortlessly, drawing her feet in and clasping her ankles. The sun lamp made a halo of her hair. "It wouldn't take much. That Hayes Planchette . . ."

"Yeah?" Sherman demanded sullenly. "And then what happens?" He stood clear of the wall, thumbs hooked in his sash. "All of a sudden, your dad's the biggest son of a bitch that ever lived, and the rest of us are a greedy crowd that got hold of something too good to be shared. And the *Pioneer* project gets kicked in the ashcan. Damn it, Marty—I'm going to pilot that ship. I've . . . well, I've got to, that's all. Everything we've ever done was leading up to it."

"Everything *Joe's* done," Marty conceded bitterly. She looked down at her ankles—then up at him. "You've been talking to him, haven't you," she said.

"Well, damn it, he's right," Sherman argued. "If people knew how long we'll take to get there, we couldn't get jailbirds to make the trip with us."

"But it's a swindle," she protested intensely. She sat

173

up straight, arch-backed, indignant. "That's all it is. A cheat and a swindle."

Sherman made a helpless, shamefaced gesture. He shifted his feet. "We can't get people any other way."

"But when they find out," Marty agured sensibly, "—and they've got to find out eventually—Joe's promised he'll turn the ship back if we can't make it fast. They'll make him keep that promise."

Sherman shrugged. "They'll have a hard time. The only promises he keeps are the ones he wants to."

"But how can he break it?" Marty wondered. "They'll kill him if he doesn't."

"Would he of made it if he didn't have it figured out?" Sherman asked. "Marty—he *always* has it figured out."

"But *how?*" Marty wanted to know.

Sherman shook his head. "I don't know," he admitted. "But he'll do it."

"But does it *have* to be like that?" Marty persisted. "Don't you think—if everybody had Dad's treatment—wouldn't there be people who'd be willing to go with us, even if they knew it might be a hundred years before we get there?"

"The right kind of people?" Sherman doubted.

"Yes. The right kind of people," she insisted. The sun lamp was bright on her shoulders. "We want sober people—not adventurers. People who know what they're doing and know what they want—and who know why they want it."

Reluctantly, Sherman nodded. She was almost right. "But it won't work out that way," he explained. "Everybody can't have it."

"What?" Marty cried, and her face was the face of a hurt, shocked child. "Why not?"

He made a futile motion of the hands. "There isn't room," he explained. "Everybody wants to live forever, and there isn't room for everybody. If it wasn't that we're going away—in a few hundred years, we wouldn't have room just for ourselves and our kids. There's only so many can live on a planet at a time. Mars and Venus —all that does is put it off. Sooner or later, that's what it comes to."

Marty hugged one leg up against her body, her knee

almost touching her chin. "But what about after we get to the colony?" she wondered thoughtfully. "What will we do about it then?"

Glumly, Sherman shrugged. "We'll have to figure something out," he said. "I don't know . . ."

"Joe's probably already thought of something," Marty said bitterly. "He . . . he's very clever about things like that." She pushed her red hair back from her forehead. "And what about here?" she wondered. "If it's going to be released after we go . . ."

"That's not our problem," Sherman said. "If he means it."

Marty frowned. "What do you mean?"

"I mean, I don't think he's going to," Sherman said.

"But he promised . . ." she protested.

"We won't be anywhere that we can call him on it," Sherman pointed out. "Has he ever given up a thing he can use?"

"But he's making the trip with us. It doesn't make any difference."

Sherman nodded. "Sure—but who's taking over? What's *he* going to do?"

"But he's not one of us," Marty argued. She didn't want to believe.

"Sure he is," Sherman told her. "You mean you didn't recognize him? It's Bob. He's playing it close, and he's been made up—I don't know how. But that's who he is, and I'll give you a guess what he'll do."

". . . of course," she murmured in a small, comprehending voice. "He'll build another ship. He'll do the same trick Joe's doing . . ."

She scrambled to her feet. "That settles it," she decided fiercely. She snatched up the first piece of clothing she could. It happened to be a sarong skirt. She wrapped it quickly around her hips.

"We'll go see that Planchette," she declared. "We'll . . ."

"No," Sherman said. He made her turn around— made her look up at him. He towered over her—large, strong . . .

"But . . ."

"The world isn't going to get it anyway," he told her. It was not a pleasant truth, but he had to tell her.

175

"Marty—there's not room for everybody, so nobody'll get it. It's the only fair way. The only decent way. But . . . Marty . . . isn't it better if people don't know? It'd make their lives hell, if they knew, getting old . . ."

"But Roger . . ." Marty protested painfully. She burrowed her face against his chest.

Sherman's big hand cradled her head. He pressed her cheek against his ribs. Firmly, he told her, "We're going. Do you hear? We're going."

He unfastened her skirt and cast it aside. He slapped her bared bottom. Submissive, she relaxed against him. He put his arms around her—rocked her gently.

"Marty," he said heavily, "all we can do is go on living—have kids—and don't fight the impossible. Feel up to it?"

Her breath was warm against his throat. "Babies? Sure," she murmured willingly. "But . . ."

Abruptly, she pushed him away. "It's not right," she protested. "We shouldn't . . ."

He stumbled back a step. He let his arms hang at his sides. He shook his head glumly. "Marty—redhead—" he said, "nothing's right. Right and wrong don't have a thing to do with it—or maybe everything's wrong. I don't know. All I know—it's a mess. And we can't do a damn thing."

He rested his hands on her smooth, bare shoulders—shook her gently, steadied her.

"It's hell," he muttered. "Hell."

Sandra called him at the office. She didn't do it often. Webber let the call come through.

She was bright-eyed and bare-shouldered. She looked more pixie-pleased with herself than he had seen her for some time. Not that he'd noticed how she looked, lately. The last couple of months, he hadn't been to their apartment much more than to sleep and eat, and he still wasn't caught up on desk work.

"What's on your mind?" he asked.

His directness unsettled her. She twitched her shoulders. "Could you come home early tonight, Joe?"

He made a quick, that-isn't-my-name-now gesture.

There shouldn't be anyone listening, but he hadn't stayed covered all these years by not being careful.

She blinked. "Lester—why did I call you Joe?" she wondered aloud.

Webber chuckled. "He was your first husband. Remember?"

Sandra's chin snapped up, startled. Then she looked away. "Would you, Les?" she asked.

"Would I what?" Webber demanded.

"Would you come home early tonight?" she repeated.

"Why?"

She shook her head. "Don't be difficult, Lester," she said patiently. "I know you're very busy. But I'd like you to come home early very much."

"I'll come home," Webber said, "when I damn well please."

He broke the circuit.

He got home, as usual, very late. "Hi," he said, walking in jauntily, as if nothing had happened.

Sandra put down the book she was reading. She stood up and came toward him.

"I'd hoped you'd come home early," she said plainly, like a disappointed child's reproach.

"Damn it, Sandy," Webber complained. "I'm busy as hell just now."

"I know," she admitted submissively. "It's all right. Whatever you want to do, Joe—it's all right."

Whatever he wanted to do. Those were the terms of their marriage. From the very beginning—from the very first day—that rule had set the limits of her rights and her freedom. Joe Webber got his way with her, always, and he always would.

"I've got a baby," she said. She spoke matter-of-factly, as if it was nothing unusual.

Webber turned. He looked up at her. "Yeah?" he said. "How long?"

"Six weeks—two months," she told him lightly. It was a petty detail.

"Well, it's about time," he said. Then he said, decisively, "He'll get born in the *Pioneer*."

Sandra's eyes showed surprise. "But he ought to come

in late February," she objected. "We don't leave until some time in March. Why can't I have him here?"

Webber shut her up with a curt, impatient wave of the hand. "We'll move up the push-off to February 10," he decided. "And we'll put you aboard a whole month before."

"Do we have to?" Sandra wondered.

Joe Webber pressed the knuckles of a fist against her soft body, down where the baby was. "Sandy," he said tightly, "I'm not letting any dame hold up the push-off just because she's got to have a baby."

Sandra retreated half a step, to relieve the pressure of his fist. "All right, Joe," she said. "But Joe—it's your baby, too."

Webber chuckled. "So's the *Pioneer*—and I've been nursing it a damn lot longer than you've had that thing in your belly."

Bob Webber was the last stay-behind to leave the *Pioneer*.

The giant ship was still in orbit, without drive and without spin. Nothing had weight. In the starkly lit, cavernous dockyard space next to the atmosphere shuttlecraft berths, Joe Webber hooked his feet in a hand grasp and said goodbye to his only loyal son.

Sandra was with him.

He wore a Captain's uniform. He had designed it himself, and it looked like a modified coverall. In fact, it closely resembled the uniform he had worn more than a hundred years before, when he commanded a ship during the First Age of Space Flight. He was smiling now, in unconcealed anticipation.

"Beat it, Son," he said. "We got to get this can moving."

Bob backed away. He floundered for another anchor hold. "Sure, Dad. Only . . ."

The Foundation was his, now. Already, the preliminary work was under way to start construction of another ship. It would be called the *Pathfinder*.

"You can do it," Webber said, confident. "Just make sure your boys stick close. Two or three to a ship, and it's rigged. Build 'em."

Bob had a dozen sons. Eight of them could be trusted.

178

And they had kids, too—some already grown up and given Perrault's treatment. Some of them, too, could be trusted. The Brent Foundation's work would go on.

"Sure, Dad. Sure," Bob said.

"Now beat it," Webber told him. "And do a good job. I'll be back to check up on you, some day."

Bob swallowed. "I'll do my best, Dad," he promised.

"You'd better," Webber snapped.

Bob looked down at his feet—anywhere where he didn't have to meet his father's implacable eyes. "Well . . ."

Sandra brushed past Webber—hugged Bob—kissed him. Her normally well-proportioned body was swelled out of shape by the baby developing in her, now scarcely two weeks from full term.

She released Bob. "Now go, Bobby," she said whisperingly. "Quickly."

Bob turned and propelled himself toward the yawning doorway of the launching chamber, where a ship was waiting to return him to the moon. In mid-flight, he turned to look back at them. Joe Webber raised a hand —hail and farewell. Bob passed beyond the doorway. He turned again, caught a grip on the catwalk rail, and scuttled out of sight.

A loud bell began clanging. The door's portals came slowly together. Their machined-smooth faces met resoundingly. The sealing plate slid slickly down into place. The warning lights—vacuum beyond—began flashing.

Joe Webber turned to go, but Sandra clutched his wrist and made him stay. After a while, the lights stopped flashing. Bob's ship was gone, and the last of the *Pioneer*'s shuttle craft had come into the berth in its place.

Sandra let go of Joe's hand. "I'll never see him again," she breathed wistfully.

"Sandy . . ." Webber began, exasperated.

"Oh, I know—it's necessary," she admitted regretfully. She kept her face turned from him—looking bleakly at the massive portals that had closed behind her firstborn son.

Joe Webber thumped her shoulder. She turned. "Let's

go," he said. He nodded toward the doorway to the *Pioneer*'s interior.

She bowed her head. She wouldn't look at him. "All right, Joe," she said.

He gave her a push toward the door, and followed. He helped her maneuver through the opening. In the corridor, he cradled her in his arms and leaped down its deep length toward the center of the ship, where the elevators were.

The corridor was deserted. Not many of the passengers, who had come aboard in the last few days, cared to venture out in no-weight. That suited Webber just fine.

They floated along the corridor. It was long and straight, and considerable effort had been spent to make it pleasing to the eye. Parkway islands lined its center, planted with shrubs and sod. On their right, the square-cut pillars of the collonade marched past. The other wall opened into bays and alcoves, with benches and casual furniture, and sometimes a hedge or a shrubbed lawn under sun-bright light.

"Could I go down to the control room with you?" Sandra wondered. "I'd like to be there . . ."

Webber shook his head. "Uh-uh, Sandy," he said. He palmed his hand against her swollen body. "Take care of Joe Junior," he told her. "We're not rigged for pregnant women down there."

"I won't name him Joe," she insisted willfully.

"He'll be Joe," Joe Webber told her, just as stubborn.

They came to the elevators just off the central plaza. Webber caught a hand grasp and stopped them. He brought her up within reach of the grasp, so she could anchor herself. He buzzed for a car.

"Get up to the apartment," he ordered. "Strap down on the bed. We've got to get this big can moving."

The elevator came, then, and he left her there.

The control room's door clicked tight behind him, sealing him inside. The room was small, designed for function. In the center, overlooked by a towering wall of instruments, four consoles crouched in a square, facing inward. Sherman sat at the biggest, faced toward the wall. The consoles to his right and left were also

180

manned. The one across the square from him was vacant.

Two more consoles huddled back against the wall, facing him. They, too, were manned.

Phil Brembeck had the First Engineer's console. He looked young and excited. Webber scowled at the sight of him; he hadn't wanted that kid here.

The other three men looked young, too, but none of them was less than fifty. They were Clan, all three of them, with Sherman blood. One of them, in addition, was a son of Webber's.

Webber floated himself into the seat opposite Sherman. He strapped in. "How's it look? Ready?"

"Almost," Sherman said.

"Check off," Webber ordered. He hunched over his console, snapping switches.

"First Engineer: Check!" Phil Brembeck said smartly.

"Two Engineer: Check!" Ralph Webber reported.

"Astro: Check!" Frank Sherman said.

"Control Feedback: Check!" said Martin Bently.

"Pilot: Check!" Sherman said, level-voiced.

As they reported, Webber checked his own console. Everything worked. The pre-plot and orbit comparator; the 360 globe radar and vision; the fireball pressure-and-temp; the magnets; the hull stress; the gravity vectors . . . and controls: the abort; the disarm; the ejector; the fireball-killer; the collision course reflex; the broached hull.

The things that might have to be done too fast to speak orders.

"Captain: Check!" Webber said, loving the words. "Don—what time have you got?"

"B minus seventeen minutes and forty . . . five seconds," Sherman answered.

It checked with his own clock. "Check," he said, and heard it echoed, one at a time, by the juniors.

"Prepare to accelerate," Webber ordered.

The men got busy.

Webber snapped on the ship's talker. "Attention," he said. "Attention."

The talker piped his words to every corner of the ship. Even the parts that wouldn't be inhabited for another twenty years.

"This is Lester Grant, Captain of this ship," he said.

"Glad to have you aboard! We'll be putting the push on in exactly fifteen minutes. Stick in your quarters. Strap down on a bed or a chair. Ten minutes from now—five minutes before we accelerate—all inship power will cut off. It's necessary. Expect it and sit tight. Deck wardens —report your floors!"

The *Pioneer* had almost a thousand decks, but less than forty were inhabited. Nor did the passengers know about those sealed-off decks. The few who sensed the disparity between the apparent interior size of the ship and published pictures of it had been more than satisfied by mention of the wealth of equipment they were taking with them. Even Planchette.

The reports of the deck wardens came in, each in turn, topship down.

"Deck fifteen plus: Secure!"

"Deck fourteen plus: Secure!"

It was routine down to deck four plus. There, the warden said, "Condition yellow, sir . . . Captain— there's a man gone out of his quarters up here. He's a doctor. Said he had to make a call. Emergency."

Webber switched from the ship's talker to direct intercom. "Who the goddamn bastard's got a bellyache?" he demanded. "Of all the goddamn times . . ."

"He didn't say, Captain. He was in a hurry."

Sherman looked up from his console. "Abort?" he wondered.

"And take a whole goddamn day to recompute?" Webber demanded. He opened the intercom again. "He's a doctor—he can look out for himself. Report yourself secure."

"Deck four plus: Secure, sir."

"Deck three plus—report," Webber ordered through the talker.

"Deck three plus: Secure!"

"Deck two plus: Secure!"

Then one plus. The Middle Deck. Then . . .

"Deck one minus: Secure!"

. . . and the countdown went on—went on until, finally . . .

"Deck sixteen minus: Secure!" was reported, and the ship was cleared to accelerate.

182

But the intercom flashed. "Captain! Middle Deck reporting. The power board shows an elevator running. Headed up."

"Damn!" Webber swore. "That goddamn doctor."

"Shall I chase him?" the Middle Deck warden offered.

Webber saw Sherman look expectantly at him, but the sweep-needle of his console clock scissored toward the B minus five mark. He shook his head.

"Don't," he told the warden. "He'll get stopped when the power cuts off. Let him sit out the push-off where he is. Teach him a lesson. Goddamn nut!"

"I didn't see it except just now," Middle Deck explained. "I . . ."

Whatever he was going to say, he got no chance to say it. The power cutoff broke communication. The control room went black.

But not totally black. The consoles glowed gently. The instruments gleamed. And every man in the control room had drilled until he knew his console blindfolded.

"Five minutes," Sherman's son at the Astro reported.

"Fuel charge released," Sherman said. "Ionized. Magnets hard. Ready to ignite."

"Spark it," Webber said.

"Four minutes, thirty," Astro read off.

Silent, intent, Sherman and the two engineers worked at their consoles. Patterns of red, green, and amber dot-lights flickered on their boards. Joe Webber watched his own instruments. The fireball reading stayed soft cold.

"Pinch it!" Webber ordered. "Goddamn! Pinch!"

"It's coming up steady, sir," Sherman said.

"Four minutes," Astro said.

"Cradle ready," Webber's son in the Two Engineer spot reported.

"Scale it down," Sherman told him. "We don't need it yet. We need the power for pinch."

"Scaling down half," Ralph Webber acknowledged.

"Three minutes, thirty," Astro reminded.

"Stand by," Sherman ordered.

"Warming," Phil Brembeck announced. He said it like the greatest moment of his life.

Webber hadn't looked from his console. The fireball was getting hot, but it hadn't sparked yet. No pressure.

"Three minutes," Astro said.

"Spark!" cried Phil Brembeck excitedly. Then, disappointed, "Died out."

"More deuterium," Sherman decided. "A c-mill."

"Two minutes, thirty," Astro said.

"Spark!" Brembeck said again. "It's holding."

Webber let his hands rest lightly on the disarm and ejector levers. He watched the temp & pressure meter.

"Two minutes," Astro announced.

"Spark critical," Brembeck said.

"Starve it," Sherman ordered.

"It's shrinking!"

"Give it enough to live on," Sherman said.

"One minute, thirty," Astro said.

"Prepare to transfer," Sherman ordered.

"Scaling up cradle," Webber's son announced.

"Bring the spark up," Sherman ordered. "But slowly."

"One minute," Astro announced.

"Power, please," Two Engineer requested.

"One—can you relax the pinch?"

"Fifty seconds," Astro called.

"Not much," Brembeck said worriedly. "A bit. Fireball swelling, sir."

"Cradle scaling up," Two Engineer reported.

"Alert for shift," Sherman ordered.

Webber's hands closed tight on the ejector and fireball-killer levers. He raised them to trigger position.

"Forty seconds," Astro said.

"Don't shift!" Feedback shouted.

"Holding!" Astro announced. He repeated it, monotonously, like the beat of a clock. "Holding! Holding!"

"What's wrong?" Webber demanded.

"The cradle's still soft. It didn't go hard," Feedback said.

"Give it power!" Webber yelled. "Bastard—power!"

"Fireball stabilized," Brembeck said hurriedly.

"Holding! Holding! Holding!" Astro said evenly, gently, again and again.

"Coming up now," Webber's son said. "Now . . . cradle ready, sir."

"Alert to shift," Sherman directed.

"Thirty seconds," Astro resumed. "Delay, twenty-six seconds."

"Fireball swelling," Brembeck said. "On the curve."

"Switch to alternate pre-plot?" Sherman asked.

"Twenty seconds!"

"No," Webber ordered. "Stick to plot. We'll make correction later."

"Tube flooded," Sherman said.

"Fifteen seconds!"

"Shift!"

A terrible silence. Then, "Transfer completed, sir."

"Cradled. Locked," said the Two Engineer.

"Ten seconds!"

"Feed it. Feed it plenty."

"Five seconds! Four!"

"Fireball swelling. Cradle resisting. Can't hold long."

"Three! Two!"

"Let it squirt."

Directly under the control room, in the bottom of the ship, a tiny star burst through its capsule of magnetic force. Its flame spewed out into vacuum. The blast nudged the *Pioneer* gently, and the blast did not stop. From the *Pioneer*'s vast storage tanks, hydrogen fed it as fast as it burned.

Things began to have weight. The lights came on in the control room.

"Under minimal drive," Sherman reported.

"Ion stream dynamos turning," Brembeck said. "Coming up to speed."

"Cradle?" Webber asked.

"Holding firm, sir," Feedback said. "Pressure dropping slowly."

"Tighten the vent, Two," Webber told his son. "You want a *brennschluss?*"

"Tightened, sir. Pressure stable, sir."

"Perceptible intake," Brembeck announced.

"Valve it into the tanks," Webber ordered. "Feedback —report."

"Fireball ninety-two percent efficient, sir," Feedback announced. "Maximum."

"Ion stream dynamos delivering full power," Brembeck announced.

Webber racked the emergency levers back in lock position. He wouldn't need them now.

"Okay, Don. Step it up," he told Sherman.

"Pre-plot tape?" Sherman asked.

"No. Vernier by hand. Make up the delay."

"Right," Sherman said. He unlocked the manual controls. "Step one on vernier," he said.

"Astro, give him the figures," Webber said.

"Never mind," Sherman said. "I can feel it."

"Check him, Astro," Webber said.

Gradually, by minute degrees, Sherman advanced the flow of fuel to the fireball. The fireball's pressure increased, and the *Pioneer*'s acceleration rose. Webber watched the hull stress meters.

"Step one complete," Sherman reported. "Acceleration, one tenth grav. Resetting for step two."

"Correction curve optimum," Astro advised. "Predict to match pre-plot orbit in the tenth step. Nice going, Don."

"I haven't done it all, yet," Sherman reminded. "How's the hull?"

"No strain," Brembeck said. "So far."

While they talked, Sherman edged through the vernier scale. "Step two complete," he said. "Acceleration, two tenths grav. Resetting for step three."

"Correction still optimum."

"Cradle magnets compensating," the Two Engineer reported.

Step by step, the *Pioneer*'s acceleration rose. By slow degrees, the sensation of weight returned. Finally, it was done.

"Step ten completed," Sherman reported. "Acceleration, one standard gravity."

"Matched to pre-plot orbit," Astro reported.

"Fireball stable," Feedback announced. "Cradle firm. Fuel flow meters re-scaled to one acceleration unit."

It was almost done. One more operation.

"What's the intake?" Sherman asked.

"Two and sixty-three hundredths acceleration units," Brembeck said. "And coming up. Ninety-nine and twenty-seven hundredths hydrogen. Valving into the tanks, sir."

"Rig for direct feed of one unit, constant, to the fire-

186

ball," Sherman instructed. "Top off the tanks with the rest, and then let it spill."

"Yes, sir," Brembeck said. There was a pause while he worked. Then, "System ready, sir."

"Thanks," Sherman acknowledged. A pause. The *Pioneer*'s acceleration slackened very slightly, then resumed. "Riding on vacuum at one standard gravity acceleration," he reported. "That does it."

Joe Webber checked over his console. "Great," he said fiercely. He snapped on the talker.

"Attention," he said. "Attention. We're moving. Acceleration, one grav. The next scheduled gravity change will be the end of the trip. All passengers and crew relieved from push-off quarters. That's it. Glad to have you aboard!"

He shut off the talker. "Four hour watches," he said. "Don—take my desk." He unstrapped from the chair. He got up and walked to the door.

"Captain, sir. Uh . . . Mr. Grant . . ."

Somebody on the intercom. Webber stopped. He turned. He went back and leaned over his console. "Who's there?" he demanded.

"Deck twelve plus warden, sir. Nick Burns," the man at the other end of the wire responded.

"Yeah? What's wrong?"

"Well, nothing's wrong, Mr. Grant. Not exactly. Uh . . . well, your wife just had a baby."

Webber glared at the intercom, grimly silent.

"Mr. Grant . . . aren't you going to say something?"

"I'm supposed to say something?" Webber challenged.

"Uh . . . well, I mean, if it was my wife, sir . . ."

"Well, she isn't," Webber snapped. "I knew she was going to have it and it was about time. Am I supposed to get excited? Am I supposed to say something? She can take care of herself."

"Yeah," the deck warden admitted. "I guess she can. That's what the doctor said when he got here. He got stuck in the elevator. Uh . . . there anything you want me to do?"

"You're dismissed," Webber told him.

"Well . . . uh, okay, sir."

"And if anybody asks, his name's Joe."

"Yes sir, Captain. But . . . uh, well, the doctor says it's a girl."

"Then spell it without the E," Webber snapped. He closed the intercom. He looked up. He saw Sherman watching him. Sherman's hammered-looking face was wooden and wordless.

"You want to go up and see her?" Webber asked. "Go ahead. I'll take this watch."

"I'd rather you went," Sherman told him plainly.

"Go anyway," Webber said. "I relieve you. Get out."

He sat down and strapped in. "The bitch," he muttered. "A god damn girl!"

One week out, Joe Webber told Hayes Planchette that the *Pioneer*'s transmitter could no longer get through to Earth. It was a lie, but Planchette had no way of disproving it.

"Am I to presume we are moving faster than light, now?" Planchette suggested.

Webber shook his head. "You'll be told," he said. "Everybody gets told. But not yet. We're moving up, but not yet."

"I have been given to believe," Planchette said penetratingly, "that we are accelerating at the rate of one standard gravity. At that rate, I imagine it will be quite some time."

"One grav is what it feels like," Webber admitted.

A week and a half out, Andrew Perrault strolled into Webber's Middle Deck office. "Got to thinking, Joe," he began.

Webber gave him the wrong-name gesture—and a dangerous glare. "Be sure we're alone," he warned.

Perrault looked around. They were alone in the office, and the door was tight-closed. His hollow-jowled face had a look of innocent incomprehension.

"So you've been thinking," Webber said.

Perrault nodded. "Been sharpening my needle," he explained. "Got to wondering when I get to stick it in people."

"Not until I tell you to," Webber snapped.

"Well, sure, Joe. Only, when's that?"

"When I tell you," Webber said. "And until then,

188

keep your goddamn mouth shut. We got to handle this thing just right. If we don't, we get killed. All of us. And we don't make the trip."

"I've lived a long time longer than I ought," Perrault mumbled gloomily.

"You're talking crazy, Doc," Webber said. It was a warning.

Perrault shrugged expressively. "Like you say, Joe," he submitted. "Only . . . well, I always sort of wanted to give it to people. Besides us, I mean. We're going to do it, aren't we, Joe?"

"Yeah. We'll do it. Keep your pants on." He paused. "You looking for something to do?" he demanded.

"Sure, Joe," Perrault volunteered. "If an old man's up to it."

"I want you to pass this around, but I don't want outsiders to hear it."

Perrault nodded glumly, and waited.

Webber punched a finger at him. "Tell 'em, when the passengers catch on, they'll be mad enough to feed us to the fireball. So they better get down to deck minus four eighty-two the minute I pass the word. And stay there."

"Deck minus four eighty-two?" Perrault echoed. "That's almost on top of the fireball. Is it safe, down there?"

"A hell of a lot safer than up here, when things bust loose," Webber promised.

Sandra came out of the baby's room. She slid the door almost shut. Turning, she pushed a stray strand of hair back from her eyes. "Joe?" she said.

Joe Webber slapped shut the cover of the report he was studying. He let it drop on the table. "Yeah? You want something?" he asked.

"Joe—what are you going to do about them?"

His gray-green eyes snapped up at her, hard, stripping her naked. "Who's them?" he demanded.

"The people going with us. The passengers. The colonists."

"What's to do about them?"

Her eyes were level and direct. "Don't play games with me, Joe," she told him. "You know what I mean. They're going to start wondering why we don't get anywhere. They'll want to know where we are. They'll want to know how soon they can . . ."

"Let 'em," Webber said.

"They'll wonder why the ship's the way it is—the . . . the gardens, and the water service, and they'll find out about all those empty decks . . . Things like that mean a long trip, Joe. And they're intelligent people."

Webber chuckled. "Yeah. Intelligent people. Smart enough to get suckered. That's how intelligent."

"Honest people," Sandra persisted. "So honest they believe everyone's honest. They won't like it when they find out you've tricked them."

"You're damn right they won't like it." He chuckled again. "Why don't you say it right out? They'll be mad as hell."

"So what are you going to do?" she asked him.

"You'll find out."

"Tell me, Joe. Now," she insisted.

Webber chuckled. "I got it all figured out," he told her. "That's all you got to know."

Two weeks out, at Webber's instigation, the passengers held an election.

It was not a bitterly fought contest. There were no significant issues, and the passengers voted believing that within the space of weeks they would be hacking their colony out of a raw, alien world.

The five elected to the Passengers' Council, therefore, were elected on the strength of professional qualifications and personality.

There was one exception—a man more versed in publicity than in the science of colony building. But, except for Joe Webber, he was the best known man in the ship.

And because he, of the five, could speak best for the group, the other four let him be chairman by tacit consent.

Hayes Planchette.

Joe Webber shoved the papers to the side of his desk when Sherman came into the office. He nodded to a chair. "Sit," he said.

Sherman sat down. His massive bull-body dwarfed the chair. "What did you want me for?"

Webber shot a glance at the door. It was tight shut. "Things are going to bust wide open damn quick, now," he said.

"I know," Sherman said. "That all you wanted?"

"That kid," Webber said. "Brembeck."

"What about him?" Sherman wanted to know, scowling. "What can he do?"

"Plenty," Webber said. "I didn't want him aboard—you got him in anyway. Okay. So it's up to you he don't make trouble."

"How?" Sherman challenged. "What kind of trouble?"

"He's the only outsider in the pilot and astro staff," Webber said. "That puts him in a spot to smell something funny before anybody else. Or we might make a slip in front of his pink little ears."

Sherman nodded, listening without committing himself. "Go on."

"Watch him," Webber ordered. "If he says anything —if he starts acting queer or he asks the wrong questions —grab him. Lock him up—one of the empty decks. And let me know."

"He's got a wife aboard," Sherman warned. "He can't be kept missing long."

"He won't have to be," Webber said. "Before they get nosy, they'll have plenty else to think about."

Sherman shrugged. That part was Webber's problem. "Okay," he knuckled under. "On one condition. As soon as we've got him locked up, he gets the treatment. No argument and no stalling. He gets it."

"Sure. Why not?" Webber agreed cheerfully. "That'll keep him out of circulation for a month."

"That's a promise you're going to keep," Sherman told him.

"You saying I don't keep my promises?" Webber demanded.

"Yes," Sherman said. "But this one you'll keep. I'll tell Doc myself." He got up and walked out.

A month out, the grumbling started. Webber let it go on as long as he dared. Then, picking a watch when

Brembeck wasn't in the control room, he boosted the ship's drive by two-tenths of grav, and revved the ship's gyro to give the hull a gentle spin.

The passengers, feeling the peculiar, subsensual changes, believed him when he announced the ship had passed the speed of light. The grumbling stopped.

But not long after, Hayes Planchette barged into Webber's Middle Deck office. Webber, warned he was coming, had cleared the papers off his desk. Slouched comfortably in his chair, smiling, he looked up guilelessly when Planchette burst in.

"What's your ulcer?" he said.

Planchette stopped with his arms stiffly straight at his sides. "I have," he stated angrily, "been refused admission to the astrodome."

"That's right," Webber said easily. He fiddled idly with his pen. "It's closed up."

"May I ask why?" Planchette demanded.

Webber gave him a scornful, jocular smile. "Look, Planchette," he argued reasonably. "We're moving faster than light, so right now the astrodome's as useful as three-legged pants. You ever looked at the hind end of a piece of light? Or seen it inside out? Well, that's what they're getting, up there, and it might as well be nothing. You can't tell a goddamn thing from it. We're flying dead-reckoning, and we can't see where we are till we get there. Now beat it. I got work to do."

Instead, Planchette rested his hands on the back of a chair. "I was given to understand," he complained, "that the mechanism of faster than light travel would be apparent to me the moment it was achieved. It is not."

"It would be," Webber said, "if I gave you a look at the gimmick—or you got a look outside."

"I insist on seeing both," Planchette demanded.

"Insist all you damn please," Webber told him. "You don't see a damn thing."

"I suggest you reconsider," Planchette stated coldly. "I speak for the Passengers' Council."

Webber snorted disgustedly. "Look," he argued. "We're going to build us a colony. In a couple hundred years, it'll be right where Earth is right now. Okay—so you think I'm going to lay it out for those guys two hundred years from now, the same thing that's so dangerous I wouldn't pass it out back home? Damn it—if I'd thought it was safe, I'd of passed it out free all over the world from top to bottom. I didn't dare, Planchette. I had to almost let you wreck the whole damn project with your bitchy suspicious yapping. You think I wanted that? You think I kept shut just for fun? I'm not nuts, Planchette. Not *that* nuts, anyway."

"I believe you made a promise . . ." Planchette said implacably.

"Yeah? What kind of a promise?" Webber demanded.

"You promised," Planchette said, "that you would prove this ship's ability to travel faster than light—that you would prove it to my satisfaction, or else you would turn this ship back."

Webber gave him an exasperated shrug. "So what's got you so nervous?" he wondered.

"I insist you prove it," the newsman said stiffly.

"You'll get your proof, all right," Webber told him. "When we get there."

"When will we get there?" Planchette prodded doggedly.

"Twenty-five days," Webber said. "At eleven o'clock in the morning."

Phil Brembeck wasn't suspicious—just curious—when he asked, "Where are the controls to the faster than light machine?"

Roger Sherman finished his coming-on-watch instrument-check before he answered, but it wasn't because he lacked a reply. He'd been thoroughly coached, by an expert. Joe Webber.

"It's got a control room of its own," he said.

"Oh," Brembeck said, and thought. "It seems sort of funny. I mean, I'd think it was better to keep all the controls in one place."

Sherman shook his head. "It isn't necessary. This thing—it's either on or off, and that's all there is to it. The ship handles the same either way—all the monster does is change the way it comes out. You might say it multiplies everything by a thousand."

"Gosh!" Brembeck marvelled. "How? I mean, does it jimmy up time, somehow?"

"That's a sloppy way of putting it," Sherman admitted.

"Could I see it, Don? I mean, I'd like to see it."

"Maybe I can rig it," Sherman said. "I'll let you know."

When the ship was seven weeks out, Joe Webber arranged for Hayes Planchette to steal the keys to the astrodome. Planchette had been trying to get them ever since he was locked out—and thought that Webber didn't know.

As soon as he had the keys, he went up for a look. Fifteen minutes later, he was down again, storming into Webber's office.

Webber was expecting him. "Have a bad night?" he asked cheerfully.

"I have come," Planchette said, "from the astrodome."

"Yeah?" Webber asked. "How'd you get up there?"

"I have my methods," Planchette said. "When facts are denied me, I am forced to find them out by other means."

"What facts?" Webber snapped. "I've told you every god damn thing you need to know."

"I have discovered," Planchette said wrathfully, "that you have knowingly and deliberately lied to me—and to every man and woman aboard."

Webber smiled, calmly relaxed. "Yeah?"

Planchette's fist waved in the air, impotent. "This ship has not even left the solar system!" he raged.

Webber chortled. "So what?"

"I demand you turn this ship around—take us back to Earth."

Smiling like a brat, Webber waggled a finger at him. "Let's get something straight, Planchette. You came straight here from the astrodome?"

"I did," Planchette stated righteously. "I could hardly believe it—that any man could perpetrate a deliberate fraud of this magnitude . . ."

"Then nobody knows about this except me and you," Webber inferred cleverly.

Planchette stopped. His face paled. He moistened his

lips and his eyes watched Webber with the unconcealed fear of a trapped beast.

"If I had any brains, I'd slit your throat and heave you into space," Webber said, pleased with himself. "Okay—so I'm nuts. Get out of here, Planchette. Go tell your buddies on the Council. Yell it to the passengers, if you feel like it. And come back in a couple of hours. Bring the Council with you."

"I'll bring," Planchette declared, "a thousand angry men and women. If you refuse to turn this ship around . . ."

Joe Webber shook his head. "Don't threaten me, Planchette," he said dangerously. "Get out. Come back with the Council. *Then* we'll talk."

Suppressed, helpless rage bulged Planchette's lips. His eyes were hate and fear and sick dismay. He turned and plodded out.

Joe Webber chuckled.

Webber got on the phone and set up a series of connections. He punched for the first one. Sherman's face blinked onto the screen.

He frowned woodenly. "Control Room," he acknowledged formally.

"The kid there?" Webber snapped.

Sherman nodded.

"Get rid of him."

Sherman flinched away from the screen. "This it?" he asked, with beetled brows.

"Yeah."

"Can I tell him?"

"Tell him anything you god damn please. But get him out of there first."

Sherman's lips pressed thin with distaste. "Right," he said.

Webber snapped off. He punched the selector. Sandra came onto the screen, the baby in her arms.

"Get downstairs," he told her. "We've got just two hours. Spread the word."

"Two hours?" she echoed.

"Yeah."

"Joe—what are you going to do?"

195

"Never mind," he snapped. "Get downstairs." He snapped off.

The next connection was Perrault's apartment, but Andrew Perrault didn't answer. In Perrault's sprawling scrawl, the screen announced, *gone for a walk.*

Webber muttered a curse. He hit the button again. Marty came to the screen.

She was naked. Water droplets glistened on her body. "Hi, Uncle Joe." She looked down at herself, cheerfully immodest. "I was taking a shower."

"Get some clothes on and get downstairs. Fast," Webber ordered.

"Can't I go like I am?" she wondered impishly. She turned slightly, the better to exhibit herself.

Webber swore.

"Has it happened?" she asked, instantly sober.

"It's going to," Webber warned. "In two hours. Get downstairs. Pass the word. And chase down your dad—he's wandering around someplace."

Now she was worried. "What are you going to do?" she asked.

"Goddammit, I haven't got time to explain," Webber argued. "Just get downstairs before they carve you up for sandwiches."

She looked down at her body again, no longer so delighted with her nakedness. "They wouldn't . . ." she protested weakly.

"Want to bet?" Webber asked. He snapped off. He punched for the last connection.

"Shuttle craft dispatcher, B division," a uniformed man responded. "Hello, Captain." He saluted casually.

"I want a shuttle ready for launching in two hours," Webber directed. "A reconnaissance job. Number *B-10-S* if she's available."

"They're all available, sir," the man answered.

"Well, that's the one I want. Have it ready."

"She'll be itchin' to fly," the man assured.

As soon as the phone screen went blank, Roger Sherman put through two calls of his own. Both times, he said the same thing as soon as a face appeared in the screen. "Control room, son. Get down here."

Ten minutes later, they were there. Relief men. They

were his sons, and he had trained them himself. He checked over his console and stood up. "Take over, boys," he said. He nodded to Brembeck. "Phil—you're relieved."

Brembeck frowned. "Why? Our watch isn't up for another . . ."

"Never mind," Sherman told him. "You wanted a look at the light speed machine—that call a few minutes ago was clearance. Now's your chance."

"Well, all right," Brembeck said doubtfully. He checked off his instruments and left the console. One of the relief men slipped into his place.

Sherman nodded Brembeck to the door. "Come on," he said.

They took an elevator up two decks. They stepped out into a deserted corridor. Brembeck looked up and down. There was nothing to see.

"Which way do we go?" he wondered.

"This way," Sherman told him, and led off.

Their footfalls echoed down the long hall. "It looks just like a cabin deck," Brembeck said.

"There isn't much difference," Sherman admitted. He stopped at a door. He opened it. "Inside," he said.

Brembeck went in. Sherman followed.

It was a two-tenant apartment, completely furnished. Brembeck stopped.

"But this isn't . . ." he objected.

Sherman closed the door. "Sit down, son," he said. "I've got a lot to tell you."

The five Councilmen were waiting outside Webber's office half an hour before the two hours were up. About half the passengers were out there, too. They looked ugly.

Webber made them wait. The crowd grew, until almost the whole thousand were out there, jamming the corridor with their bodies, fouling the air with their breath.

Joe Webber looked them over on his peephole screen, a satisfied smile on his face. He took a mini-recorder from his desk and dropped it in a pocket.

When the two hours were up, he let the Council come

in. He welcomed them with smiles and handshakes. The forefront of the mob advanced dangerously. Webber stopped them with a glare and a raised hand. He banged the door shut and toed the lock-knob in the sill.

Outside, the mob faced the door, sullenly quiet. Leaderless now, they were no danger. Webber swung to the Council. "Inside," he ordered, nodding across the anteroom.

They looked that way, following his glance. He slipped a hand into his pocket to start the recorder.

He led them into the sanctum and shut the door. Unobtrusively locking it with his heel, he waved to the crescent of low-slung, armless chairs set in front of the desk. "Grab a chair, men," he invited.

They looked around warily, then sat down. The chairs were built for slouching. The five had to sit with their legs stretched out in front of them, their hands in their laps. Webber chuckled to himself. Let them try and look big and imposing and dangerous, sitting down there practically on the floor. It couldn't be done.

He hopped up on the prow of his swept-wing desk. He looked down at them, his heels swinging eighteen inches off the floor.

"Hell," he exclaimed delightedly. "We don't even know each other."

"This is not a social visit, Mr. Grant," Hayes Planchette stated frigidly.

"The name's Webber," Webber said. "Joe Webber. *Captain* Webber." He pointed at a leather-faced, weather-stained Councilman. "Who're you?"

"Mark Radin," the man said. "I understand you refuse to turn back."

"The *Pioneer* is going out," Webber told him implacably. "What's your business?"

"I'm a hunter," Radin said. He looked up at Webber as if squinting into the sun. But his eyes were steady. "I know guns, and I know how to use 'em," he said. "I can drop an elephant at a quarter mile, or a lion at a dozen feet. I can knife it, if I have to. Anything else you want to know?"

"Do you admit," demanded a round-faced, bald-spotted man, "that it will be years before . . ."

Webber interrupted. "I didn't get your name."

198

"Paul Ritter," the round-faced man said automatically. "Do you admit . . ."

"How do you fit in?" Webber interrupted again.

"I was to direct the reconnaissance teams," Ritter said, offense in his tone.

"Oh. Yeah. The mapmaker," Webber said carelessly. "Well, we'll have a use for you someday."

"Mr. Grant," Planchette demanded loudly. "How long will this voyage take?"

"The name's Webber," Webber said.

"He asked you a question," another man said. He was lean and tanned—young, with a long, narrow jaw. "We don't care what your name is."

"It's Webber," Webber snapped. "What's yours?"

"John Burke," the young man said. "I'm a mineral geologist—and I sure as hell can't work very well with nothing but metal decks underfoot."

"Well, relax," Webber told him. "We'll have plenty of kids in a few years. You can teach 'em the business. And we'll get there, someday."

"When?" Burke prodded.

Webber shrugged. "Fifty—seventy-five years. Something like that."

"But we'll be old men," the last Councilman protested. He was medium tall, small-boned, and delicate-faced. "Maybe dead."

"What's *your* name?" Webber wanted to know.

"I am Arthur Moresby," the slight man answered primly. "And before you ask, I am an ecological zoologist."

Webber made an annoyed face. "What's that?"

"I study animals in terms of their needs," Moresby told him precisely. "I investigate the ways their environment meets those needs."

"Well, you ought to feel right at home," Webber decided. "You can check up if the *Pioneer* can keep us alive that long. I'm betting it can."

"That is a more difficult problem," Moresby objected. "Men control their environment."

Webber shrugged. He didn't care to argue the matter. "Well, now that we know each other, maybe we can get down to business."

"We insist you turn this ship around," Planchette declared.

Joe Webber shook his head. "I worked a hundred years for this," he said stubbornly. "You don't make me quit that easy."

"But you promised," Planchette protested, aghast.

"I had my fingers crossed."

"We don't care if you had 'em braided," Burke snapped. "We're talking for a thousand people. You got us aboard with a stack of promises and lies. Well, we don't like it."

"We want to go back to Earth," Moresby said.

"If you don't knuckle under, we'll take over the ship," Burke threatened.

"Yeah?" Webber mocked, unimpressed.

"Either turn back now," Radin told him, "or do it with a gun in your back."

Webber chuckled. "What guns?"

Open mouthed, they stared at him. Then they looked at each other. "What about it?" Ritter asked, looking at Radin.

"There's guns aboard," the hunter said. "There's got to be."

Webber smiled, pleased with himself. "Yeah. But who's got 'em?"

That stopped them cold. None of them had anything to say.

"It figures out this way," Webber told them. "You can come along and like it. Or you can hate it. But god damn it, you're coming. Sure—maybe it'll take a little longer than you figured. So what? You signed on to make a colony, out there. Well, god damn you, that's what you're going to do."

"You can't do it," Burke said stubbornly. "There's a thousand of us. You can't stop us. We'll take over the ship . . ."

"I got the crew on my side," Webber said.

Burke hesitated only a moment. "Well, how many is that?" he challenged.

"About twenty, counting everybody," Webber said cockily.

"Do you think you can stop us with twenty?" Ritter doubted belligerently.

Webber nodded confidently. "Why not?"

"Even armed," Radin maintained, "you can't win. Our chance will come. You can't stop us forever."

Webber pointed a finger at him. "Look," he said. "I can keep you aboard as long as I like, and you don't have anything to say about it. Who d'you think built this ship?" He tapped his chest. "I did. And I hand-picked every man and woman aboard. You included. You don't have the chance of dirt in a laundry. Not a god damn chance."

"You're bluffing," Ritter accused.

"Not a god damn bit," Webber said. He slipped down off the desk. "I'll prove it."

He went around behind the desk. He snapped a toggle on the control board. The wall parted behind him. He looked up at the Council and smiled at their startled faces.

"Yeah," he said. "I got a back way out." His gray-green eyes were narrowed like a cat's. He jerked a thumb over his shoulder. "Let's go."

He stopped the recorder.

Ritter stood up. "Are you afraid to face our people out front?" he demanded.

"I'm not scared of any son of a bitch with two legs," Webber told him. "Is that any reason to let 'em troop after us everyplace?" Scornfully, he turned away from them. "You coming or ain't you?" he demanded over his shoulder.

He led them along a dim, narrow passageway. Another passageway branched off, and they followed him down a flight of stairs. They went down several decks. Finally, they emerged on deck four minus, in the middle of that deck's food and air-regeneration gardens.

"I do not like this sneaking around in secret passages," Planchette declared.

"Shut up," Webber told him. He led off. "This way."

The place was deserted. They walked along a curving aisle toward a colonnade glimpsed through the gaps between the sandwiched trays of growing things. The air was fresh and cool here, and the plants grew thick and lush in the fertile soil. Webber plucked a handful of berries without breaking stride, and crammed them into his mouth.

They passed through the open colonnade into a corridor. He led them along it to the central plaza—to the deck warden's office. Still they saw no one. Webber went to the phone. He set up a combination and punched it through.

A young man's face appeared on the screen. "Control room," he reported. "Relief Pilot Gilbert Elston in charge. Waiting your orders, Mr. Grant."

"Where's Rog?" Webber demanded.

For a moment, the young-looking pilot stared speechlessly at something beyond Webber's shoulder—where the five angry men of the Council stood, looking on. "Who?" he asked.

"Rog," Webber repeated. "Your dad."

"Captain, I . . ." The young man was making hand signals frantically.

Webber laughed. "It's okay, Mike," he said. "The mask's off. I'm Joe Webber—you're Mike Sherman. We use our own names from now on. Now—where's your old man?"

Mike Sherman swallowed. "He had me come down and take over," he explained awkwardly. "Then he took his engineer and went somewhere. He hasn't come back yet."

"What's he doing?" Webber demanded pettishly. "Tucking the kid in?"

"I don't know," Mike said helplessly. "He didn't tell me."

"Hell," Webber muttered. "Well, I want elevator shaft B-12 opened up so we can get down there. Can you do it without wrecking the ship?"

"I think I can, sir," Mike said soberly. "Dad taught me everything he knows. But what about . . . ?" He gestured toward the men behind Webber.

"Just some tourists I'm showing around," Webber said. "Get it open."

He reached out and snapped off. In the moment as he turned, he started the recorder. "Okay. Come on," he told the Councilmen.

They went out into the plaza. It was roughly octag-

202

onal, with corridors radiating outward from it. "Look around," Webber told them. "I want you to see this."

He crossed to a wall. It was blank metal, without even a weld seam to mar its polish. He felt along it, up over his head, then slapped the metal smartly with the flat of his hand.

The corridor nearest them closed. Great sliding sheets of steel extruded from the walls, the ceiling, and the floor. They interleaved, sliding over each other with oily slickness like gigantic scissor blades. The outermost face came down like a curtain and compressed the paved floor.

"That's Spänn process steel," Joe Webber told them. "You'd have a god damn hell of a time trying to bust your way through it."

Hayes Planchette stalked up to the barrier. He felt it and peered at it closely. "This is part of the compartment system, I presume."

"Yeah," Webber said. "The ship's full of these things. And they're tight. We can shut 'em from up here, or downstairs."

Planchette crossed to the wall where Webber had slapped. He felt there—felt nothing. He slapped. Nothing happened. He tried another spot. Then another. Impatiently, he banged the wall.

"Give up, Planchette," Webber told him. "You can shut 'em from up here, but you can't get 'em open again. The only place you can spring 'em is downstairs. The control room."

"I see," Planchette said, gritting his teeth.

"Yeah," Webber said. "And there's something like five hundred decks between you and us. And every way to get down there is plugged at every deck. Sidewise and downwise. Everywhere."

"So many decks?" Moresby wondered.

"She's a big ship," Webber said simply.

"You're saying we can't get down there," Ritter inferred.

"With the tools you got, yeah," Webber said. He started off. "Now come on. I got something else to show you." He stopped the recorder.

They boarded an elevator. Webber opened the push-

203

button selector panel and rearranged the wires inside. He worked fast, dexterously, and he stood close so his body and his hands concealed the changes he made. Then he slammed the panel shut and punched the selector for deck sixteen minus.

The elevator dropped. It was nearly as if the floor fell out from under them. The almost-weightlessness produced looks of intestinal upset on the Councilmen's faces. Cat-poised, Webber watched them. He smiled.

"Like I said," he said, "it's a long way down."

They stepped out, finally, on a nameless deck. Six young men met them. They wore crewmen's uniforms. Their high-velocity pistols looked like business.

Planchette gawked at the nearest one, zeroed in on his belly. "What's the meaning of this?" he blustered. "I demand an explanation."

Webber was the last man out of the elevator. "It's okay, kids," he said.

Hesitant, the crewmen put up their guns. "They carrying anything?" one of them asked.

Webber shrugged. "Wouldn't hurt to find out."

The one who had spoken nodded to his companions. They circled around the Councilmen and frisked them from behind. They were very thorough. Ritter started to protest, but the spokesman unlimbered his pistol again. Ritter shut up.

"Everybody get down all right, Ken?" Webber asked.

"Yes, sir," the spokesman acknowledged. "Except Harry, up in the shuttle berths. He said you gave him a job to do."

Webber nodded. "That's right. Where he is—right now, he's safe enough."

The five crewmen finished the frisk job without having found anything. They moved away from the Councilmen, their hands empty.

"They're clean," Ken reported.

"Swell," Webber approved. "Neat piece of backstopping, Ken."

"Just looking out for our own skins," Ken said plainly. "You wriggled us into this rig-up. We'll go along with you, but we know damn well we've got to look out for ourselves."

"Yeah," Webber said absently. "Okay. You're dismissed." He swung back to the Council. "Now come on. I got a lot to show you." He started the recorder again.

He took them on a quick tour of the deck. It was exactly the same as all the other decks, with residence apartments, food and air-regeneration gardens, a water reclamation plant, and a livestock zoo.

The tour came to an end outside a cage of clucking hens. "I wanted to show you guys this deck is just like all the others." Webber said. "This is *our* deck."

"I fail to see your point," Ritter said.

"We got five hundred decks between us and you," Webber reminded him. "And they're blocked. All of 'em. And we got everything we need down here. We don't need you for anything. You can't get down here, and you can't smoke us out."

He let them think about it for a moment. Then he turned on his heel and walked past them. "Come on," he said, and bumped the nearest of them—Burke—on the arm.

"Where are you taking us now?" Moresby wondered.

"The control room," Webber said. "Let's go. You ain't seen nothing yet."

They nodded woodenly to each other and shuffled after him. He kept the recorder running, this time, but they didn't say a word.

He smiled. They were starting to get the idea.

They went down in an elevator, but it was only a short drop this time. He led them along a corridor and through a series of titanic metal doors which parted as they approached and bumped shut behind them.

The doorways were narrow. They went single file. No door would open until the one before it had sealed. Webber stopped between the jaws of one of them. It was a yard thick, and the butt face had a mirror polish.

"These things are tough," he said proudly. He slapped the smooth butt-edge. "Damn tough."

He smiled. "You want to know how tough?" he asked. "Well, we got a hydrogen engine down here. That's the same as a bomb, except we keep it controlled. Only they don't *stay* controlled all the time."

"They explode," Planchette contributed.

"That's right," Webber said. "And the bigger your engine, the bigger the blast. And we got the biggest there is. If it ever blows up, it won't leave much where it was. But these doors . . . well, we figure it can't get through these doors. They'll stop it. That's how tough."

They were impressed. He could tell by their faces—their meat-dead, dry-fleshed faces and their wary, shifting eyes. "Don't worry about it," he advised wryly. "If it blasts, you won't live long enough to feel it."

He started on, then looked back at them. They hadn't moved.

"What's the matter? Ain't you coming?" he prodded. "Come on. You want to live forever?"

They didn't look eager, or happy, but they came.

Three men were on watch: the pilot, his engineer, and a feedback man. The control room was silent, and they didn't look up when the jaws of the innermost door split open. Only their consoles were important.

The Councilmen stopped just inside. They stood close together, as if huddled for warmth. Behind them, the massive doors bumped quietly together. The seal-plate settled into place.

"Well, what d'you think of it?" Webber asked proudly.

They looked around with numb incomprehension at the overwhelming galaxy of instruments and controls.

"How . . . how far is the engine?" Moresby wondered nervously.

"The fireball's about twenty yards straight down," Webber told them. "We're right on top of it, like a bird on an egg." He turned to the pilot. "Rog show up?"

"Not yet, sir," Mike Sherman said cautiously.

Webber nodded. "Okay. Lock the doors," he ordered.

The engineer did something at his console. "Doors locked, Captain," he reported.

Webber didn't acknowledge. He swung to the Council. "Quite a place, huh?"

"It is impressive," Planchette conceded reluctantly. "However . . ."

"Yeah?" Webber challenged before Planchette could make his objection. "You're a technical man. How'd you like to squat in the engineer's seat for a while?"

"I do not have the training . . ." Planchette demurred cautiously.

"Hell, it's easy," Webber persuaded, grabbing his arm and steering him around behind the engineer's console. "Get up, Bart," he said. "This guy wants to sit down. You're relieved."

The engineer looked around. "To *him?*" he wondered.

"Hell, why not?" Webber wanted to know.

Bart looked doubtful. "Well, if you say so, Mr. Grant."

"It's Webber," Webber said. "Get up."

The young man checked his console quickly, then slipped out of his chair. "Don't let him touch anything," he said worriedly.

"He's got a technical education," Webber said, oozing confidence. He prodded Planchette. "Okay," he said. "Sit down."

Gingerly, Planchette settled into the chair. He kept his hands off the console as if it were electrified. Webber stood close behind him. "Strap in," he ordered.

Fumbling unfamiliarly, Planchette found the straps and buckled them.

"Okay," Webber said. "Now all you got to do is keep the fireball tame. Ever diddle a piece of bomb before?"

Planchette shook his head, wetting his lips. He huddled his hands in his lap.

"Nothing to it," Webber assured him cheerfully. "You know how it works?"

Planchette gestured helplessly at the console's massed dials, knobs, pip-lights, and levers. "How?"

"Magnets," Webber said. "But if you get 'em too strong, they wrench loose. If you slack 'em, they can't hold the bomb. So you keep 'em balanced against the fireball pressure. And you jimmy *that* by how much hydrogen you feed it. Simple, huh?"

Planchette sat without moving, his eyes scanning back and forth across the console. It took a man months of intense drill to learn it. Pip-lights winked sporadically. Dials trembled. The knobs, the levers, the studs lay enigmatically spread before him, close enough to touch.

"But how . . . ?" he fumbled dumbly.

Webber chuckled. He looked like a cruel, small boy.

He walked around to the Number Two Engineer's console. Now, on routine watch, it was vacant. He sat down, checked it, and turned it on. He increased the flow of hydrogen to the fireball.

"Fireball pressure up," the feedback man sang out. "Compensate."

"That's you, Planchette," Webber said.

"But . . ."

"Juice up the magnets," Webber urged him impatiently.

Planchette's hands poised indecisively over the console. "Which . . . ?"

"Everything's marked," Webber told him, as if he couldn't understand why Planchette hadn't done anything. "Just be careful you don't shut the vent. Then we'd *really* blow up."

Planchette stared at him. He wet his lips. His jaw trembled.

"Watch your instruments," Webber barked. "They're what tells you what to do. You trying to find out what it's like to get vaporized?"

"Mr. Grant, I . . ." Planchette stammered helplessly.

Webber turned up the hydrogen flow very slightly. "By the way," he said nonchalantly. "We've got a special name for where you're sitting. We call it the sweat seat."

"Fireball up to margin pressure," the feedback man called. "Compensate, please."

"*How?*" Planchette cried explosively. "Tell me how!"

Webber didn't seem to hear. "The engineer that makes a mistake is a dead engineer," he said implacably. "There isn't a piece left of him."

They could feel the fireball's heightened pressure. It drove the *Pioneer* hard. The acceleration needle crept around to 1.85 gravs. Everything was heavier. Sweat streamed down Planchette's face like water.

"Shall I hike it some more?" Webber asked persuasively. "Shall I make it two gravs?"

"No! Don't!" Planchette gasped fearfully.

"Why not?" Webber argued. "Can't you compensate? Hell—the magnets are made to take four!"

208

"I can't!" Planchette confessed horribly. "I can't!"

"There's nothing to it," Webber persuaded impatiently. "How about it? Let's make it two gravs."

"No! Please! Don't!" Planchette begged. "Mr. Grant, I . . ."

"The name's Webber," Webber said.

"I can't! I can't!" Planchette screamed. "Stop! Don't! Please! Please! Mr. Grant, I . . ."

He brought up his fists above the console, a meaningless shriek emitting from between clenched teeth. The duty engineer darted forward and grabbed his wrists. They struggled. Then, with a shudder, Planchette wilted. He sagged against the seat strap. His breath came in blubbering heaves.

The control room was as quiet as judgment.

Joe Webber cut back the hydrogen flow. The terrible acceleration relaxed back to one grav. "Fireball pressure down," Feedback announced. "One acceleration unit."

"Get up," Joe Webber told Planchette heartlessly. He jerked a thumb. "You washed out."

Planchette didn't seem to comprehend. His eyes were vacant. The silence was awful.

"Get him out of there, Bart," Joe Webber told the engineer.

Bart bent over Planchette and unbuckled the chair strap. He helped Planchette to stand—helped him stumble away from the console. The bigger man submitted numbly.

"Take over, Bart," Webber said.

Bart handed Planchette over to the Council. He went back to the console and slipped into the chair. Quickly, he began to make adjustments.

Webber got up from the Two Engineer's spot. He walked up to the Council and looked up at them with his hands on his hips. "Any of you other guys want to try it?"

None of them answered. They shifted their feet and avoided his gray-green eyes.

"Know anybody on your side that can do any better?" he demanded.

Still no answer. They looked at each other, then down at the floor.

Webber stopped the recorder. Brushing past them, he walked to the door. The jaws parted. He went through. Beyond, he stopped and looked back.

"Well, c'mon," he urged. "I ain't got all day."

They took the elevator up again. None of the Council asked questions. They were beyond asking questions.

Hayes Planchette looked tired. He swabbed his face with the palm of his hand. He squeezed his nose. He didn't seem to care what happened around him.

The elevator stopped at deck sixteen minus. Webber stepped out. "The rest of the way, we walk," he said.

It was a long, exhausting walk to the shuttle berths. Webber made them walk fast to keep up with him.

When they got there, the door was sealed. Webber banged on the panel. After a moment, it opened a crack. "Who's there?" the man inside asked.

"Just me and some rubbernecks," Webber said. "Open up, Stan."

There was a hesitant pause. Then the door opened.

Like all the other crewmen, Stan Fawcett looked young. He stood back away from the door, and as soon as the last of the Councilmen was inside, he stepped forward and closed it.

Webber started the recorder again. "The shuttle ready?" he asked.

Fawcett turned around. "Yes sir," he said. He was not a big man, but his muscular limbs and his chunky face were obvious signs of his Sherman ancestry.

"Stand by to launch," Webber ordered. He started on toward the yawning open portal of the launching chamber.

"Yes sir," Fawcett said again. "But . . . Mr. Grant, there's nothing out there. Why . . . ?"

"That's Webber," Webber corrected. "We're going out for a joy ride. Back in an hour."

He motioned the Council to follow him. They stumbled on the tracks laid down for cargo handling machines. Webber chuckled.

"What did you say your name was?" Planchette asked, disbelieving.

"Joe Webber," Webber said. He stopped and turned

210

to face the Councilmen. "Seems to me, you haven't been listening too good, Planchette."

"But he was . . ."

Webber nodded, smiling. "Yeah. That's me. I'm a hundred and fifty years old."

He didn't explain. He walked into the launching chamber. The catwalk rang under his feet.

The reconnaissance shuttle was different from most spacecraft. It was slimmer, and not as tall. Its nose dome, instead of a needle-tipped cone, was a bullet-round, transparent hemisphere. Its intakes, instead of circling its body like a collar, were housed in two scoops that protruded like bulbous wings.

The shuttle stood upright, cradled against the catwalk. It loomed huge over Webber, mirror-polished and bright. Its dark entrance port stood open like the mouth of a cave.

Not pausing, Webber walked inside. He waited in the valving chamber for the Council to catch up. The light was dim in there.

When they were inside, he sealed the entrance port. Brushing past them, he scrambled up the ladder to the cockpit. They followed.

By the time they were all in the cockpit, he was buckled in the pilot's power-assist frame. He motioned them into observer's chairs. There were six of the chairs, and they were spaced around the transparent nose-dome's circumference, facing outward. "Strap in," he instructed.

They hesitated, looking around. Light from the launching chamber drowned the cockpit's own dim lighting.

"Where are you taking us?" Burke demanded.

"A hell of a lot farther than you'd care to walk," Webber snapped impatiently. "Plant your cans. We're going to launch this boat."

They sat. Submissively, they fumbled with their buckles.

Webber snapped on the dockside talker. Stan Fawcett's face appeared on the screen. "Standing by," he reported.

"Launch us," Webber ordered.

"Yes sir," Fawcett responded. He half turned from the screen, and though the screen did not show his hands, the show of intentness on his face was sign enough of the work he was doing. The lights in the launching chamber died, and for a long breath they were in darkness.

Hayes Planchette's yelp of surprise announced the opening of the launching doors. They looked out at a million stars—unblinking stars like scattered bits of icy fire.

The shuttle lurched. Still gripped in its cradle, it glided lightly, slowly sidewise through the launching doors. Then the cradle let go.

Instantly, they dropped. The *Pioneer's* dark flank flashed past, abreast of them and going faster all the time. Nothing had weight. Planchette howled precipitously.

"For the love of God!" Moresby cried. "What have you done?"

The gap between the shuttle and the *Pioneer* widened, and then, with a blink and a blinding flash, the starship was gone. All around the small craft were the stars. The Milky Way was splashed across the sky like a tattered path. Far ahead, driving swiftly away, the *Pioneer's* fireball was a fierce, bright star surrounded by a black, large bulk that blotted out the stars beyond. As they watched, with awe and horror, the shape grew smaller, and the star less bright.

Glowing faintly, reaching up from infinity, the *Pioneer's* ion trail wake pointed up toward the vanishing ship. It, too, drew slowly away as the shuttle craft drifted off from the *Pioneer's* line of flight.

Webber touched a control. With slow, deliberate speed, the shuttle's nose turned toward the glowing beam—and kept on turning until the shuttle again lay parallel to the glowing wake.

They looked back the way they'd come. High overhead, a very bright star burned.

"Take a good look," Webber told them.

The ion trail faded in distance, but it seemed to radiate from the eye-piercing star at the zenith.

"You guys got any idea where we are?" Webber asked.

"I know we're still in the solar system," Radin said.

"The solar system," Webber told them, "is damn big."

He let that sink in. Then he asked, "Where's the sun?"

For a long moment, none of them spoke. Maybe they didn't breathe. Then Moresby pointed at the brilliant star. "My God!" he gasped. "Is *that* the sun?"

Webber chuckled. "Yeah."

The Council, very suddenly, faced infinity.

"Now here's a tough one," Webber said. "Where's Earth?"

There was a long, unbroken silence.

"What's the matter?" Webber prodded. "Eyes no good?"

Moresby waved a vague hand. "Is it . . . is it somewhere back there?"

"You know," Webber sneered, "you're getting almost smart. Let's try one more. What sort of a chance do you think you've got of getting back there without a man that knows how?"

"But . . ." Moresby protested.

"I'll tell you something else," Webber said. "There ain't a book in the ship that'll help. I made sure of it. Like I made sure the only guys that know how are on my side."

"You planned this!" Ritter suddenly accused. "You deliberately planned this!"

"What did you think I was doing?" Webber demanded. "Playing it by ear? Listen, you. I planned this for a hundred years. You hear that? A hundred years. I didn't miss a thing. And I *won't* miss a thing, either. I've got you aboard, and god damn it, you'll stay aboard till we get there."

"How long . . . ?" Ritter wondered.

"Fifty years. A hundred. Who cares?"

"But we'll die. We'll be old men," Moresby protested.

"You guys don't listen very good," Webber told them. "I said I've been planning this a hundred years."

"But you couldn't have . . ." Moresby argued. "You . . ."

"Why not?" Webber wanted to know. "I'm a hundred and fifty years old. Why couldn't I of done it?"

"But it's . . . it's impossible," Moresby explained.

Webber chuckled. He started the ship turning again. "We better head back," he said. He watched the sky-scape wheel until the ship was again turned away from the sun—pointed out toward the *Pioneer*'s far destination. The big ship's ion trail glowed more faintly now, and they had drifted farther from it. But still it pointed the way.

"Still think you can take the ship over?" Webber taunted. Far ahead, the *Pioneer*'s fireball was a fast-fading star. "You can't get down to the control room, and you can't starve us out. You can't fly the ship, and you don't even know where to fly it. Still want to go home?"

"We don't seem to have any choice," Burke admitted ruefully.

Webber started the hydrogen engine. He had no engineer to help him, but the shuttle had been built so one man could fly it alone. It wasn't as easy, but it could be done. The small craft leaped upward.

"You got plenty of choice," Webber said. He stepped up the fireball's pressure. The shuttle drove hard.

"I'll make you a deal," he proposed. "Any of you guys want to go back—I'll give you a shuttle. I'll give you a bunch of 'em—up to six, if you need 'em. You can fly back in them."

"Who'll pilot them?" Radin demanded.

"That's your problem," Webber said. "I got just enough men in the ship to keep it running."

"I don't think we care for your offer," Ritter said coldly.

Webber shrugged. It made no difference to him.

"Offer!" Burke spat contemptuously. "You call that an offer?"

"Take it or don't," Webber told him. He couldn't care less.

He cut down the fireball's feed. It was giving two gravs, now. Working the gyros, he edged the craft closer to the *Pioneer*'s fading trail.

"I'm a hundred and fifty years old," he repeated deliberately.

"You're insane!" Planchette accused with sudden comprehension.

"We got a thing that does it," Webber said. "There's

214

about forty-five of us, counting women and kids. If you're real good and don't make us trouble, maybe you'll get it, too."

High above them, far ahead, the *Pioneer*'s fireball slowly brightened. The black mass of the ship was getting bigger, too.

"Just one thing," Webber added. "The treatment ain't permanent. It's got to be done every couple of years. So you better behave."

No one spoke.

"Hell, you're getting a good deal," Webber argued. "All you got to do is don't make trouble, and you'll live forever. What's wrong with that?"

"Nothing. Absolutely nothing," Ritter conceded with a helpless sigh. "You have us trapped, Mr. Grant. Completely trapped."

"The name's Webber," Joe Webber maintained.

Ritter laughed. It bubbled out of him abruptly. He didn't stop.

Webber slipped a hand into his pocket and stopped the recorder. When he played back the tape on the *Pioneer*'s talker, that hysterical laugh would be the last thing the passengers heard.

He chuckled. "*Now* who's crazy?" he wanted to know.

"Had your appendix out?"

Brembeck nodded.

"It'll grow back," Sherman told him. "And any teeth you had out. And if you ever broke a bone, we'll have to break it again and put you in traction, so it'll mend the right way. You'll be sick as a dog for about a month. It's not any fun, but . . ."

He paused, and kicked a chair leg with his right foot. "This was steel, once," he said. "It's worth it."

"Then we're not going faster than light?" Brembeck wondered. "It'll be years before we get there?"

Sherman nodded. "A good many years," he confirmed grimly. "The only thing to make up for it—you'll live to see it. You'll still be young."

The young man shook his head bewilderedly. "It's sort of hard to believe. I mean, you're . . . you're really Roger Sherman? You really . . . ?"

"Yeah," Sherman said. "I crashed the *Jove*. A hundred and ten years ago."

"Gosh," Brembeck marvelled. "You don't *look* that old." Then he said, "Would you tell me about it?"

"I don't like to talk about it," Sherman said, looking away. Then he turned back, stubbornly decisive. "Hell," he muttered. "It's the least I can do."

He sat down and told Brembeck about it. To the young man, it was a tale of high adventure—to Sherman, it was a small bit of hell he had somehow lived to tell about.

That was how he told it. Grim and unsparing.

He explained the situation—how the *Jove* had been their only chance of getting down, and how poor that chance had been. How they'd decided to take that chance, even though the ship wasn't built to cut air—was built only for space, and had neither the hull nor the power to hit atmosphere. And anyway they didn't have much reaction mass left.

He told of the terror and tension of the hours as the *Jove* ripped through atmosphere time and again, slowly losing her orbital speed, falling faster and faster, her hull heated dull red. Brembeck listened raptly all the way, from the beginning of that nightmare flight to the moment he was fished out of the Pacific by the men from the search plane.

"I didn't figure it right," Sherman finished. "Almost right, but that isn't good enough. I figured we'd dropped enough mass. We hadn't. I thought the air would slow us up more than it did. I made some excuses at the time, but that's all they were. Excuses. I slopped the job. That's all there is to it."

"But nobody blames you," Brembeck protested. "What else could you do?"

Sherman looked at his fist, white-knuckled in his lap. "I shouldn't of tried it," he said. "I should of dropped more weight. I don't know where it would of come from, but I should of dropped it. Another thousand pounds and maybe I could of done it. I . . . Oh, hell," he muttered. "Anyway, I crashed her."

"You were lucky," Brembeck said.

"If you mean because I got out, I guess you can call it lucky," he said. "I'm not so sure."

216

"Sure, it's lucky," Brembeck argued. "I mean, if you hadn't got out, you wouldn't be here, now. You wouldn't be making this trip."

Sherman studied him intently. "You call that lucky?" he wondered. "I figured you'd be mad."

"Well, it'll . . . it'll take a little getting used to," Brembeck admitted. "But . . ."

"You don't mind it?" Sherman asked quizzically. "After the way we've lied—and . . . and swindled you— and, well, you're a prisoner, now. You know that? You don't mind?"

"No, sir," Brembeck said respectfully. "It's an awful surprise, but . . . shucks, as long as I've got to stay aboard ship for a while, it doesn't matter much just where. I mean, I always wished I could of lived back in the old days . . . the reaction mass ships . . . This is— well, this is almost as good. I mean, even if it's a long ride, well, we *are* going there. And after all, that's the important thing."

"That's how we figured it in the old days," Sherman nodded. "They were long rides then, too."

"Yeah. That's right," Brembeck admitted. "I never thought much about that. Uh . . . was it like this, back then?"

Sherman nodded. "Yeah. It was a lot like this. I'll tell you about it, sometime."

"I'd like to hear about it," Brembeck said earnestly.

"They'll be plenty of time," Sherman told him. "Lots of time."

"Yes sir," Brembeck said. "Uh . . . just one thing . . ."

Sherman anticipated him. "I'll try to get your wife moved down here," he said. "We may have to keep you locked up quite a while."

"Could you do that?"

"Somehow," Sherman said. "I'll manage."

"Uh . . . thanks, Mr. Sherman."

Sherman grinned. "Call me Rog."

"Yes sir," Brembeck said thoughtfully. "Uh . . . sir —Rog—it's been an . . . an honor to work with you." Timidly, he offered his hand.

Sherman gripped the hand warmly. "You're not done

yet," he promised. "We need men like you. I'll keep the job open."

Cocky, bouncy, like a boy strutting home from a ball game he'd won, Joe Webber strolled along the corridor.

He'd done it. It was easy. Playing the tape on the ship's talker, with his commentary, had taken all the squawk out of them. They couldn't do a thing, and they knew it. He had them just where he wanted.

Oh, there'd still be trouble, of course. A few hotheads to cool. Some stubborns to be softened up. And the Clan would have to stay down here on Bottom Deck a few years. But the tough part was over. He'd done the job. The *Pioneer* was going out.

Not bad for a hundred years' work.

He took a swipe at a hedge. The resilient twigs scratched his hand. He whistled tunelessly through his teeth.

He felt real good. He was going to walk into his apartment, and Sandy would be there with the baby, and everything was going to be swell.

But they were waiting for him. Not just Sandra and the baby, but Sherman, and Marty, and Andrew Perrault. They sat in low chairs facing the door, stone silent as if sitting in judgment.

And Sandy had a pale look, as if something awful was going to happen.

Webber stopped just inside, all at once cold.

"Shut the door," Sherman said.

Numbly, Webber closed the door and stomped the lock stud with his heel. Then he turned back. "Well, what d'you want?" he demanded.

"We don't like it, Joe," Sherman said.

Webber scowled. "Yeah? What don't you like?" he asked defiantly.

"You've kidnapped a thousand people," Marty accused him. "You've made prisoners of them."

"We think it's sort of wrong, Joe," Perrault explained clumsily.

"What the hell!" Webber protested. "I didn't *make* 'em come aboard."

Marty nodded. "No. You were too clever for that," she

218

admitted bitterly. She stood up. Her eyes were unwaveringly level to his.

"You tricked them," she said. It was an indictment. "You took advantage of them. Oh, they wanted to come. They wanted to help build our colony. I think they'd still like to do it, even now. But they don't want to sit doing nothing for a hundred years. You even promised them they wouldn't have to."

Webber made a disgusted, whimpering sound. "God damn it," he complained. "They wouldn't of signed on if we'd told 'em the truth."

"We're not going to argue that," Marty said calmly. "It doesn't change things. You've lied to them. You made them a promise you never intended to keep. You've made them prisoners."

"For crissake," Webber protested. "You knew I was going to do it. How come you wait until now to start bitching?"

"I guess we didn't think much about it," Marty conceded. "Maybe we didn't *want* to think about it. And we thought you'd somehow persuade them to accept it, instead of forcing it on them, and . . . and we thought you'd let them have Dad's treatment, sort of to make up for it."

"They'll get it," Webber contended. "I told 'em so, didn't I?"

"But you're making a whip of it," Marty explained. "You're using that horrible lie that it isn't permanent. Joe—don't you realize the terrible things that does to a person? You're . . . you're making slaves of them."

"But we got to keep *some* control on 'em," Webber protested. "They'll run wild."

Marty shook her head stubbornly. "We have them aboard, and we have control of the ship. We don't need any more than that."

"We got to make sure," Webber insisted. He tried persuasion. "Look—we had space flight once. It wasn't much—a few trips to the planets, and the orbitbase, and a station on the moon. But it was a start, and it would of got bigger. But then people ganged up and killed it because they couldn't see any money in it for themselves. Well, it won't happen this time. You hear me? It's not going to happen."

Marty shook her head slowly, despairing for him. "Someday they'll kill you, Joe," she warned.

He laughed harshly. "I'd like to see 'em try!" he sneered.

"You're so blind, Joe," she persisted. "So terribly blind. Can't you see how wrong you are?"

He made a disgusted sound and turned away from her. He stalked toward a corner of the room. Then he whirled.

"Okay. You're so full of the right way to do things," he challenged. "What do you want to do now? You want to turn back—crawl back to Earth on our hands and knees because the people upstairs don't like the deal they got? You want to do that?"

Marty seemed to gather herself for a retort full of fury and fire, but Sherman set a calming hand on her shoulder. He stepped past her. He towered hugely over the small man.

"No," he said grudgingly. "We'll go along with that much. Because you've already done the damage, and because we want to make the trip. But we're going to change some other things."

"Yeah? What?"

"First of all, they get Doc's treatment," Sherman dictated. "They get it now, and they get told it's permanent."

"Yeah?" Webber argued. "Then what happens when we get the colony set up? Do we keep on giving it out to 'em as fast as they come, until there's no room to sit down, it's so crowded? Till you got to blow a guy's brains out every ten minutes or you don't get enough to eat? You think *that's* the right thing to do?"

"I'll bet you've got an answer," Sherman said ironically.

"Sure," Webber said. "We'll pack 'em in ships and go out and make us a whole bunch of colonies. You think I'm gonna be satisfied with one lousy goddamn little colony? We got plenty of time, Rog, and there's lots of stars out there, just waitin'. Billions! You think I'm gonna sit on my hands?"

Sherman shook his head. "They wouldn't stand for it," he said. "They'll never let you put them in a ship again, once they get out."

"Okay. So what are *you* going to do?" Webber challenged.

"We haven't decided yet," Sherman admitted. "We've decided only one thing—you don't give the orders any more."

"Why not?" Webber demanded.

"We don't like the way you did things," Sherman told him bluntly. "We're taking over."

"How would you of done it?" Webber wanted to know.

Sherman made a helpless gesture. "I don't know," he said. "But it would of been a lot different."

"Yeah," Webber jeered. "And you'd be makin' the trip by yourselves."

"Maybe," Sherman conceded. "That's something we'll never know, now. But it might of been better, that way."

Webber laughed unpleasantly. "You didn't dare buck me before now," he said viciously. "You know why?"

"I'm listening," Sherman said stonily.

Webber smiled insidiously. "Because any other way, you couldn't be sure," he accused. "And you didn't have the guts to do it yourself."

Sherman nodded. "Maybe you're right," he admitted, as if with a bitter taste in his mouth. "But this is as far as we'll go. We're giving them Doc's treatment. Now. And we're telling them it's permanent, so you'll never be able to pressure them. And we're taking you out of command."

"Go ahead, you bastard," Webber sneered. "See if I care."

He spun around—pointed at Sandy. "You! You bitch!" he accused. "You let 'em in here!"

She looked pale and frightened, but she didn't move.

Marty walked up to Webber and looked down at him. "I think you *do* care," she said soberly, and her grave brown eyes searched deeply into him, as if she could see something buried there that she could pity.

Sherman turned to Perrault. He grinned. "On your feet, Doc," he urged grandly. "Quit loafing."

Clumsily, Andrew Perrault climbed to his feet. "Honest, Rog?" he wondered owlishly. "Honest?"

Marty hugged his arm warmly. "We won't ever use it

221

again, Dad," she promised, bubblingly happy. "We'll *give* it away."

Perrault looked around, blinking, awkward. "I don't hardly know what to say," he confessed.

"Neither do I, Dad," Marty laughed. "Isn't it wonderful?"

He watched them go out. He looked like a small, sulky boy. When the door was shut again, he kicked the wall. Hard.

"Just another goddamn passenger," he muttered bitterly.

"They left the good part," Sandra said softly.

He'd forgotten she was there. He whirled. "Yeah? What good part?"

"We're still making the trip," she reminded him simply. "We'll still make the colony."

Webber muttered something under his breath. He didn't answer her.

"Joe . . ." she offered timidly. "Joe—we've got a long trip ahead. It'll get awful quiet. Would . . . would you like me to stay? I'd like to stay, Joe."

He turned away from her. "Yeah. Stick around," he grumbled.

. . . yeah. They'd left him that much. The *Pioneer* would make the trip. They'd find their star. They'd colonize their new world. Maybe they'd even—some of them—go on, and settle other worlds, and keep on going, on across the galaxy.

Just like he'd planned.

But . . .

But it wouldn't be *his*.

He wasn't big any more.

IF YOU ENJOYED THIS BOOK YOU WILL WANT TO READ THESE OTHER GREAT SCIENCE FICTION ADVENTURES FROM LANCER

DON'T MISS THIS IMPORTANT ANTHOLOGY

FIRST FLIGHT
MAIDEN VOYAGES IN SPACE AND TIME BY

**L. SPRAGUE DE CAMP • A. E. VAN VOGT
ALGIS BUDRYS • THEODORE STURGEON
BRIAN W. ALDISS • ROBERT HEINLEIN
ARTHUR C. CLARKE • JUDITH MERRIL
POUL ANDERSON • LESTER DEL REY
Edited by DAMON KNIGHT**